Root of All Evil?

A Pastor Stephen Grant Novel

Ray Keating

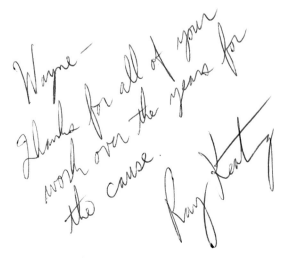

Wayne —
Thanks for all of your
work over the years for
the cause.

Ray Keating

This book is a work of fiction. Names, characters, places, events and incidents either are the product of the author's imagination or are used fictitiously. Any resemblance to actual persons, living or dead, events or locales is entirely coincidental.

For more information:
Keating Reports, LLC
P.O. Box 596
Manorville, NY 11949
keatingreports@aol.com

ISBN-13: 978-1479112197

ISBN-10: 1479112194

For

Beth, Jonathan and David,
my family whose love provides strength

and

Matt Carolan,
my friend who helped introduce me to
the world of ideas

"No one can serve two masters, for either he will hate one and love the other, or he will be devoted to the one and despise the other. You cannot serve God and money."

- Matthew 6:24

"For the love of money is a root of all kinds of evils. It is through this craving that some have wandered away from the faith and pierced themselves with many pangs."

- 1 Timothy 6:10

"He who had received the five talents went at once and traded with them, and he made five talents more... And he who had received the five talents came forward, bringing five talents more, and saying, 'Master, you delivered to me five talents; here I have made five talents more.' His master said to him, 'Well done, good and faithful servant. You have been faithful over a little; I will set you over much. Enter into the joy of your master.'"

- Matthew 25:16, 20-21

Prologue

No one who knew Paige Caldwell would ever call her shy or modest. But secretive? Most certainly.

For a CIA agent, she was something of an enigma. Her job demanded the ability to blend into a crowd. Yet, her striking beauty and self-confidence meant that Paige drew attention. Of course, she used all of this to her advantage in both her professional and personal lives, and sometimes in acts of playful self-indulgence.

As a neighbor approached, tugged along by his golden retriever, Paige opened the front door to her Old Town Alexandria townhouse wearing nothing more than a men's dress shirt, with the three top buttons undone.

The neighbor failed to avert his eyes as Paige grabbed mail from the box, and then crouched down to pick up a newspaper. She pushed back her long, black hair, glanced up and said, "Good morning, John."

He stammered, "Ah, m-morning."

"How's Marie?"

"Who? I mean ... Marie ... yes, she's great."

Paige smiled, winked one of her gray-blue eyes, stepped back into her house, and shut the door. Watching through a window, she giggled at the neighbor glancing over his shoulder as the dog relentlessly dragged him back home.

She flipped through the mail, and stopped at an oversized, tan envelope with her name and address written in calligraphy. She opened it.

"Gracious Savior,
Grant Your Blessing"

Jennifer Emma Shaw
and
The Rev. Stephen Wayne Grant
request the pleasure of your company at their marriage
on Saturday, June 11,
at four o'clock in the afternoon

St. Mary's Lutheran Church
Manorville, NY

In lieu of gifts,
Jennifer and Stephen request that you consider
donations to either

LCMS World Relief
and Human Care
or
The St. Luke's School
Education Trust

"Well, that didn't take very long, Stephen," Paige said aloud. "Good for you." Her smile carried a hint of sadness.

A voice called from upstairs. "Liebling, are you coming back to bed?"

Paige dropped the invitation on a table, and the shirt on the floor.

"Of course, lover." She ascended the stairs.

Chapter 1

U.S. Senator James "Jimmy" Farrell rated exceptional in various ways.

His path into the world's greatest deliberative body was rather unique, as were his politics for a senator from New York.

His death would be extraordinary as well.

Jimmy Farrell had been a tough, bare-knuckles, hard-drinking political leader of the Staten Island Conservative Party for several years. When the statewide party couldn't stomach backing another liberal Republican in a presumably losing campaign against a powerful, incumbent Democrat, Farrell volunteered to be the Conservatives' sacrificial lamb.

But the campaign took two unexpected turns. First, it was revealed that the married incumbent Democrat had engaged the services of a long list of prostitutes. Three days later, several media reports pointed to the Republican personally benefiting from contracts awarded while he was mayor of a small, upstate city.

It all played into old notions of Republicans being consumed by money, and Democrats obsessed with sex.

More hookers and more dollars flowed forth from the media on a daily basis during the final weeks leading up to the election. After the polls closed, having garnered 36 percent of the vote, Jimmy became the second Conservative to win a U.S. Senate seat from New York.

Farrell understood the unique circumstances of his victory, and the history of his state. James Buckley was the Conservative Party candidate who won the 1970 Senate race because Democrat Richard Ottinger and Senator Charles Goodell, a liberal Republican appointed by Governor Nelson Rockefeller after the assassination of Senator Robert Kennedy, split the state's left-wing vote. Buckley served only one term. And since New York was arguably more liberal now, Senator Farrell was a sure bet for one term – that is, barring additional, unforeseen scandals.

In office, Farrell made no compromise. He spoke his mind, and voted his principles. No sacred cow existed that he would not slay, and no political third rail avoided his touch.

Backed by a handful of conservative Republicans, Farrell even led opposition to a highly popular effort – proposed by Republicans and backed by Democrats – to begin shifting U.S. foreign economic aid from government projects to helping entrepreneurial start-ups in developing nations.

Farrell declared on the floor of the U.S. Senate: "We shouldn't be subsidizing businesses, big or small, at home, and we certainly shouldn't be doling out U.S. tax dollars to businesses in foreign countries. I want to end government economic aid altogether, no matter who gets it." He mysteriously added, "I believe ominous forces are looking to cash in on America's naïve generosity."

It was not surprising that the Senator from New York drove both Democrats and Republicans over the edge, with some accusing him of literally being crazy.

But crazy or not in his politics, Jimmy Farrell certainly was a predictable creature when it came to his day-to-day personal life.

While Congress was in session, when not required to be in the Senate, Farrell often could be found dining, drinking and holding court at The Dubliner Restaurant and Pub, just a block from Union Station. His favorite meal was the Guinness Burger – sirloin marinated in Guinness, served on a potato pancake with Welsh cheese and onion straws. The New York Senator, however, was far more expansive in his beverage selections, being open to all of the draft beers offered – from Guinness Stout to the Dubliner Irish Lager.

Members of his staff periodically tried to get Farrell to limit his attendance at the pub. Their arguments included the potential political negatives of spending so much time in a bar. That fell on deaf ears, as Farrell seemed to revel in his one-termer status. As for pointing to drunk driving risks, Farrell reminded staff that he never drove himself around D.C. In fact, the responsibility for driving Farrell fell to different aides on varying hours and days. That reality apparently was the true impetus behind his aides' urgings, as each dreaded the duty of getting their boss out of The Dubliner and back to the Watergate condo he rented.

It turned out that Jimmy Farrell's last night on Earth was the final evening for one of his legislative aides as well.

Once the bullet ripped into and lodged in Larry Payton's brain, his vital signs quickly faltered. By the time his body was dumped on Second Street along the tracks behind Union Station, no spark of life remained.

Just after midnight, a blue-eyed, blond-haired, stocky, bushy-mustached man, dressed in a black suit, white shirt and thin black tie, entered The Dubliner. Few took notice, as he resembled many drivers seen around the nation's capital. He asked a bartender where he could find Senator Farrell.

The barkeep said, "Around the corner, in the dining room. There's a group of older gents."

One of those gentlemen spoke loudly. His animated hands helped tell a tale, with the beer in his right hand periodically sloshing over the rim of a pilsner glass.

Farrell's light gray hair was thick and wavy, with a few traces of its original sandy brown remaining, while his complexion was pock marked and ruddy. The Senator's current facial redness was partially due to five lagers consumed over the past two hours, and partially to the extra sixty pounds his five-foot-eight frame had to carry.

The man in the dark suit approached the table, and waited as Farrell's story continued. After the Senator and two others erupted in laughter, the stocky fellow introduced himself as "Mr. Audia," told the Senator that Larry had an emergency, and he had been sent to drive Farrell home.

Jimmy offered his presumed driver a beer, but it was refused. Audia told the Senator that he would be waiting in the car outside, ready to leave whenever Farrell was.

Farrell said a bit unsteadily, "Okay, thanks, I'll be out in five minutes."

Twenty minutes and one more beer later, Farrell emerged into the warm night air and Audia waved him over to the car, and opened the back door.

As Audia turned the dark sedan onto Massachusetts Avenue, Farrell focused more closely on his surroundings. "Hey, this is my car. Why are you driving my car?"

"Oh, I'm sorry, Senator Farrell. Didn't Larry explain?" He pulled the vehicle over to the curb.

"Larry? No. Explain what?"

Audia pulled a pistol from the gym bag resting on the seat next to him, and turned around. He looked Farrell in the eyes.

The alcohol consumed by the Senator delayed his ability to focus on the weapon. "Hey, what the…"

"Oh, that's right, Larry's dead." Audia smiled and fired the weapon.

A tranquilizer dart hit Farrell just below the neck, immobilizing the senator almost immediately.

Audia turned around, shifted the car into drive, checked his mirrors, and pulled away from the curb. In a matter-of-fact, almost soothing voice, he said, "Unfortunately, Senator Farrell, you will be joining Larry in death shortly. But first, I will get some information from you that my client needs."

The fear on Farrell's face eventually faded away, as his eyes rolled back and closed.

Chapter 2

"Wakey, wakey, eggs and bac-ey, Senator Farrell," chirped the seemingly carefree hired gun. "Come on, rise and shine."

Senator Farrell moaned, and struggled to open his eyes. He finally focused on the smiling face of Mr. Audia. Farrell then discovered that he was unable to move. Restraints around his calf muscles, wrists and chest made him one with a wooden chair.

"What the hell is this?" asked Farrell.

Audia, sitting about five feet away and directly across from Farrell, replied, "Give it a second, Senator. I'm sure you'll remember what happened. After all, it was just two hours ago. In the meantime, I apologize. I don't actually have eggs and bacon. Still way too early for breakfast. But that was how my mom used to wake us up as kids."

Audia looked back down at a magazine resting on his crossed leg, and flipped a page. "You know how some people enjoy politics? I'm sure you do, Senator. For me, I guess it's ironic. Probably seventy percent of my clients, and therefore seventy percent of my targets and earnings, come from the world of politics in some way or another. Yet, I can't say that I have any real interest in politics. It's so plodding, petty and mind numbing. So, the political jobs are just about the money. But the corporate world, now that fascinates me. Sure, that's about making money, too. But they find interesting ways to get people to spend. Less bureaucracy as well. Easier to get things done."

Farrell shook his head, and seemed to gain some added clarity. "You picked me up from The Dubliner. You had a gun." A look of horror transformed Farrell's face. "Oh Christ, and you said Larry was dead. That you killed him."

"See, I knew you'd remember," said Audia without looking up from his magazine. "And what else did I say, Senator?"

Farrell swallowed hard. "That you were going to kill me as well."

"Correct. Excellent, Jimmy." Audia paused, and turned another page of the magazine. "By the way, you're a U.S. senator, so you should know. What's a good French restaurant in the D.C. area? The *Washingtonian* here," he pointed at the periodical resting in his lap, "likes Marcel's a great deal. What do you think?"

"I think you're a sick bastard. That's what I think."

Audia closed the magazine and placed it on a wooden table, next to a silver tray housing various medical instruments, including a syringe. Audia looked into the eyes of his captive. "That was not very nice, but understandable, I suppose. Can I call you 'Jimmy'? Well, you don't really have a say at this point, so Jimmy it is."

Farrell's voice shook. "What do you want?"

"I told you that earlier, Jimmy. My client needs information, and you are going to give me that information." Audia actually smiled pleasantly at Farrell.

The Senator stiffened a bit. "What makes you think I will tell you anything? Why should I? You said that you're going to kill me."

"True, you are going to die tonight. But you also will tell me everything I want to know." He turned and picked up the syringe, and looked at it closely. Audia tapped it and squirted a bit of the liquid into the air. "You might call this a kind of truth serum. It will quickly bring down whatever defenses you might have left after several beers and a tranquilizer dart." He laughed. "You know, Jimmy, you really shouldn't mix all of these drugs. Not good for you." Audia rose and circled behind Farrell. He grabbed a hunk of the Senator's gray hair, and yanked his head to the left. He leaned in close to Farrell's ear. "But if you have some unknown training or inner strength, which I highly doubt, Senator, despite your rep for being tough, then I have additional means for extracting information." Audia re-directed Farrell's head once more so that the Senator could see scalpels and forceps of varying sizes resting on the tray.

Audia then plunged the needle into the New York Senator's neck.

The well-paid assassin returned to his seat. "This will only take a few minutes, Jimmy."

Less than a half hour later, Audia had gotten what he wanted from Senator Farrell without any resistance.

Audia smiled. "Thank you, Jimmy. We'll be retrieving that laptop of yours. But in general that was easy, right? I told you it would not take long. Isn't that drug a miracle worker? You tell me what I want to know, and while you realize what you are saying, there's not a damn thing you can do to stop yourself."

"What now?" Farrell managed.

"You die," Audia said. "What the hell do you think is going to happen? I'm going to go soft and let you go? Ha!" He continued: "But I promise that your death will be exceptional, fittingly different for a U.S. senator."

Audia moved alongside Farrell. He grabbed the strap across the front of the Senator's chest, placed the other hand behind the chair, and gently tipped Farrell back and down.

While being lowered, Senator Farrell had his eyes closed, whispering a prayer – the "Hail Mary." He stopped when his neck rested in a carved inset so that it could not move.

Audia said, "Come on, Senator, open up. I don't want you to miss this."

Farrell opened his eyes, and was staring up at a large metal blade hovering several feet above.

"A guillotine. That's different, right? I'm really getting into this whole French thing of late." Audia let a rope slip from his left hand. Farrell's eyes bulged in fright. His mouth opened and a tiny portion of a scream escaped before the plunging blade efficiently detached the Senator's head from the rest of his body.

Chapter 3

Politics and marathons consumed Skyler Tobin's life.

Her political passion led her to work in Congress, to live just off Capitol Hill, and to be willing to join any Republican campaign in which the candidate had at least a 50-50 chance at winning. While only 29 years old, she was considered a campaign veteran with 20 races under her belt, ending up on the losing side only three times.

Meanwhile, she trained incessantly and was highly competitive when it came to running marathons. She had a marathoner's thin, bony body, topped by short, bleached blond hair.

In Tobin's world, this politics-marathon combination left no time, and no interest, for romantic pursuits or staying in contact with family and old friends.

Skyler seemed tireless in running either campaigns or marathons. In fact, her colleagues called her "The Machine." While at least some of those co-workers meant it in a less-than-complimentary way, she wore the moniker like a badge of honor.

As dawn was breaking, "The Machine" was running on Capitol Hill. Each day started this way, followed by a return to her apartment for a shower, digesting the morning news and commentary, and heading off to work in the Rayburn House Office Building.

But this morning, the ritual would be broken at the foot of the Robert A. Taft Memorial and Carillon.

Other than hearing bells striking on the hour and sounding on the quarter hour, most people seemed to be unaware of the Taft Memorial, just to the north of the Capitol Building. Of course, most didn't know who Taft was either.

"The Machine" knew the bare basics.

Taft served as a U.S. senator from Ohio, Skyler's home state. He was a leading critic of FDR's New Deal programs, and was the conservative alternative to Thomas Dewey and to Dwight D. Eisenhower for the Republican presidential nods in 1948 and 1952, respectively. But Taft lost each time. He became Senate majority leader in 1953, but died later that year after being diagnosed with cancer.

Tobin, though, was unaware of Taft's isolationist leanings, which were quite different from the internationalism common among many Republicans since the start of the Cold War. All Skyler really needed to know was that Taft was "Mr. Republican." That fact led to her running a lap around the memorial each morning. She told others, "It's my personal salute to a great Republican."

As the skies began to brighten, Tobin started climbing the steps up to the 100-foot tower. But she stopped. At the base of the 10-foot bronze statue of Taft sat a black gym bag, with the top unzipped and laid open. Skyler could see something light colored moving slightly in the morning breeze.

She approached slowly, and once within view of the bag's contents, she let out a small scream before covering her mouth. Skyler Tobin turned away, took a breath, and then turned back and walked closer.

The gray hair was matted with dried blood. The mouth was agape. And the dead but open eyes seemed like they wanted to spring from their sockets.

"Oh, my God," she whispered, staring at the decapitated head of Senator Jimmy Farrell.

Skyler finally yelled, "Help. Someone, help!" She pulled her iPhone out of its belt holder, and dialed 911. "My name is Skyler Tobin. I'm at the Taft Memorial on Capitol Hill. There's been a murder."

She listened to the 911 operator.

Skyler replied, "Yes, I'm sure it's murder. It's Senator Farrell from New York. His head is in a gym bag."

* * *

Within minutes, the Capitol Police and FBI swarmed the area. The Capitol Building was sealed and the surrounding area cordoned off for several blocks.

FBI Special Agent Ryan Bates arrived at the feet of Senator Taft, staring down at the head of Senator Farrell. The tall, thin Bates ran his right hand through sandy hair sitting atop an oversized head. He took a deep breath, looked up and scanned the area. More accentuated breaths followed. Getting sick appeared to be a real possibility. His already light complexion grew paler.

A fellow agent, who was watching, asked, "Ryan, you okay?"

He nodded unconvincingly, as the Taft Carillon rang out that it was 6 AM.

Chapter 4

Jennifer Shaw sat in the back of a white, SUV stretch limousine sipping a glass of Moet Imperial champagne, laughing with friends.

As the former wife of the adulterous Long Island Congressman Ted Brees, and the soon-to-be bride of Pastor Stephen Grant, Jennifer was trying to maintain a low-key lead-up to the wedding just over a week away. She asked her best friend, confidant and matron of honor, Joan Kraus, to keep that in mind for this bachelorette party.

Over a recent lunch, Jennifer warned, "And no male strippers."

Joan responded, "You sure? After all, marrying a pastor means you probably won't have this kind of opportunity again."

"I'll survive."

"You're no fun," said Joan.

The result on this warm, clear Friday night was a just-finished, two-hour dinner for six women at a waterfront restaurant in Westhampton Beach. Now, the SUV moved along Dune Road, passing huge homes perched precariously on the ocean.

With Joan seated to her right, on Jennifer's left was Pam Larson. The perky, blue-eyed, blond, former cheerleader grew perkier with each sip of the bubbly. Pam had confessed at dinner that she rarely drank alcohol. No one at the table seemed surprised.

Despite having a dozen years on the 24-year-old Pam, Nicole Freeman matched the perkiness, with some flightiness and chattiness thrown in for good measure. Rounding out the party was Jennifer's cousin, Vicki Dart, along with one of her business partners, Yvonne Hudson.

Vicki, while sweeping back long brown hair, looked at Jennifer and asked, "Well, Sis, what's our next stop?"

"I have no idea. Joan's in charge."

Joan said, "Actually, I just handled the dinner." She smiled, and sipped her champagne.

"What do you mean?" Jennifer's stare at Joan narrowed.

"Well, when I spoke to Yvonne, she volunteered to take care of the entertainment."

Jennifer's narrow gaze shifted. "Yvonne, you didn't."

Yvonne's thin body, fair skin and rather sharp facial features closely mirrored Jennifer's. The difference came in hair color – Jennifer's dark auburn versus Yvonne's blond frosting.

Yvonne mocked innocence by batting her eyelashes. "Whatever do you mean?"

"You know I collect very sharp objects – daggers and swords."

"Yes, my dear, I am well aware," said Yvonne.

Nicole chimed in: "Ooo, does this mean there are going to be big strong men removing their clothes?" She laughed and gulped down more champagne.

"Really?" Pam suddenly looked worried. "I'm a church organist and youth director. I can't be sticking dollar bills in men's underwear." She turned to Jennifer. "Can I?"

Before Jennifer could answer, the limo stopped. The window separating the partygoers from the driver was lowered. In a heavy New York accent, the driver announced, "Hey, ladies, we're here."

Jennifer asked, "Where is here?"

"Thank you, Vincent," replied Yvonne. "Shall we ladies? The entertainment awaits."

Vincent came around, and opened the door. First out was a clearly enthusiastic Nicole, followed closely by Vicki and Yvonne.

Pam downed the rest of her champagne, put down the flute, and declared, "Oh well, let's see what happens." And out of the car she went.

Jennifer remained seated.

Joan leaned in and whispered, "Trust me."

The two friends looked at each other.

Jennifer smiled and nodded. "Of course." They followed the other women out into the night, with the sound of ocean waves in the distance.

"This doesn't seem like the right place," commented Nicole with more bewilderment in her voice than usual.

Six attractive women, dressed in short, fashionable dresses and high heels, appearing ready to hit a nightclub, stood in a driveway looking at a very large, gray-shingled beach house. No lights could be detected through the sizeable windows.

Yvonne said, "Oh, it's the right place." She walked confidently to the front door, and opened it. Turning back to the others, she called, "Well, coming girls?"

Joan pushed Jennifer into the lead. "We most certainly are."

Jennifer looked skeptically at Yvonne, and took a few tentative steps into the dark home. "Okay, what's going on?"

Lights suddenly flooded a huge great room, quickly followed by shouts of "Surprise!" echoing in the air. Another ten women had been waiting in the dark.

Jennifer greeted additional friends from church, two assistants from her firm, and three clients of that business.

One of those clients was Carla Young, a New York City money manager and owner of this beach home.

Carla threw her arms around Jennifer, and said, "Welcome, my heroine."

"Wow. Why would I possibly be your heroine, Carla?"

"Not only do I value your firm's work, but... And I know I shouldn't bring this up at your bachelorette party and that it's old news, but I have to. That press conference was poetic justice."

After Jennifer's first husband, Congressman Ted Brees, confessed to having a lengthy affair with his chief of staff, Kerri Bratton, and stated his intention to leave his wife, Jennifer decided not to play the political good wife. Instead, she held a press conference exposing her soon-to-be-ex-husband as a liar and a cheat.

Though receiving similar kudos over the nearly two years since, Jennifer was still not completely at ease with her decision to hold that press conference, an insecurity that she had confided to Joan on a number of occasions.

Carla quickly plowed ahead. "But never mind that. You must be wondering about your bachelorette party coming to my home? Let's head over there."

All furniture in the great room had been moved out, so that a stone fireplace and floor-to-ceiling windows were joined by a stage. Four microphones on stands, a drum set, an electric guitar and a base guitar waited on the stage.

The short, petite, and tanned Carla shuttled Jennifer onto the stage, and positioned her between the two center mikes. "We have special guests just for you, Jen." She turned Jennifer to face the audience of fourteen, and reached up from behind to place her hands over Jennifer's eyes.

Leaning her head around the taller Jennifer, Carla announced, "Ladies, please hold your appreciation as they take their positions, and until I allow our guest of honor to drink in the scene."

Nonetheless, one yelp, a giggle and a few gasps leaked out.

With Jennifer's eyes still covered, a soothing male voice crooned, "Jennifer Shaw, we've reunited for you. I hope you remember this little song."

Drums thundered. Guitar strings screamed. Carla pulled her hands away, as Jennifer jumped in surprise. This 36-year-old woman's face transformed into that of a teenager's stunned look, shocked and overjoyed at who surrounded her.

Call Us Men, so hot during the early nineties, had not played together in more than a dozen years. Yet, here they were, starting out with their number one single "Don't Be Dancing With That Guy."

The lead singer, Tony, indicated that Jennifer should dance with him. After some prodding – though not very much – Jennifer kicked her high heels off the stage and, to screams of delight from her friends, danced on stage with the band she had been infatuated with during high school and college.

Chapter 5

At the same time that two Cole Haans flew through the air in a Westhampton beach house, Stephen Grant debated whether he should throw away the two cards in his hand.

He decided to go with a jack and a seven, both hearts, coolly tossing two chips into the middle of the green felt table. "Call."

The dealer said, "And the flop." He turned three cards over in the middle of the table: ten of spades, ten of hearts, and eight of hearts.

Well, this might work out, Grant thought.

In his time with the Navy SEALs, then the CIA, and subsequently, for nearly eleven years now, as a pastor, Grant gained expertise in reading people. A gambler would call it picking up on another player's tells.

The gray-haired, slightly overweight man to Grant's immediate left, in a yellow Hawaiian shirt featuring surfers and palm trees, wasn't interested in hiding anything. After seeing the flop, his exhale exposed disappointment. The quick attempt to recover with a swig of beer, a joke and a smile signaled a bluff. "Fifty, if any of you have the courage." Tom Stone was a man ill at ease with deception of any kind.

To the left of Stone was a short, well-built man dressed in khaki pants and a buttoned-up, dark brown polo shirt.

He intensely stared at the flop, and then checked his hole cards. Grant knew a right hand running through his very short blond hair meant a good hand, while a bet followed by a hand cradling a chin or covering a mouth, as if in deep thought, indicated a bluff. But the man's displeasure was apparent to all. With a grunt, Ron McDermott said, "Fold."

Next in line was a tougher read. It wasn't because the athletic, early twenty-something was a young poker wizard who'd perfected his game online. To the contrary, Scott Larson had little idea of what was going on, and clearly felt uncomfortable with poker altogether. But that made him a wild card at the table, not bound by poker strategy or common sense. "Um, I guess, call." It was more question than conviction on the part of St. Mary's young choir director.

The lawyer was next to make a decision. Grant failed to detect any tells. But that was because George Kraus took few, if any, risks. His conservative attire – light blue button-down shirt and dark blue pants – and the conservative cut of his brown hair were both perfect reflections of his style of play. He only bet when possessing a competitive hand. "Too rich for me." He tossed his cards aside.

The last two at the table, however, truly challenged Grant.

A fit, crew-cut, raspy-voiced man oozed confidence, and he picked his fights carefully. Grant could barely distinguish between a bluff, and a bet made from a position of strength. This guy was very good. The only hint Grant picked up on was that a bluff tended to come just a bit quicker than other wagers. It didn't matter this time. Sean McEnany declared, "I'm out as well."

Finally, to Grant's immediate right was a gentle, calm black man. He appeared younger than he actually was, with only some specks of gray in his hair, hinting at 60 not being far off. Grant knew Glenn Oliver was a poker veteran. At the table, his smooth, relaxed actions never varied, no matter what his hole cards happened to be. "Fifty, and another thirty."

Grant already knew what he was going to do. But per his set ritual, he paused, looked each player still in the game in the eyes, and then bet. "I'm in for the eighty. Call." The odds were not good, but he could not walk away from a potential straight flush.

Tom called, but Scott folded, and seemed relieved to do so.

The turn rewarded Grant with the nine of hearts. *Nice.*

Another smile and bluff came from Stone. And another raise from Glenn. Grant tossed in the 90, but the raise pushed the bluffer to fold.

The river card mattered not. Grant knew he had the hand won, even if Glenn had pocket tens.

Glenn bet 75. Grant saw that and raised another 75. His raise was called.

Grant revealed his straight flush – all hearts seven through jack.

"Nicely played," said Glenn, who turned over his pocket tens.

"Ouch, tough break, Glenn," Grant said.

"If my quick math is right, that was the biggest pot. Nine bucks," said Sean, who was playing dealer and host for the night.

Stephen had been in Sean's basement once before. That time, Grant quickly passed through this main room with its Vegas look, including the poker table the eight men sat at now, a big screen television, assorted comfortable chairs, a billiards table, and a well-stocked bar. Behind a shelving unit in the adjacent utility room was a metal door, protected by high-tech security, leading into a computer and communications room. On that occasion, Sean McEnany, former Army Ranger and current vice president with a firm doing contract corporate and government security, provided Grant with some valuable information in the midst of a crisis. McEnany remained something of a mystery to Grant, but he also had become a friend, and someone Grant felt like he could rely upon for help at St. Mary's.

Tonight, Sean provided the supplies and setting for Stephen's bachelor party, featuring a huge spread of hot and cold party food, a wide choice of beer and other alcoholic beverages, a steady, background stream of current-day country music – Grant's favorite – and poker.

Grant responded to Sean's remark on taking the pot. "The night is still young, and besides, I don't think this would put me in a higher tax bracket."

"Apparently your soon-to-be-wife will, though," remarked Tom Stone, with a smile, which generated a particularly robust laugh from Ron McDermott. Stone, an Anglican priest at St. Bartholomew's Church, and McDermott, a Roman Catholic priest at St. Luke's Church and School, were Grant's closest friends, with the three making a rather unique ecumenical trinity.

McDermott added, "Ah, Stephen, the burdens of marrying a wildly successful career woman."

"Somebody's got to do it, and it's obviously not going to be you, Ron," Grant parried.

George Kraus, who always seemed so serious, observed, "Pastor, I still don't think you need to give up your church salary. Doesn't seem right to me. The church should pay you."

"George, don't worry. It's something that Jen and I will be able to do, and are happy to do."

"And it's allowing us to bring on a second pastor," added Glenn, who spent a good deal of time at St. Mary's as the head of buildings and grounds.

"Ah, Zackary Charmichael. Fresh out of seminary, right?" asked Tom.

"That's right, a newbie," replied Grant.

Stone added, "Newbies, ugh. I'll say a prayer for you."

Ron interjected, "For him? How about a prayer for Zackary Charmichael having to deal day in and day out with Pastor Grant? Now that warrants prayer."

"Funny," said Grant.

"Okay, gentlemen, this not only is the tamest bachelor party I've ever thrown, but the church talk has got to go," interrupted Sean.

"Sorry, are we cramping your style, Sean?" asked Stephen.

"I'll be alright." Sean got up from his seat, and started heading over to the oak bar. "If you need another draft, bring your mug over to the bar. Or grab a bottle from the fridge. Who was drinking the G&T?"

George answered, "That's me, and I'll have another."

Sean said, "Sounds good. And for Scott, who does not drink and clearly feels uncomfortable with poker, how about another Coke?"

"Thanks, that'd be great, Mr. McEnany."

Sean stopped and looked at Scott. "If you ever call me 'Mr. McEnany' again, I will hurt you. Understood?"

Stephen came to Scott's defense. "Hey, give Scott a break. He volunteered to be the designated driver tonight. And I think we're corrupting him with drink and poker."

"By the way," Ron commented, "I was watching *Prohibition* the other night, that Ken Burns documentary. And I found out that the only two Protestant churches that didn't support a ban on intoxicating beverages were the Episcopalians and the Lutherans." McDermott looked at his two friends – Stone and Grant. "Knowing how corrupting you can be, I'm not surprised." Then McDermott took a big gulp of beer to go with his smirk.

Chapter 6

Ninety minutes after surprising Jennifer, Call Us Men finished playing their hits, as well as the non-hits that only hard core fans like Jennifer longed to hear. The group mingled, signed autographs and took photos with each guest at the bachelorette party.

The stretch SUV limousine left Carla Young's beach house just before 2:00 AM, arriving at Jennifer's home 25 minutes later.

Her tan, Tuscany villa-style home with terracotta roof sat on a two-plus acre strip along an inlet in Center Moriches on Long Island's south shore. Since the mini-compound – with separate garage, Jacuzzi, pool and bungalow, tennis court, putting green and dock – had been owned by her family before she married Ted Brees, no doubt existed that Jennifer would be keeping it in the divorce.

Pam Larson, who was far drunker than the number of drinks she had consumed would seem to dictate, was guided to a room and poured into bed. Joan and Nicole quickly disappeared to their respective accommodations, too. That left Jennifer, Vicki and Yvonne sitting around a table in the cool night air on the patio, enjoying a bottle of Pinot Grigio.

"I'm tired, but not interested in going to bed," said Jennifer. "This has been a wonderful night. Thank you so much." She raised a glass to her cousin and her business partner.

"Your expression when first seeing Call Us Men was priceless, Sis," said Vicki.

Jennifer smiled. "I still can't believe you were able to get them to come. It was amazing. I felt like a teenager again."

Vicki observed, "It was all Yvonne and Carla."

"No," corrected Yvonne, "it was all Carla. She was an investor, I think, in the company that gave Call Us Men their first deal." She continued, "By the way, if you don't mind me asking, why do you two call each other 'Sis'? I thought you were cousins."

Jennifer answered, "We are cousins. But growing up, we spent most summers together, and our grandmother said at some point, 'You two are like inseparable sisters.' We liked that, so we started calling each other 'Sis,' and have done so ever since." She looked at Vicki. "Right, Sis?"

Vicki replied, "Absolutely, Sis."

Yvonne took a sip of wine. "Do you mind if I ask another personal question, Jen?"

"Fire away."

"Well, I don't want to put a damper on things, but since I care, I have to ask: Are you jumping into this wedding thing kind of quick? I mean you were only divorced – how long ago? – a year and a half?"

Jennifer smiled. "Yes."

"Don't you think you're rushing things?" asked Yvonne.

Jennifer mockingly responded, "Gee, maybe you're right. Let's call the whole thing off."

"I'm serious."

"I know you are. But you have nothing to worry about," assured Jennifer. "Getting married 18 months after a divorce sounds like an unhealthy rebound, and if you were doing it, I'd say the same thing you just did. But over the

past nearly two years with Stephen, I've never felt so..."
She paused. "I'm not sure, exactly, how to put it." Jennifer
took a sip of wine. "I've never been more sure of anything
in my life."

"Didn't you feel that way at first with Ted?" said
Yvonne.

"Actually, no. I certainly thought I loved him. But when
things came apart, I recognized that there was an
underlying unease, like each of us were acting like a
married couple. As it turns out, of course, he was just
acting. But even for me, I was stretching things, convincing
myself that we had a good marriage and part of this acting
was just the politics. You know, having to behave a certain
way because he was in the public eye. But we wound up
doing the same thing in private as well. There was a lack
of depth."

"And how do you know that you and Stephen have this
depth?" Yvonne responded.

"It's not just one thing, but several. I've never been more
at ease with anyone in my life. Take this the wrong way
and it could sound really sad for a couple just about to get
married, but we're comfortable together."

Yvonne let out a small, disapproving grunt.

Jennifer continued, "Oh, shut up, and let me finish. At
the same time, no man has ever made me feel more
excited, special, and respected. He's a bit of a romantic as
well, and by the way, darn hot."

"True. Six feet, fit, black hair and those green eyes. He
is hot," chimed in Vicki.

"Glad you approve, Sis," said Jennifer. She looked back
at Yvonne. "In addition, Stephen is a good man. Again, I
know how that can sound. And it sure doesn't mean that
he's perfect. Far from it, and I let him know that. But I
know I can count on Stephen in a way that I never could
Ted."

"Okay..." started Yvonne.

Jennifer, however, interrupted. "Most importantly, though, we have the same idea of what marriage ultimately is – a gift from God. Our faith makes us one, and it completes us, together."

Yvonne got up from her chair, walked around the table, and leaned down to Jennifer. She squeezed her partner's hand, kissed her on top of the head, and whispered, "I'm happy for you. Forget I even asked. And quite frankly, I'm jealous."

Chapter 7

It was atypical for the Reverend Dr. Harrison Piepkorn, president of the second largest Lutheran church body in the U.S., to make a special trip from St. Louis to Long Island to perform a wedding.

Piepkorn confessed ulterior motives.

Sure, it's nice to preside at the marriage of a fellow pastor. But Piepkorn also wanted to thank Pastor Stephen Grant for faithfully serving in his stead at an historic ecumenical event nearly two years ago, as well as for Grant's effort, though ultimately in vain, to protect the late Pope Augustine. But there was more. It had been unique, to say the least, to receive requests from the Vatican and the United States government to have Grant replace him at that gathering. At the time, Piepkorn had been given some information about the previous CIA career of Grant. But on this journey, he finally had the opportunity to talk with the man face to face.

During their dinner two nights before the wedding, the pastors hit it off, though Piepkorn's curiosity about Grant probably failed to be fully satiated.

But for those in Grant's post-CIA life, none had gotten the full story. Nor would they ever get most, or even some, of the details. The only question for Grant was: How much would he eventually reveal to Jennifer?

The mid-June weather – sunny and warm with a light breeze – was about as perfect as it got for a late afternoon wedding.

Standing at the top of the front steps of the Tudor-style St. Mary's Lutheran Church, Stephen had to restrain himself from going inside to make sure all was set, as he usually would, if it were not his own wedding.

Glenn Oliver, one of Stephen's ushers, was watching. He said, "No need to check on things. All is well. President Piepkorn has a certain air of authority, after all."

Stephen smiled, "Indeed, he does."

His other usher, Ron McDermott, asked, "Are we getting nervous?"

"Actually, it's more a sense of relief that the time has arrived."

Tom Stone, the best man, added, "But with cars now arriving, the bride will not be far behind. So, I am going to take you inside to wait for the ceremony to get under way. Can't see the bride before the wedding, of course."

The two men walked through the narthex and into the sanctuary. The room combined dark wood beams, off-white walls, ceilings rising to points, and etched glass windows along the sides featuring moments in the earthly life of Jesus. Behind the altar hung a large Crucifix, and at the other end, behind the choir loft, was a large, circular window with Jesus as the teacher etched in it.

Stephen and Jennifer decided against any decoration inside the sanctuary, so as to not detract from the room's purpose and beauty.

Tom and Stephen moved to the right of the altar, and into a small room where the Altar Guild normally did their work. The two eventually were joined by Glenn and Ron after they finished ushering guests into the pews, and Jennifer and her bridesmaids were ready to enter.

When Pam Larson started playing the organ, Tom said to Stephen, "It's time for your march to the gallows, my friend." He winked at Stephen, and pointed him to the door. Stephen, Tom, Ron and Glenn took their positions in front of the altar.

The first bridesmaid, Yvonne Hudson, walked down the aisle in a light blue, V-neck, knee-length, chiffon dress, followed by the similarly dressed Vicki Dart, and then Joan Kraus, the matron of honor, in a one-shoulder, sleeveless, knee-length, also light blue dress.

But each striking woman, along with the more than 300 people, including some fifty not directly invited, receded into the background for Stephen. All he could do was try to focus on the back of the church, searching for a glimpse of his soon-to-be bride.

Finally.

Stephen saw Jennifer in a strapless, white gown, pearl earrings, and a diamond bracelet on her right wrist. She carried a cascading bouquet of blue stargazer lilies, Dutch iris, calla lilies, wildflowers, and blue and white baby's breath.

Stephen Grant, former Navy SEAL and one-time highly skilled CIA operative, was not prepared for the sudden weakness that struck his knees. While Jennifer smiled and seemed to glide forward, her eyes warmly focused on him in this sea of family and friends.

George Kraus, in a neat, black tuxedo similar to the ones Stephen, Tom and the ushers donned, positively beamed as he escorted Jennifer down the aisle. He kissed her lightly upon arriving in front of the altar, and then guided her next to Stephen.

Stephen's experience during the ceremony was unlike anything he previously experienced in a church. Part of his brain engaged appropriately in what was going on, but the overriding effect was being disconnected from all around him, except Jennifer.

After vows and rings were exchanged, and they were declared husband and wife, Pastor Piepkorn, with a hint of

his South Carolina upbringing, said, "The almighty and
gracious God abundantly grant you His favor and sanctify
and bless you with the blessing given to Adam and Eve in
Paradise, that you may please Him in both body and soul
and live together in holy love until your life's end."

All replied, "Amen." That seemed to snap Stephen back
to being fully engaged with his surroundings.

Stephen and Jennifer rose from kneeling positions.
Piepkorn smiled and said, "You may kiss the bride."

The wedding guests applauded, and as the couple's kiss
persisted, a few cheers even broke out.

Jennifer mischievously whispered, "We'll pick this up
later."

"We certainly will, Mrs. Grant," Stephen replied.

After the Lord's Prayer and a final blessing, Jennifer
and Stephen turned to the congregation as Pam Larson
began playing and the choir started singing Bach's "Jesu,
Joy of Man's Desiring." The newlyweds proceeded down the
aisle.

As he walked with his new wife's arm interlocked with
his own, joy, excitement and anticipation swirled for
Stephen. But his happiness overwhelmingly came down to
a deep sense of fulfillment.

This is right. Thank you, Lord.

* * *

The simple but elegant reception was a tribute to
Jennifer's style and humility.

Long Island wedding receptions are not known for their
understatement. Rather, they often turn out to be
ostentatious, not to mention loud, affairs.

Jennifer shunned the local wedding factories, and chose
a charming restaurant on the North Fork nestled on a
small pond. The owner was willing to close for the night to
host the reception, as the 250 wedding guests would easily

top his average dinner attendance. Beyond the ambiance, Jennifer appreciated their entrée options of duck breast with sautéed pears, seared sea scallops, spinach and mushroom stuffed chicken breast, or marinated and grilled strip steak.

Rather than a band, she selected a DJ who, per her instructions, kept the music in the realm of new country, recent but not too recent pop and older rock, with some Big Band and swing sprinkled in, covering the musical preferences of the newly married couple.

Everything inside the restaurant was ready, and the wedding party took time to stop by the pond for photos.

While looking forward to the reception, Stephen found himself wanting to extend this time with Jennifer and the wedding party. These were their closest friends, and Grant reveled in the moment together.

Tom kept up a steady flow of jokes of widely varying quality, with his wife, Maggie, on the side trying to make sure her husband did not get carried away.

Ron and Glenn seemed to be engaged in a good-natured disagreement over the Mets and Yankees. Ron was defending the troubled Mets, with Glenn merely noting the Bronx Bombers' typical excellence.

Meanwhile, Jennifer was posing with Joan, Vicki and Yvonne for photos.

Hmmm. Fifteen years ago, not only couldn't imagine getting married, but wouldn't really have had anyone to be in a wedding party.

Since finding Jennifer, Stephen came to realize that it was she, especially when smiling and laughing as was the case now, who spread a beauty onto things around her.

Jennifer broke his wonderment. "What are you thinking, my love?"

"Well, if it doesn't sound too corny, I was admiring your beauty, and appreciating our friends. There was a time, not all that long ago, that none of this was in my life, and I didn't really care. Now, I see blessings."

"You're right, that is corny." She kissed him. "And it's sweet." She gently rested her head on his shoulder, until the photographer called them over for some final shots.

A few minutes later, the entire group started back to the restaurant and reception.

As they strolled on the green grass, Maggie said, "Jennifer, I have to apologize again for missing your bachelorette party."

Jennifer replied, "Maggie, please, two kids sick. Don't worry about it. Everyone better?"

"They're good. Thanks. But my husband here remains in trouble."

Tom protested, "Oh, come on. You practically commanded me to go to Stephen's bachelor party that night, if memory serves."

"But I missed a private performance of a reunited Call Us Men." With Tom not looking, Maggie smiled at Jennifer.

Tom continued, "But how could I have known...?"

Ron interrupted, "Really, Tom. What kind of husband are you, anyway? You can play cards anytime, but how often will Maggie get the chance to hear Call Us Men?"

Maggie added, "Probably never again."

"Hear that, Tom? Never again. That's terrible." Ron shook his head in exaggeration, and then laughed. The others joined in.

Tom moved closer to Ron, and said, "Threw me right under the bus. Thanks, buddy."

Ron said, "Hey, what are friends for?"

"I won't forget this," replied Tom.

* * *

At the reception, Jennifer and Stephen moved from table to table, making time to speak with all of their guests.

They approached what Jennifer during the planning process had come to call the "Seminary Table." Here were the five men with whom Stephen had spent most of his time at the seminary in Fort Wayne, Indiana, along with their respective spouses.

Stephen noticed that no one seemed to be talking. "Why so quiet, group?"

Pastor Graham Foster, probably Grant's closest friend throughout much of seminary, answered, "Our brothers disapprove of where my congregation is being led, but it's certainly nothing to concern yourself with, especially on a day of such blessings."

The rest of the table unenthusiastically agreed with Foster, and more pleasant introductions and interactions that had begun earlier on the receiving line were expanded.

Only one of the pastors in the group was older than Grant. That was Jacob Stout. Known as "Big Jake" at seminary, he was a retired high school teacher and football coach. Even in his early sixties now, he was an imposing, solid six foot three. As Jennifer started speaking to each individual, Stout pulled Grant to the side.

"What's up, Jake?" asked Stephen.

In a whisper, Stout said, "Do you know how far Graham has gone down the path of 'ka-ching Christianity'?"

"What is "ka-ching Christianity'?"

"You know, prosperity preaching."

"No, that's not Graham," protested Stephen.

"It wasn't Graham at sem, but when have you spoken with him last?"

Stephen reflected, "Well, other than happy birthdays and passing FYIs via email, I guess it's been several years."

"Well, his church down in the D.C. area has become all about focus groups and marketing fads. Lots of getting right with God so you can receive blessings from God. And he's got a new book coming out. Guess what the title is?"

Grant said, "Should I be afraid to guess?"

Before Jake could answer, Jennifer returned to Stephen's arm. "Can I interrupt, Pastor Stout, and take my husband?"

"Of course, Jennifer. And you have to call me Big Jake."

"He must like you, Jen. Very few get the thumbs up on 'Big Jake.'"

Stout said, "What's not to like?"

"You're absolutely correct, Jake," agreed Stephen.

"Flattery, gentlemen, will get you everywhere."

Before moving on to the next table, though, Graham stepped in front of Jennifer and Stephen. "Can I just speak to you both for a brief moment?"

Grant noted that his friend looked a heck of a lot better than some dozen years ago. He was no longer a bit overweight, but instead, muscular, even chiseled. His formerly unkempt blond hair was now gelled and spiked. And his slightly crooked and tad yellowish teeth were now perfectly aligned, almost blindingly white, and shown off by a broad, seemingly ever-present smile. He even sounded different.

"Naturally, Graham," answered Jennifer.

"Stephen, don't take this the wrong way, but I was reluctant to provide a gift to either the LCMS World Relief or the school you suggested in the invitation."

Stephen began, "That's alright, Graham…"

But Foster continued, "If you don't mind, Margo" – he looked over and, of course, smiled at his wife still seated at the table – "and I decided to give a sizeable donation, in your names, of course, to an international group I'm involved with that works to help Christians in developing nations start up their own businesses."

The economist in Jennifer immediately emerged. "That's interesting."

"It most certainly is," said Graham. "I don't want to monopolize you two, but when you get back from the honeymoon, give me call, and I'll provide all of the details. Or, better yet, it would be just super if the two of you could visit us in Washington some time soon."

"I'm in D.C. regularly with my business," said Jennifer.

"That's wonderful. Do you get back on the old turf any more, Stephen?"

"No, actually, I haven't been in Washington in a few years."

"Well, you will have to come, visit New Jerusalem, and stay with us. By the way, my first book is being published shortly. I'll send a copy. Now, get back to the rest of your guests."

That is a new Graham. He was never that fit, nor that smooth. And what's the deal with the smiling and the teeth?

Chapter 8

Once it was reported that Senator Jimmy Farrell's decapitated head had been found, Long Island Congressman Ted Brees began planning and maneuvering to be appointed to the now-vacant U.S. Senate seat.

Brees and his chief of staff, Kerri Bratton, who also happened to be his top political adviser and lover, gushed in private at how everything surrounding Farrell's death aligned neatly for Brees.

The other New York senator was from upstate, so it was likely that Farrell's replacement would come from the New York City metropolitan area. For good measure, just like Brees, New York Governor Robert Shimansky was one of those moderate-liberal Republicans who occasionally got elected in a Blue State like New York.

Now, as his former wife was getting remarried, Brees sat at a small, dark cherry wood table in the Breakfast Room of the Governor's Mansion in Albany, waiting for Governor Shimansky.

"Good afternoon, Ted," Shimansky said as he entered the bright and airy room with large windows. "Sorry to keep you waiting."

The fashion and physical differences between the two men did not reflect their close political alignment. With his neatly cut brown hair, slight tan, and perfectly tailored light gray suit for his five foot, ten inch frame, the 42-year-old Brees looked like he just fell out of a men's clothing catalogue. Meanwhile, though the calendar said Shimansky was only seven years older than Brees, he looked as if he had two decades on the Congressman. Shimansky was short, a bit overweight, bald, and dressed for a regular-guy late Saturday afternoon at home in jeans and a University at Albany dark blue sweatshirt.

"Good to see you, Bob," said Brees. They shook hands and sat across from each other at the table.

Shimansky got down to business. "So, let's talk Jimmy Farrell."

"Terrible. What a way to go."

"Yeah, you can say that again. I wouldn't wish that on anyone," said Shimansky. "But I've got to say that I'm not exactly torn up that he's dead. I couldn't stand that son of a bitch. There's no way he should have been a senator from New York. And he wouldn't have been if the media hadn't crucified our guy during that campaign for some petty bull shit."

"True enough," replied Brees.

"Anyway, dead is dead, and now I have to pick someone to take his seat. But since this is a congressional election year, as you know, my pick would have to run for the seat this November."

Brees added, "Yes, but even a few months of incumbency can be a big political advantage."

"Damn right," said Shimansky. "The Conservative Party jack asses are demanding that I appoint one of them because Farrell was a Conservative. I had to kiss Conservative ass to get this office, but I'm done. When it comes to a Senate seat, they can go screw themselves. I make our Republicans happy by picking a Republican, and most of the rest of the state either doesn't see any real difference between Republicans and Conservatives, or they don't care. Farrell's victory was seen as a freak event at the time, and other than the few Conservative faithful, no one else is going to take me to task for appointing a fellow Republican."

"I agree," said Brees.

Shimansky laughed. "I'm sure you do. Okay, here's the deal. I think you fit the bill for what we need. You're moderate on the social crap. I've noticed that with this economy and concerns over federal debt, you've stepped up the rhetoric to show you're tough on spending and borrowing. All good."

"Thanks," said Brees.

"Now, you know I would never tell you how to vote?"

"Of course."

"But there are three issues that I would hope the next senator from New York would support. Number one: While spending obviously needs to be cut, New York cannot afford to see any further reductions in federal dollars coming back here. After all, we send a heck of a lot more down to Washington than we get back. Making that balance of payments even worse would be unacceptable."

Brees chimed in, "I have the same worries, Bob. In the House, I've fought hard for our fair share in the first CD. If I were senator, it goes without saying that I would continue the same effort for the entire state."

"Good, I thought so," said Shimansky. "Number two: The banks and Wall Street. That schmuck Democrat Stan Wilson has been hammering away on Wall Street in the Senate, and all I hear are threats of moving more operations out of state. We need some balance from this other Senate seat, someone that will work to block the really bad legislation, and thereby open some important opportunities for campaign support among these firms and individuals."

"Bob," assured Ted, "New York is still the financial capital of the world, and any senator from this state should be working to strengthen that position."

"Okay, the last item will seem odd, but it's almost personal."

With a new look of caring concentration, Brees leaned in, "What is it, Bob?"

"You're onboard this effort to begin moving much of our foreign economic aid away from giving money to governments in developing nations, and instead, getting it into the hands of start-ups and small businesses in these countries?"

"Yes, it gets big support from both sides of the political aisle, and polls off the charts. Last survey I saw, 74 percent of likely voters agreed with the idea."

"Right. And it's supposed to get rolling as a pilot project, beginning in one nation and, depending on how it does, expanding from there?"

"Yes, that's the plan, at this point," answered Brees. "But anything can happen, as you well know, in committee and once on the floor."

"I understand that there's a debate over a few possible nations to kick things off."

"The California and Arizona delegations, for example, are pushing Mexico. They argue that it will help stem illegal immigration. Others are pushing an African nation, though they haven't settled on which one as yet, hoping to score some race-card political points. Among more conservative Republicans, they've latched on to Belarus as a way to help bury the last remnant of communism in Eastern Europe. A Christian group's been working the values and free enterprise angle there as well."

Shimansky reported, "I don't know if you were aware or not, but my family was from Minsk. In fact, I was born there."

"I knew you were from Eastern Europe, but did not know where exactly."

"When I was a baby, my father and his brother decided to escape the hells of communism. As told to me, it was an undertaking seemingly doomed to failure. In fact, my aunt, uncle and two cousins were captured and executed."

Brees said, "I'm sorry."

Governor Shimanksy continued, "But somehow – due to dumb luck, some bribes, a series of close calls, and perhaps a little help from above – we eventually found our way into West Germany. My parents risked it all, wound up in the United States, changed their son's first name to Robert, and now he's the governor of New York."

"That's amazing," said Brees. "You should write a book."

"I just might one day. But in the meantime, you can see why it's important to me that Belarus be the choice for this pilot aid project. The new Prime Minister is sending signals that an openness is possible, and he's talking in friendly ways to international businesses."

Brees smiled. "What kind of Republican would I be if I were not ready to strike a blow to undermine the last, lingering bit of communism in Eastern Europe?"

Shimansky said, "In that case, Senator Brees, let's contact our staff and pick a good time for a press conference announcing my selection."

Chapter 9

The gleaming, white Gulfstream G650, with blue and silver striping running along its side below eight round windows, sat patiently on the tarmac. The lights glowed and the Rolls-Royce BR725 engines were ready to thrust this ultra-luxury private aircraft into the night sky over Republic Airport in East Farmingdale, Long Island.

As the couple destined for a honeymoon in California's Napa Valley approached, waiting was a beautiful, brunette flight attendant in a short, light blue uniform with "Casino Beach" and a small palm tree embroidered just above the left breast. She extended a hand of welcome.

"Mr. and Mrs. Grant, my name is Candy Welles," she said with a bright smile. "Congratulations on your marriage."

"Thank you, Ms. Welles," replied Stephen Grant.

"Yes, thank you very much," added Jennifer Grant.

"Please, it's Candy, and follow me," instructed Candy, as she ascended the eight steps into the plane.

The just-married Grants followed her into the cabin. The carpeting was white and plush. They moved past a white leather seat on the left and a well-appointed bathroom on the right, into a small kitchen area, and then through a door into a sitting area featuring six more white leather seats, along with a small couch and a flat screen television.

Candy said, "If you would both buckle in and get comfortable, Captain Barnes and First Officer Church will have us airborne in just a couple of minutes. Once at a cruising level, I'll return with more information. If that is alright with you?"

Stephen noted that Jennifer was a bit distracted, so he replied, "That would be wonderful, Candy. Again, thank you."

Candy went forward and took the seat across from the lavatory, while Stephen and Jennifer buckled into seats next to each other.

Stephen commented, "This is the most comfortable airplane seat I've ever been in. In fact, it could be the most comfortable seat I've sat in anywhere." He took his bride's hand in his. "Your father has a nice little plane here, Jen."

"My father knows how to treat himself well," she responded.

"Yes, well, a private flight to and from Napa Valley, and a week at a spa combine to make for a very generous wedding present," observed Grant.

"Even if he didn't make the actual wedding," she added.

"Okay, given your shaky relationship with your father, how about we just treat this as an anonymous gift, otherwise this honeymoon might get off on the wrong foot?"

Jennifer looked at Stephen, and her slight frown melted away into a smile. "You're right. I'm sorry." They leaned in and kissed, with their lips eventually separated as the G650 bolted forward on the runway.

A few minutes later, Candy returned with a tray of chocolate-dipped, fresh strawberries and a 1996 bottle of Dom Perignon. She poured flute glasses for both Jennifer and Stephen. "I trust you'll enjoy this. It's one of the best Dom vintages."

"I'm sure we will," said Stephen. They both sipped the expensive bubbly.

Candy continued, "I'm here to provide whatever you might need during our flight, which should take about four-and-a-half hours. But I, of course, will maintain your privacy. After all, this is the beginning of your honeymoon." She smiled. "I'll be in the forward attendant seat listening to music or watching a movie with headphones on, and this door will be closed. If you need anything at all, please touch a button on any chair, and I'll be signaled." She pointed to the back of the room. "Through that door is the stateroom. Does all of this meet your expectations and needs?"

Jennifer said, "Candy, this far exceeds any and all of our expectations or needs. It is much appreciated."

"Wonderful." Candy smiled again, and closed the door behind her.

"Flying on one of the most expensive and fastest private aircrafts in the world with a flight attendant named Candy. You can't make this stuff up," chuckled Stephen. He took a deeper drink of the champagne.

Jennifer looked at him. "And…"

"And my smart, exciting and seductive traveling companion happens to be my wife as well."

"Nicely done, my husband."

"I thought so."

Jennifer placed her glass in a holder next to her seat, stood up and strolled about the cabin. She stopped to look out one of the windows.

Grant could not take his eyes off her. *I am the most blessed man alive.*

"I have to see what the stateroom looks like," Jennifer said. She opened the door. "Oooh, nice. It's bigger than you might think, Stephen."

Grant was taking another sip of champagne, and was about to respond when he heard the door click closed behind him.

Well, Mrs. Grant, what are you up to?

He smiled, as his anticipation grew.

Grant rose, decided to kick off his shoes, walked to the door and opened it. He was surprised to see the bed empty. But as he took a step into the room, the door was pushed closed from behind. Jennifer moved forward, pressing her body against his, and wrapping her arms around him.

"Tell me, Stephen," she whispered looking up into his eyes, "are you a member of the mile-high club?"

"I am not."

"Nor I," she replied. "Should we join?"

"You read my thoughts."

Chapter 10

Having landed at Napa County Airport – or "Skyport to the Wine Country" – in the wee hours of the morning, and with the time difference, Jennifer and Stephen had no plans for Sunday at The Meritage Resort and Spa in Napa Valley.

They did manage to attend a Catholic Mass held in the hotel's unique Our Lady of the Grapes chapel, with a soaring wood-beam ceiling. The rest of Sunday was spent sampling wines in the Meritage's Trinitas Tasting Room, uniquely built in a cave, followed by time alone in their room overlooking the vineyards, along with some room service.

On Monday, the newlyweds set their sights on lunch in the resort's Siena restaurant. As they entered the expansive, bright, light colored room, Jennifer looked at a group of four men. They were seated around a table positioned under a large painting of six racehorses making the turn on a dirt track.

After sitting down at their own table, Jennifer whispered, "That's Senator Ellis."

Stephen said, "Who?" He glanced at the table Jennifer was indicating with a tip of her head.

"U.S. Senator Duane Ellis. Liberal Democrat. His family owns a winery somewhere around here. I think that's what

Clive or Yvonne mentioned. He's on the Foreign Relations Committee. We've disagreed on more than a few occasions."

Yvonne Hudson and Clive Vadis were Jennifer's partners in a research firm that served money managers and other investors, focusing mainly on economic, political and legislative trends.

Stephen said, "Have I mentioned how much I love politicians?"

"Just a few times. And I'm not all that fond either, especially given the ex."

"That's a group in need of redemption."

"Not that we're generalizing, Pastor Grant?" Jennifer smirked.

"Of course not," Stephen replied.

"Well, I still have to deal with politicians on a pretty regular basis."

"I did my time with Congress at the agency, but I am fully supportive of my bride's career."

"Good, because here comes Senator Ellis," Jennifer whispered.

Duane Ellis had the relaxed look that often comes with inherited fortunes. His dark blue, summer weight suit, light blue shirt and seersucker tie fit perfectly, which gave the impression that he was not as overweight as he actually was. And his dark, wavy, combed-back hair had a hint of Elvis Presley.

"Jennifer Brees, my favorite conservative economist. How are you?"

Jennifer and Stephen rose to meet the Senator.

She replied, "Senator, it's wonderful to see you, but it's Jennifer Grant now, and this is my husband, Stephen."

Obviously unconcerned by his mistake, Ellis shook hands with Stephen. "A pleasure to meet you, Mr. Grant. You're a lucky man to have such a beautiful and formidable spouse."

"Yes, I know. Thank you, Senator."

Ellis turned back to Jennifer. "It's interesting that I should see you here. I'm meeting with two leaders of the business community in Mexico and a Mexican economic development official about this new foreign aid initiative being debated. You know, possibly shifting our aid emphasis away from handing money over to foreign governments, and instead helping their economies by getting funds to worthy start-ups and small businesses. It polls off the charts. If memory serves, you testified against increasing foreign aid in our committee, so I assume you're onboard with this?"

Jennifer said, "Actually, I'm not a fan, Senator."

"Really? Why?"

Stephen thought the Senator's surprise seemed legitimate.

Jennifer diplomatically answered, "Senator, I'd be more than happy to meet with you and discuss the issue, but might it wait until after I get back from my honeymoon?"

"Your honeymoon?" He glanced at Stephen and back at Jennifer. "How foolish of me. No business talk now, of course. I apologize."

"No reason for an apology," Jennifer reassured.

"I'm going to leave you two alone, and get back to my guests. Please enjoy everything that we offer here in the Napa Valley, and congratulations."

As he turned to go back to his table, the three heads of the others in his party were looking in the direction of Stephen and Jennifer. That's when Stephen recognized one of the guests from Mexico. It had been many years, but it definitely was the same man.

In a low voice, Stephen said to Jennifer, "You're not the only one who knows a person at that table."

"Really?"

"The man in the tan suit."

"Yes."

"He was a player in one of the leading DTOs that ..."

"DTOs?"

"Oh, sorry, drug trafficking organizations. Anyway, the U.S. was cracking down on Colombian drug cartels smuggling cocaine in the late eighties and early nineties, so the cartels subcontracted with various Mexican DTOs. That gentleman was in the leadership of one of those DTOs. I reviewed his file while at the agency."

"Who is he?"

Stephen worked to access a part of his memory that had been archived when he left the CIA behind and became a pastor. Then he found the right file.

"Manny. That's it. Manny... Manuel Rodriguez." Grant was pleased with himself.

Jennifer said, "So, you're telling me that Senator Ellis is meeting with a Mexican drug runner working for a Colombian drug cartel?"

"Actually, from what I read after leaving the agency, the Mexicans pushed out many of the Colombians, and now control most of the cocaine coming into the U.S. Mr. Rodriguez either left that world behind and became legitimate, or he has risen to such power in the drug world that he has the air of legitimacy."

Jennifer smiled and shook her head.

Stephen asked, "What is it?"

"I'm pretty sure that no other Lutheran pastor on the face of the planet has ever had this kind of conversation with his wife."

"Well, I wouldn't bet on that. There are at least a few other pastors that I know of from military or law enforcement backgrounds."

"Okay, what are you going to do now?"

Stephen looked at his menu. "Since I'm still very hungry, I'm going to start with the oysters on a half shell, followed by the chicken and avocado club. Then I'll put in a call with my former colleagues, just to make sure they're aware of Mr. Rodriguez's presence. After that, I took the liberty of making a reservation for a hot-air balloon ride."

Jennifer smiled. "Have I said that I love you today?"

Chapter 11

It was about a half hour since the meeting with Senator Ellis ended, and Manuel Rodriguez was heading toward San Francisco on I-80 W in a black Mercedes SLS AMG Roadster with the top down.

Reaching inside his jacket, Rodriguez pulled out an encrypted mobile phone. The call went directly to Lydia Garcia just south of Monterrey, Mexico.

Speaking in Spanish, Garcia answered and demanded, "Status, Manuel."

"I just left the meeting with Senator Ellis, and he unfortunately had nothing to add to what we already know. It remains a contest between Mexico and Belarus, with an outside chance that an African nation could emerge as a late competitor."

"What about the others in the meeting?"

Rodriguez laughed. "Carlos Luis ably represented the business community, and Jose Mora did well as the government representative."

"Good."

"Did you expect otherwise? After all, the lives of their families are at stake."

Lydia warned, "Do not assume anything, Manuel."

"Yes, of course."

"Stay focused. This could mean hundreds of millions, even billions, of dollars coming from the very American government trying to shut us down."

Manuel replied with a bit of annoyance in his voice. "I know, I know."

"Well, apparently you need some reminding, as you often are too interested in expensive cars and the loose American women that seem to come with them."

With that comment, the call was ended.

Lydia Garcia was a rare combination in the illegal drug business – both a woman and one of the most ruthless and powerful Mexican drug lords.

Manuel tossed the phone onto the seat next to him, and spoke out loud to himself, "Lydia, you are far too serious, not knowing how to appreciate our success." He chuckled. "And let's hope that the young woman I'm going to meet in San Francisco tonight is as loose as you presume."

Manuel spotted a narrow gap between the SUV in front of him in the center lane and a car in the left. The Mercedes Roadster accelerated smoothly and quickly, moving between and beyond the other two vehicles just as they whipped past the tiny, 9-hole Joe Mortara Golf Course on the Solano County Fairgrounds.

Chapter 12

In the FBI's J. Edgar Hoover Building on Pennsylvania Avenue, Ryan Bates entered the office of Supervisory Special Agent Rich Noack.

Noack turned away from his computer terminal, and pulled his chair forward to face Bates. Even when seated, the six foot, six inch, bald Noack dominated the room. He said, "Grab a seat, Ryan."

"Thanks. What's up?"

"I just got a call from Pastor Grant."

"What's he been up to since the Pope Augustine mess and the terror attacks?"

"On his honeymoon actually in Napa Valley."

"Nice."

"Get this. He married the ex-wife of Congressman Ted Brees. Grant saves Jennifer Brees in the shootout at his church, and winds up marrying her."

"Well, Congressman Brees rubbed me the wrong way, so good for her."

"Yeah, Ted Brees is an asshole. Unfortunately, I read this morning that he's been picked by Governor Shimansky to fill Senator Farrell's seat."

Bates shifted in his seat. "Hmmm. Interesting."

"Anyway," Noack continued, "Grant couldn't get a hold of Caldwell over at CIA, so he called me. He's staying at a resort in Napa and stumbled across Senator Duane Ellis meeting with three people from Mexico about this foreign aid for businesses thing that's being kicked around on the Hill. Seems Grant recognized one of the Mexicans, identified him as Manuel Rodriguez. Grant remembered seeing a CIA file in the early nineties on Rodriguez being part of the cocaine trade, and wanted to give us a heads up."

"What's the deal on Rodriguez? Is Grant right?"

"That's what you're going to find out. We have Senator Farrell beheaded – a known practice of Mexican drug gangs – and another U.S. senator meeting with a potential veteran of Mexico's cocaine trade. Get on this quick, Ryan."

"Will do. But I'm going to grab something first from Starbucks to get recharged. You want anything?"

"Something wrong with FBI caffeine?"

"Tastes like crap, and I need something more. Still feeling the weekend."

Noack said, "You wuss." He laughed and shook his head.

Bates stepped out of the office, but then froze when Noack called, "Wait."

Bates leaned back in, "Yes?"

Noack sheepishly said, "Get me a grande Mocha Frappuccino, no whipped cream."

"Right. And you called me a wuss?"

"Hey, I said no whip."

Washington, D.C.'s summer humidity had arrived early, and Bates sweated as he walked away from the FBI building. He pulled a burn phone out.

A male voice answered, "Yes."

Bates said, "They're focused on Rodriguez."

"Thank you."

"You know, I don't like this. It's not what I signed up for."

"No, it isn't. But that's the reality at hand," the voice responded coldly, and the call ended.

Bates entered Starbucks, and dropped the phone in one of the trash cans.

Chapter 13

An unmistakable joy emanated from Ted Brees.

On Wednesday morning, he was joined in the well of the U.S. Senate by the Vice President of the United States, and was sworn in as the junior senator from New York.

The swearing-in was re-enacted later in the old Senate chamber for photographs, colleagues, family and friends, including Kerri Bratton, of course, and Governor Shimansky, who made the trip from New York.

At the subsequent press conference, after thanking Shimansky and the "good people of New York," Brees was asked what his priorities would be while serving in the Senate.

He said, "My goal stays focused on contributing however I can in the effort to return this nation to greatness. Coming into the Senate at this juncture, three issues have my attention in the near term. First, we've got to get federal spending under control, and balance the budget. That's critical. But we also cannot neglect our needs, and that includes making sure that New York gets its fair share of aid for critical projects, especially given how much New Yorkers send to Washington in terms of tax dollars."

A hand shot up from a reporter, but Brees said, "Bill, I'll take your question in a second, let me just touch on the other two points quickly. It is crucial to strike an important balance when it comes to Wall Street. We have to make sure that the excesses of the recent past do not occur again, but at the same time, our financial firms cannot be crippled, with jobs lost, due to misguided and costly regulation. Third, and finally, I think it's time to rethink how U.S. foreign economic aid works, and that's why I'm onboard with the focus shifting to helping entrepreneurs and small businesses rather than governments. And while I think this is how we should proceed eventually with many nations, I support kicking things off in the East European nation of Belarus. That would make a powerful statement to a people who have waited far too long for the arrival of greater freedom and prosperity."

Governor Shimansky smiled. He glanced at a short man with thick glasses in the audience, who nodded with a smile.

In contrast, on the other side of the room, Jose Mora, the Mexican economic development officer back from his California visit with Senator Ellis, showed a strained look, taking a handkerchief from his pocket and patting his forehead.

Brees paused, "Now, for questions. Like I said, you're first, Bill."

Chapter 14

The narrow, three-story Belarus embassy stood inconspicuously on New Hampshire Avenue in northwest Washington, D.C.

Aleksandr Kachan, the short man with thick glasses, wearing an ill-fitting brown suit, knocked on the ambassador's office door.

It was Kachan's superior, Minister of Trade Vadim Slizhevskiy, who called out in their native Belarusian, "Come."

Kachan entered.

Slizhevskiy was sitting in a leather chair, across from Ambassador Oleg Rumas. On the desk between the two men rested two glasses and a bottle of vodka. It wasn't the vile swill that placated the average, oppressed Belarusian. Instead, it was a high-priced, numbered bottle of Kauffman Vintage Vodka.

The contrast between Trade Minister and Ambassador was striking. Slizhevskiy was loud and overweight, with unkempt gray beard and hair. Rumas, on the other hand, was quiet, neat, slim and fit, with short, thinning black hair and small, round glasses.

Slizhevskiy waved Kachan over. "Report."

Kachan said, "Ambassador. Minister." He nodded at each. "Governor Shimansky delivered. Senator Brees said all of the right things, sir."

"Good, good, Alek. Now go," ordered Slizhevskiy, waving him off without looking at his aid.

Kachan seemed surprised and unsure, but disappeared.

Rumas poured a small amount of vodka into each glass. Slizhevskiy grabbed the glass and swallowed the clear liquid quickly. Rumas watched the Trade Minister closely, while consuming the vodka at a far more measured pace.

Slizhevskiy declared, "These conservatives in the American Congress are doing so much on our behalf." He laughed, picked up the bottle, and poured another for each.

"It is a delicate balance, Vadim," replied Rumas coolly. "The Americans appreciate the Prime Minister's talk of openness, and are hopeful that this talk, combined with aid to Christian business owners, will strengthen what they call the oppressed Christians in our country. Make no mistake, conservative and religious beliefs run deep in this U.S. President. Empowering unregistered, subversive groups in our country, as well as in places like China, is a real mission for him. But this thinking enslaves and blinds him." The ambassador sipped from the glass. "The Prime Minister's plan to have ultimate control over these U.S. aid dollars is sound, but risks still exist that it could spin beyond our control."

"That Pastor Foster, and his funders and political allies who control this Entrepreneurship & Values group still worry me, even with his assistant working on our behalf."

"Indeed, my friend."

Slizhevskiy took another swig of vodka, and shrugged his shoulders.

Rumas added, "You are managing this entire effort with great skill, Vadim, and I will relay this to the Prime Minister when next we speak."

"Thank you, Oleg."

"You are welcome, and now, I must get back to other pressing matters."

"Of course, as should I." Slizhevskiy put his dark gray suit jacket on, and pushed the knot of his tie higher. He poured and downed a last drink of vodka before leaving the room.

Rumas picked up his phone.

A deep voice answered, "Oleg, I trust all is going well."

"Yes, Anitoliy. Vadim is ably working the politics, the bribes. Farrell's replacement, a Ted Brees, is onboard. All is moving forward."

"Good. Vadim is a drunk and a buffoon, but has his moments. Manipulating capitalists in this manner is so much more rewarding than what we tried to do with the Soviet KGB, don't you think, Oleg?"

"I heartily agree, Mr. President."

Anatoliy Snopkov, the relatively new president of Belarus, laughed, wished his longtime comrade well, and hung up.

Chapter 15

George Kraus and Pastor Grant took a last look into the bay of the small moving truck.

"Are you sure that's it?" asked George.

"Nothing else," replied Grant, as he pulled down the door and latched it closed. They got into the cab, with Stephen behind the wheel.

"This is the easiest move ever."

"Well, we moved a few things before the wedding, but almost all the furniture is staying here for our new pastor."

"Don't get me wrong, Stephen. I'm not complaining about moving a chair and desk, three bookcases, some books, DVDs, sporting equipment, and wall hangings." While talking, he ticked each off with a finger. He held up nine fingers to make his point. "The last time I helped someone move, I strained my back. No risk of that today."

"Thanks again for helping, and for picking us up at the airport last night."

"Not a problem. It's not always easy, but I can get away from my own law firm on occasion – even on a Monday afternoon. It sounds like you and Jennifer had a great honeymoon, by the way."

"It was fantastic." Grant started the truck, and paused to look at the house he had lived in for more than a decade.

"It's hard to believe that I lived in that house longer than any other place since high school."

"You grew up in Cincinnati, right?"

"Yes, our home was about twenty minutes outside the city." Grant had not thought about his days growing up in quite some time. *Mom and Dad would have loved Jen, not to mention me being a pastor and St. Mary's.*

George asked, "Which is stranger – moving out of here or moving into Jennifer's house?"

"Moving has never been much of a problem for me. And while I obviously appreciate St. Mary's providing a parsonage, this place never really felt like home to me."

George said, "Not surprising."

As he shifted into drive and the truck began moving down the street, Stephen raised an eyebrow and said, "Why do you say that?"

"Well, from what I could tell, you didn't spend much time here. I always assumed it was too quiet, too much alone time."

"You're surprisingly perceptive for a lawyer, George."

"Yeah, that's funny. But with two teenage daughters, I don't necessarily understand your aversion to quiet, alone time."

"And now you are the funny one."

"Yes, but what about moving into Jennifer's?"

I've known you for a long time, George – poker, golf, ball games – and this is your most talkative and inquisitive.

Grant answered, "I was more concerned that Jen might be uneasy, given that she and Ted lived there, not to mention the attack and what she was forced to do. But she's pretty amazing, being more concerned that I would be uncomfortable. That house has been in her family for a long time. It's very much Jen's home."

"So, this doesn't bother you?"

"It seemed a bit odd, at first, when she talked of living there. But once I came to understand what the house meant to her, it was easy to put aside my concerns. I pray it comes to feel like *our* home."

"It will," said George.

"Again, why so sure?"

"Because, Pastor Grant, if you have the real thing in your marriage – and I have no doubts about you and Jen – then wherever your wife and family are will feel like home. You just referred to the place where you grew up with your parents as 'our home,' but I never recall you doing the same with the parsonage. I believe you will quickly feel at home in this house because that's where Jen is, and she values it."

"Okay, I now see why you're a lawyer. You pick up on things, don't really miss much."

"Thanks, I think."

"You know, George, I think you've been the quietest person I've ever known, and that's saying something coming from a person who used to work at the CIA. But all of a sudden, you offer this assessment of home and marriage. What gives?"

George paused, as if choosing his words carefully, which was typical for him, and for some lawyers. "I've long thought of you as more than just my pastor, Stephen, but as a friend. At the same time, Jennifer and Joan are very close, tighter than most sisters I've seen. Jennifer is family, and now you're family, too."

"So, we're like brothers-in-law?"

George responded simply, "Yes."

"Okay, bro. And I think you're right on what feels like home, and moving into Jennifer's house."

The short trip from the parsonage to Stephen's new home was soon at an end. They turned onto the short, suburban road, and approached one of the nicest houses in the neighborhood, a house that could not be seen behind high hedgerows. The wrought iron gate was open, and Stephen steered the truck between two light stone columns onto a concrete driveway inset with triangular, earth-tone tiles laid in large circles. The vehicle rolled alongside a large yard on the two-plus acres stretching along an inlet from the nearby Moriches Bay. They parked in front of the 4,200-square-foot house, across from a three-car garage.

"Of course, the various amenities here probably make it a heck of a lot easier to feel at home as well," added George with a wry smile.

"Again, funny," said Stephen. "Since we're now family, I can tell you to get your ass out of the truck, and start moving things, bro."

Chapter 16

Pastor Grant took a deep breath.

First full day back and a council meeting. Perhaps not the best planning on my part.

Given the heartfelt congratulations on the wedding, it didn't bother the ever-punctual Grant that the council meeting got rolling about 15 minutes late. After an opening prayer, Grant's report was brief, as were the others presented by council members seated around the long cherry-wood table in St. Mary's large library/conference room.

The chair squeaked and strained under a shifting 320 pounds as Everett Birk, the church council president, leaned forward. "Thanks for the reports. Let's turn to open business."

Everett looked at the council secretary. Drew Frazier was a longtime member at St. Mary's, but had only been on the council for a few months. When they needed to fill the council secretary spot and Drew volunteered, Grant was unsure. The 66-year-old Frazier, a retired postal worker, always seemed to be around the church to help with projects, but that assistance came with a price. Even counting some highly cynical people he worked with at the CIA, Grant did not know anyone as negative as Drew Frazier. No matter what was undertaken at St. Mary's, even as Drew helped get the job done, he would criticize the project. Drew could be counted on to find the downside of just about anything. If not careful, a person could get sucked down his drain of pessimism.

But when Drew volunteered to take the secretary position, and no one else expressed interest, Birk and Grant had no other option than to graciously accept the offer. Birk told Grant at the time, "He's always complaining about what the council decides. Maybe having Drew on the council, involved in making the decisions, will make him more supportive."

At the time, Grant chose not to further verbalize his doubts, merely saying, "Let's hope so."

Drew looked at his notes. "The first item is ... um ... the pothole in the parking lot."

Glenn Oliver, chairman of the buildings and grounds committee, replied, "Filled. Fully repaired."

As he checked off the item, Drew mumbled, "'Bout time."

Everett quickly said, "Thanks, Glenn, to you and your team. Great work." Everett looked at Drew, who had not taken his eyes up from his list. "What's next?"

Drew said, "The only other items have to do with Pastor Grant's compensation and the arrival of Pastor Charmichael."

Birk looked to a thin, pale woman with straight blond hair and oval glasses. "JoAnn, why don't you sum things up for us?"

The timid voice of JoAnn Brown, church treasurer, matched her appearance. "Yes, I'd be happy to, Everett. As presented in our meeting six months ago, Pastor Grant informed the council that after he got married to Jennifer that he no longer wanted to take any compensation in terms of salary and benefits from St. Mary's, though remaining in his position and carrying out the duties of a full-time pastor. Pastor hoped that part of his salary would be used to bring on a second pastor. The council and congregation later agreed that St. Mary's needed a second pastor, and wound up calling Zackary Charmichael, but left Pastor Grant's compensation as a line item on the eventually approved budget. The council asked Pastor Grant to pray and think, once again, about his offer, and to report to the council tonight."

Everett said, "Thank you, JoAnn." He turned to Grant, who was sitting next to him. "Well, Pastor, still intent on going through with this?"

"I have thought and prayed about it some more, spoke to Jennifer, and we still think it's the right thing to do. As I said before, without getting into the specifics of my family's finances, this is something that Jennifer and I can afford to do, and feel like we should do."

Everett said, "Anyone else have something to say on the matter?"

With a grim face, Drew said, "I do."

"Alright, Drew, go ahead," replied Everett.

"I've expressed some reservations about this before. But the more I've thought about it, I'm actually insulted by this."

Grant made sure to contrast the anger in Drew's voice with a calm in his own. "Insulted? Why?"

Before Drew could answer, Sean McEnany made his own irritation clear. "How could you possibly be insulted by such a gift to the church? It doesn't make any sense."

Drew replied, "Well, that's the way I feel. This comes across as another case of the 'haves' flaunting it over the 'have nots.' It's just wrong."

Sean bore down on Drew. "Really? So, any gifts to the church above a certain level or from certain people are suspect to you, Drew?"

Drew seemed to physically waver a bit, as all council eyes were on him, and no one came to his aid. "Well, how do we know how Pastor Grant and his wife are able to do this? How do we know where this money comes from? I've heard rumors that Wall Street is involved."

With his anger mounting, Grant was going to interject, but let Sean continue.

Sean said, "Oh, no, not Wall Street. What is this 'Occupy St. Mary's'? Are you accusing someone of doing something illegal or immoral, Drew?"

"No. Of course not."

"Well, what is it then? Do you want to check on what everyone does for a living, see if it fits your little check list or criteria, and make sure that they do not make too much money, before taking any gift to St. Mary's?"

"Um, no, well, not exactly."

Sean nearly exploded, "Not exactly! What does that mean? I work for a corporate security firm, Drew, is that okay with you? Am I somehow not worthy to head up the evangelism committee at this church? Are my earnings too dirty to go to St. Mary's?"

Drew said, "To be honest, I have problems with corporations getting rich off regular people."

Grant worked to keep his temper in check, as Drew was not just attacking him, but more directly, Jen.

Remember, you knew he would find the negative in pretty much everything. He's on the dark side, like a Sith. Darth Drew. Lord, forgive me. Alright, I have to assume that Frazier is not malicious. He's just an idiot.

Stephen decided it was time to speak up. "Please, our intent here was not to cause any strife or discomfort. As we talked about this months ago, Jennifer and I could simply put my salary back in the collection plate each week. We just thought this would be the easiest way to save St. Mary's the full cost of my compensation. Just like anyone else with the means to give to the church, this is what we want to do. It's important that all of you understand there's nothing more at work here, no ulterior motives.

Perhaps we made a mistake in how we're doing it. If so, I apologize."

It was Suzanne Maher's turn to say something. St. Mary's vice president had sat stoically, not moving her thin, saggy, 80-year-old body. "You have nothing to apologize for, Pastor Grant," she said in formal fashion. "Your gift to St. Mary's is very generous, and should be accepted with grace. Quite frankly, it is Mr. Frazier who should apologize."

Suzanne had an air of authority that came with the combination of her age, intellect and confidence; an unfailing willingness to help people in need at St. Mary's; and an occasional tendency to question or even challenge Grant on doctrinal issues. Stephen had long been grateful for her willingness to aid others, as well as her appreciation for the details of Holy Scripture and church teachings. But her tone when correcting and challenging, along with some annoying nitpicking, earned her the private nickname of "St. Mary's enforcer of doctrine."

Everett said, "Now, we've always had a policy on this council of encouraging a full discussion. Nothing is meant to be taken personally, I'm sure, and apologies should not be necessary."

Suzanne had not removed her stare from Drew Frazier. "I disagree, Everett. There is a line that should not be crossed, and in my view, it was crossed. Mr. Frazier, since envy most certainly is a sin, perhaps you should also be thinking about confession."

Whoa! Harsh, but thanks, Suzanne.

Drew Frazier was speechless. He offered no apology.

Suzanne Maher resumed her statue-like position, with perhaps a touch of smugness evident between the many lines on her face.

Everett Birk noted that Pastor Grant had made his decision, and barring any unforeseen expenses, even with the addition of Pastor Charmichael, St. Mary's just might end the budget year with a surplus "for a change." He moved on to the details of what still needed to be done for the arrival this week of Zackary Charmichael, and his Saturday ordination and installation as assistant pastor at St. Mary's.

The issue of Pastor Grant's compensation, or lack thereof, was settled ... at least, for now.

Chapter 17

In May, the 27-year-old Zackary Charmichael finished his final year at the seminary in Fort Wayne, Indiana; took a few weeks back home in Seattle with his parents, sister and brother; and for the past week and a half, drove in his black Toyota Camry across the country.

He took in Yellowstone National Park, Mount Rushmore and the Badlands. He poked around parts of the Great Lakes, and then made a beeline across much of Pennsylvania to spend a day in Philadelphia.

On Thursday, Charmichael drove the 165 miles from Philly to Manorville, NY. While it should have taken no more than three-and-a-half hours, he unfortunately hit the Long Island Expressway just in time for the afternoon rush hour. Charmichael pulled into the driveway of the three-bedroom ranch that served as the parsonage for St. Mary's Lutheran Church an hour later than planned.

Waiting for him were Stephen and Jennifer Grant.

After getting out of the car, Charmichael took off his rectangular, brown-rimmed glasses, rubbed his eyes, and stretched his thin, five-foot-seven-inch frame. His thick, light brown hair was unkempt, but in a seemingly purposeful way.

While coming out of the house to greet Charmichael, the first thing Grant noticed was the brown t-shirt with a heavily armed and armored character that read: "While You're Reading this T-Shirt, We're in Your Base, Stealing Your Flag."

Stephen said, "Zack, it's great to see you. Welcome to Long Island and to St. Mary's."

As they shook hands, Zack replied, "Thanks, Pastor Grant."

"Ah, remember what I said before, it's Stephen. No formalities. And no senior pastor or assistant pastor, just pastors. Got it?"

Zack smiled. "Right. Absolutely. Sorry about being a bit late. But when I hit the Long Island Expressway, things more or less came to a stop."

"Rush hour on the LIE can be an experience. You'll find that Long Island drivers are ... how can I put this generously? ... probably more aggressive than you might be used to."

"You can say that again. Some of them seem a bit ... well ... crazy."

"Yeah, as it's often put in New York, they're freakin' nuts – and I cleaned that up. This is your first time on Long Island, right?"

"Yes. First time ever in New York."

"I'm not from New York either. Long Island's great, but it takes some getting used to. We'll get you acclimated. With very few exceptions, the people at St. Mary's are wonderful, and make it very easy."

"Thanks, Stephen."

"We're also all ready for your ordination and installation on Saturday. Most of the pastors in the circuit will be there, along with Dr. Brett Matthews, our district president. What about your family?"

"They all fly in tomorrow."

"Excited?"

"That would be an understatement. I feel incredibly blessed."

"Don't worry. We've got everything set at St. Mary's. Just take it all in and enjoy it. You're right, it's a true blessing. Now, shifting gears, you're probably a bit tired. Do you want to unload the car now, or have something to eat first? Jennifer is inside, and she made some dinner. Just salad and sandwiches that can be eaten anytime."

"I'm not tired at all. I could go for bringing things inside, and then eating, if that's okay with you?"

Stephen said, "Let's do it."

Zack noted, "There's not much. I appreciated St. Mary's paying for shipping most of my stuff."

"The boxes you sent are inside. You were cheap to move, and everyone was excited to hear you were coming, especially when they heard what Everett and I had to say after our meeting in Fort Wayne."

Zack opened the back doors of the car and popped the trunk. "Mainly clothes and things my parents found necessary to purchase for the parsonage in the back seat. Books and electronics in the trunk."

Stephen looked at the equipment and related paraphernalia in the back of the Camry. "You're an Apple guy?"

"Yes, a MacBook and iPad."

"We're going to get along just fine on the computer front then."

"I do much of my devotional, theology and sermon reading now on that iPad. I've got all the biggies from Concordia Publishing on it – *The Lutheran Study Bible*, *Treasury of Daily Prayer*, *Concordia*, and others."

"What are in the book boxes then?"

Zack smiled a bit sheepishly. "I like artwork on paper, so those are graphic novels – Batman, Justice League, Avengers, Captain America, some others."

Stephen glanced to the other side of the trunk. "And video games, I see."

"Yeah, Xbox 360. I love playing."

"That explains the t-shirt. *Halo,* right?"

Zack smiled broadly and his rate of speech accelerated. "Absolutely! My biggies are *Halo, Madden, Batman Arkham Asylum, Golden Eye.* What else? Um, also love the Tom Clancy games, *L.A. Noire* and *Star Wars: Force Unleashed,* of course. I just started getting into *Assassin's Creed,* but I haven't decided yet if it's anti- or even pro-Christian, or well, just a fantasy game. Do you play?"

"I guess you'd call me a 'noob.' I've only dabbled due to Scott Larson. I think I mentioned that he's our choir director, and his wife, Pam, is our organist and youth director. They basically cover all things music and youth at St. Mary's. You'll meet them tomorrow. But Scott is your man on gaming."

"That all sounds great. Looking forward to meeting them."

They both grabbed boxes and went to the house.

Barely inside the door, Stephen introduced Jennifer. She greeted Zack with a smile, hug and kiss on the cheek. "I am so glad to meet you, finally."

Zack said, "It's great to meet you, Mrs. Grant."

"While I'm excited about being Mrs. Grant for nearly two weeks, you will never call me that again. It's Jennifer or Jen, whichever you like."

"Okay, Jennifer, and congratulations to both of you on the wedding."

Jennifer said, "Thank you. Now take a look around at your new home, and I'm going to help bring in your things." She went out the front door.

Zack started to look around, and suddenly seemed bewildered.

Stephen asked, "Anything wrong?"

Zack looked in the kitchen to the left and the living room to the right with his mouth open.

"There's a hallway through that door, with the bathroom and three bedrooms," instructed Stephen.

"Three bedrooms?"

"Yes. You sure there's nothing wrong?"

"Wrong? What could be wrong? I've had limited living space for the last eight years, and this is the size of my family's house. I actually share a bedroom with my brother, or I used to. This is a bit overwhelming, actually."

Stephen smiled. "Well, at the risk of sending you over the edge, I've cleared out all of my stuff, so the rest stays for you to do with as you will."

"All of the furniture?"

"Yeah. I told you that before, right?"

"Oh, um, yes, I guess you did. But it didn't really register." And then Zack spotted the 42-inch flat screen television hanging on the living room wall. He pointed at the television and looked at Stephen. "That, too?"

Stephen said, "I trust it works with your Xbox."

"Works? It's perfect."

I think he's getting emotional over the TV.

Zack looked around again. "Stephen, I can't tell you how great this is."

"Well, I'm glad you're happy. How about we bring the rest of your stuff in, and then eat? I'm getting hungry."

Zack almost yelled, "Absolutely!" He raced to open the door for Jen, and then darted out to retrieve more from his car.

Jen quietly said, "He looks happy, and enthusiastic."

"More than you know," replied Stephen. "Apparently, the television removed any doubts that might have lingered. Perfect for *L.A. Noire.*"

"For what?"

"You're not a gamer, my sweet. You just wouldn't understand."

Jen rolled her eyes. "And you do?"

Stephen smiled. "Haven't a clue."

As Zack carefully removed his Xbox 360 from the car, Jen leaned close to Stephen's ear, and whispered, "I've got other games in mind for you later tonight, Stephen." And she kissed his ear lobe.

"I love you."

She replied, "As I believe Han Solo said: I know."

"Nice movie reference."

"Thanks."

Zack came in the door with the gaming hardware.

Looking into the box still in her arms, Jennifer said, "It appears we've got another sports fan. Judging by these bobbleheads and wall signs, it's the Mariners, Seahawks, and Canucks, Zack?"

"Big time."

Stephen said, "Well, if I can marry a woman who for some strange reason loves the St. Louis Cardinals, it should be a breeze for this Reds and Bengals fan to work with a follower of northwest teams."

Zack replied, "What about hockey? I'm passionate about my Canucks."

Stephen smiled, observing, "'Passionate about my Canucks' – I don't think those words have ever been uttered on Long Island before."

Zack laughed, "Probably not."

"I've adopted the Islanders, and given their longtime woes, I therefore try not to talk hockey too much. But it'll be real easy to get tickets when the Canucks come to town."

"Nice. When I graduated from seminary, one of the gifts my parents promised was an annual subscription to NHL Ticket, so I can catch all the Canucks games."

"I guess they really are your Canucks," Stephen observed.

Chapter 18

After getting married, going on his honeymoon, and welcoming Zack Charmichael to St. Mary's, Pastor Grant was trying to get back into some kind of normal, day-to-day rhythm.

On a Friday morning like this, along with Mondays and Wednesdays, that meant getting together with Father Tom Stone and Father Ron McDermott for devotions, breakfast and general conversation – when their schedules permitted. On rare occasions, these gatherings would shift to a local golf course.

For several years, despite coming from three different Christian denominations – the Lutheran Grant, the Catholic McDermott and the Anglican Stone – the men shared a deep traditional Christian faith that embraced what they had in common while acknowledging differences. The three had grown to become the closest of friends, strongly supportive of each other, their families, and ministries.

It was a few minutes before seven, and Grant was the first to arrive at the Moriches Bay Diner on Montauk Highway. The establishment of windows, mirrors and chrome was about five minutes from his new home. While the menu was diverse, Grant appreciated the satisfying diner comfort food.

He ordered a Diet Coke while waiting for his friends.

Tom Stone arrived next, wandering over to the table.

"Tom, my best man, good to see you."

"And you as well, Stephen. How's married life?"

"Great. Almost feel like a different man after being single so long. I see you're mixing up the wardrobe. Replacing the usual Hawaiian shirt and cargo shorts with a polo shirt and Hawaiian shorts. What brought on such a bold move?"

"You're just jealous that you lack my fashion sense."

"Tom, you know many things, including theology, but fashion is not one of your strong points."

Ron McDermott appeared and made Stephen slide over deeper into the booth. "Stephen, welcome back. Tom, ugly shorts."

Though far more serious than Tom, Ron nonetheless had a dry sense of humor. Tom Stone and Ron McDermott had a tight friendship, which probably surprised many people given their different demeanors and style choices. When not on official church duties, and if it was over fifty degrees, Tom could be found in shorts, while it was rare to not find Ron in clerical garb.

Tom replied, "Good to see you're both as annoying as ever. I would have hated to see that things had changed in any way since our last morning meeting."

"No worries. Same old," said Ron.

The three men placed their orders with the waitress, and then each pulled out their respective volumes of *For All the Saints: A Prayer Book For and By the Church*, which had been their devotional choice for more than two years now.

Stephen often wondered what other diners thought when the three read Holy Scripture and prayers. Did it get some people thinking and reflecting about God, even for a few minutes? Were some uncomfortable? He had no doubt that more than a few were annoyed.

However, probably five or six times over the past few years, a person approached their table to talk, usually not sure what to say. One actually sat down with them, and three others wound up returning to regular churchgoing, with two now attending at St. Luke's and one at St. Bart's.

When their prayers concluded, Ron said, "Almost two weeks now, is married life still agreeing with you?"

Stephen said, "Let's just say that I understand how lucky I am."

"You are, indeed," said Tom, after taking a sip of his coffee. "It's pretty clear that you made out far better than Jennifer did in this marriage."

"Tom is absolutely right," added Ron.

"Thanks. You're both right, but you don't have to be so honest."

Ron said, "And what about Zackary? He arrived, correct?"

Stephen nodded. "Got here last night."

Tom asked, "Still as impressed with him as you were when at the seminary?"

"Yes. Jen and I helped him move in, and had a nice dinner. Jen was taken by his enthusiasm."

"Get a feel for his interests outside church?" asked Tom. "Does he share any of your affinities for shooting, archery, golf, history, or movies? He's not a Cincinnati sports fan, is he?"

"Mariners and Seahawks, and a big Canucks fan."

Ron said, "Canucks, really? I've never met a Canucks fan."

Stephen continued, "He's also a passionate gamer – sci-fi, military and spy games, it seems."

Tom and Ron looked at each other with slight smiles, and then at Stephen.

Ron said, "Military and spies, huh? Does he know anything about the past exploits of his new boss?"

Stone and McDermott knew about Grant's previous employment with the CIA, including a limited, vague inclination of what that might have involved, along with his more recent adventures regarding gun-toting killers.

Stephen instinctively glanced around and lowered his voice. "He knows that I once worked for the CIA, and about the shooter at St. Mary's. Anyone reading the news knows that much. But he knows nothing more, and there's no reason why he should come to know anything more."

"No plans to bring him onto your local team?" Tom chuckled at his own comment.

Stephen looked at his two friends closely, quietly.

"Yes, yes, we know," relented Tom.

"Of course," added Ron, who then changed the subject. "On another matter, I could use some thoughts or ideas on something going on at St. Luke's."

"Sure," replied Stephen.

But the waitress then arrived with their breakfast orders. For Stephen, it was a short stack of pancakes, while Ron chose two eggs sunny-side up, sausage and an English muffin. Tom wound up going with the biggest breakfast on the menu – French toast, two over-easy eggs, bacon, sausage, ham and toast.

Noting Tom's choice, Ron observed, "I thought Maggie was still pushing you to eat better?"

"She most certainly is. Last night, we had a variety of steamed vegetables and a small piece of broiled fish. It left a lot to be desired, let's just say." As they started eating, Tom added, "Don't tell her what I'm eating, by the way."

Stephen feigned outrage. "Are you asking us to lie for you?"

Tom replied, "Well, no, I mean. Oh, just don't volunteer anything, alright? I should have known I couldn't count on you guys." He shoved a big piece of French toast dripping with syrup and butter into his mouth, and suddenly seemed quite happy. He looked at Ron, and with food still in his mouth, managed to utter, "Okay, so what's up at St. Luke's that you need our powerful insights?"

Ron said, "Don't get carried away. Father Burns has told me that he'll be retiring at year-end, and he's worried about the school." Father Stanley Burns was the senior parish priest at St. Luke's Roman Catholic Church and School.

Stephen asked, "Is the school in trouble?"

"Actually, no, at least not in our view. We're in the black, but our enrollment has declined a bit over the past few years."

Stephen said, "The economy, or something specific to the school?"

"I'm confident that our school is well run, and barring the rare but inevitable pain in the ass, the parents are strong supporters."

Tom chimed in, "With five children having graduated from St. Luke's and one still attending, I can attest to both – strong parental involvement and good staff."

Ron continued, "Thanks. So, I think it's the bad economic stretch combined with the high property taxes around here. A lot of families simply are unable to make the sacrifice to send their kids to a parochial school when forking over so much in taxes for public schools."

Stephen added, "And you guys have been far more proactive than some other parochial schools with the education trust and its scholarships."

"By the way, thanks again to both Jennifer and you for suggesting contributions to the trust in lieu of a wedding gift. I know I said it before, but that was incredibly kind and many of your guests were quite generous."

"You're welcome. We're more than happy to help. St. Luke's is an important school to have around in a culture like this."

Ron said, "Father Burns has worked hard to communicate that our school is a central mission of our church. He always points out that we're passing on the faith to our children, and what could possibly be more important than that?"

Stephen replied, "I'm always amazed when I hear about pastors and congregants who miss that key fact, and are even hostile to a church school."

Tom interjected, "What exactly is Stan worried about?"

Ron said, "As everybody knows, a good number of Catholic schools have been closed in recent years, and some of those schools were not in bad financial shape either."

Tom continued, "Ah, so you two are trying to think pre-emptively."

Ron said, "Right. Any thoughts?"

Stephen started to say, "I'm not sure if I have anything unique to contribute, but how about ..."

But Tom interrupted. "Money." He then took another satisfying mouthful of his breakfast.

Ron replied, "Yes, well, that's fine. But we've got an excellent fundraising system for a preschool through eighth grade institution."

"No, I mean big money. Big endowment-type money." He wiped his mouth clean with the napkin.

With a touch of exasperation slipping into his voice, Ron said, "Sounds very nice. And where would we find such a treasure? Know anyone with big bucks just aching to give it away?"

Tom smiled, and with a large gulp, finished the remaining coffee in his cup. "As a matter of fact, yes, yes I do."

Chapter 19

It would be hard to find two Republican members of the U.S. Senate who were more different.

Ted Brees was a liberal on most social issues, like guns, abortion and the environment. But on economic topics, he was mixed, generally favoring tax relief, willing to talk about getting "spending under control," but more interested in bringing home the bacon. He also was ready to go to bat to protect businesses important to New York — which in recent times amounted to little more than parts of the financial industry.

On the other hand, Senator Trevor Tenace of Virginia was an outspoken, enthusiastic conservative. He made clear, in fact, celebrated, his Southern Baptist roots, pro-life and pro-gun-rights stances, and support for lower taxes, less regulation and generally smaller government — unless increased government spending was directed at national defense or one of his pet projects.

The walls in Tenace's richly paneled Senate office were populated with photos of the Senator hunting, fishing, playing golf and posing with various NASCAR drivers and pastors, along with assorted plaques and certificates from taxpayer, pro-military, pro-Christian, and pro-family groups. Those same organizations distrusted the likes of Senator Ted Brees.

The two did have something in common, however. Both were young, handsome, and nattily dressed, with Brees in a blue, double-breasted Brooks Brothers suit and Tenace in a grey plaid suit from Ralph Lauren.

Yet, here they were in a meeting on a substantive topic of mutual interest and importance.

"I'm glad we were able to meet for a bit, Ted. I haven't had the chance to welcome you to the Senate."

"Thanks very much, Trevor."

"It's ugly business, though, what happened to Jimmy."

"I certainly wish my Senate career started in any other way."

"Of course," replied Tenace, with a smooth voice just hinting at his southern Virginia roots. "Well, as for the reason for our talking, this is one of the very few issues where Senator Farrell and I disagreed. I think this is a rare case where government could make real improvements in people's lives. You've said you're onboard with shifting to a small business goal on foreign aid?"

"Yes, and I think you're right about the impact." Brees also volunteered, "And it's the right call to have the pilot program geared at Belarus, rather than Mexico."

"I have to say, Ted, I was a bit surprised to hear that you were in the Belarus camp, rather than Mexico."

"It seems to me that a more immediate impact would be seen with a nation like Belarus, especially given the signals that this could help liberate a too-long enslaved nation under communism, or in recent times, some kind of communist-lite. Besides, if this succeeds the way I expect, Mexico can be next on the list."

Tenace smiled broadly. "I completely agree. Now, there's a relatively new private nonprofit called Entrepreneurship & Values in Action. They've started doing this kind of work with private dollars. Rather than offering traditional charity, they make investments in start-ups and small firms. They're only at work in three or four countries, but one has been Belarus."

"That's ideal," observed Brees.

"Again, I agree. However, while the group is not explicitly Christian, it's run by Christians, and they tend to provide investments to Christians looking to get businesses off the ground and growing. Does that create any discomfort for you?"

"Look, Trevor, I don't want this to sound patronizing or cynical. I'm not particularly religious, as you apparently know. But I know you are, and I understand our Republican base and have tremendous respect for our people of faith. I also understand the difference that Christianity can and has made in undermining totalitarian regimes, helping to liberate people. If this Entrepreneurship & Values in Action group is getting the job done, then it makes sense to work with and through them. And quite frankly, given the tremendous bipartisan support this effort has, providing aid with the help of a faith-based organization only strengthens our political base."

"Fair enough," said Tenace. "Sounds like we're working together on this. I'm looking forward to it."

"Me, too."

Tenace noted, "We're moving fast. A couple of things. First, I'm calling a quick hearing in the Foreign Relations Committee."

"Good."

"Second, you should meet a pastor here in the District. He's a key mover and shaker behind the EVA, very passionate. He really has become the *de facto* leader."

"Sure, who is he?"

"Pastor Graham Foster from the New Jerusalem Church."

Chapter 20

Déjà vu? I really feel like this has happened before.

Stephen Grant was in a chaise lounge, with a writing pad and an open Bible on his lap. But his attention was drawn to Jennifer, who was floating and swimming in the pool.

"You know, I think I had a dream like this once," said Stephen.

"Is that right? Tell me more," said Jennifer. She swam over to the side of the pool where Stephen was sitting, crossed her arms on the edge, and rested her chin, waiting for the story.

Stephen dug into his memories. "Sometimes I can't recall a dream from last night, but this one sticks with me from a couple of years ago. It's weird. This is exactly what we were doing. You swimming, and me sitting here."

Jennifer said, "Ah, excuse me, Pastor Grant. But did you say this dream was about two years ago?"

"Yes."

"Well, that would have put me still married to another man. Tsk, tsk, shame on you. Dreaming about married women."

Grant sighed, "Not funny, Mrs. Grant."

Her laugh and brown eyes pulled him in, as always.

Grant smiled. He got back to the dream as Jennifer slowly drifted back in the water. "I had a pad and the Bible on my lap, just like this. And I also had the same feeling as I do now."

"And what feeling is that?"

"Comfortable, and at home."

She swam back toward Stephen. "Do you mean that?"

"Very much, Jen."

"That makes me happy. I know you've told me over and over that you're good with living here. But I've been worried that you were just being ... well ... Stephen, the good pastor willing to suffer in silence. You've experienced just as much change as I have, Stephen, from longtime bachelor to married man moving into a home his new wife already owned, not to mention giving up your salary at church because of what your wife earns. Lesser men might be threatened, no?"

"Or, they might kick back, quit working and enjoy the ride on the pretty wife's dime."

"Amusing. But I'm serious and ... concerned. Do you resent any of this?"

"Jen, we've talked about all of this before. And if I had a problem, I would let you know and we wouldn't have decided what we did. I thought we settled this, especially the salary thing, when we talked about being truly one in all aspects of our marriage?"

"I know we did. And I agree. But I worry, just a bit."

"Well, no more worries on this, my love. The only thing that stuck in the back of my head – far back in my head – was whether this would truly be *our* house. But tonight, I have no doubts."

Jennifer said, "Good, because it would eat away at me if you had doubts."

"None. By the way, I had a chat about this with George when we were moving stuff on Monday."

"Really? Did he offer any sage observations?"

"Actually, yes. He basically said that our marriage was the real thing, and that wherever we were would feel like home to both of us."

Jen swam back to the edge of the pool, and looked at Stephen. "He's a smart man."

Grant returned her smile, and said, "I could not agree more."

Jennifer floated onto her back, and said with a laugh, "You better agree, or you'd be in trouble."

Jennifer's mobile phone from her home office sat on a table next to Stephen. Its ring broke into their playful exchange.

Jennifer said, "Don't bother, let the machine get it."

Okay, here's the dream again. Too weird. Is this a message, Lord, that I'm where I should be?

Stephen picked up the phone and looked at the small screen. He recognized the name. "Are you sure? It says that Kristin Madsen, who I believe is a U.S. senator from the state of Texas, is calling you."

Jennifer shifted into a more serious tone, and said, "I should take that."

Stephen decided to play secretary while his wife got out of the pool. He clicked the answer button. "Dr. Jennifer Grant's office." He listened, and winked at Jennifer, as she shot him a don't-be-an-idiot look. "Of course, Senator Madsen. I'll put her right on."

He handed the phone to Jennifer, who said, "Krissy, how are you?"

Stephen picked up a pen and looked at the pad on his lap, and said just loud enough for his wife to hear but not the Senator, "First, it's Call Us Men, and now Krissy. Aren't we important?"

Without a noise to give away her actions to Senator Madsen on the other side of the line, Jennifer spun a barefoot around and kicked the pen out of his hand.

Ha, nicely done.

Jennifer stuck her tongue out at Stephen, then smoothly proceeded away toward the house. Into the phone, she said, "No, nothing so lavish as a new employee. That's just my husband, either trying to be helpful or cute. I'm not sure which."

After being gone for 15 minutes, Jennifer returned. "I've just been invited to testify before the Senate on a new foreign aid proposal. Feel like going to D.C. for a couple of days?"

"When?" asked Stephen.

"After church on Sunday, back on Tuesday afternoon."

"Well, with my usual Monday off, barring any unforeseen funerals, I can probably do that."

"By the way, Krissy wants to meet you."

Chapter 21

St. Luke's Roman Catholic School usually was a place of kinetic energy. But at this moment, a rare, still quiet engulfed most of the red brick, two story building that stood across the street from St. Luke's Church and rectory.

The school year had just finished the previous day, weekend activities had declined dramatically with the arrival of summer, and St. Luke's summer camps would not kick off until July Fourth passed.

Nonetheless, the three people carrying the ultimate responsibility of running this preschool-through-eighth-grade institution were meeting on a Saturday morning in a small, bland, unassuming conference room adjacent to the principal's office.

Father Stanley Burns, Father Ron McDermott and Mrs. Carol Fleming, the school principal, were finishing a discussion of how the school year had gone.

"All in all, I'd say this was a successful year," concluded Mrs. Fleming.

"Agreed," said Father McDermott.

"Yes," added Father Burns, though his voice sounded distant.

"But...?" said Mrs. Fleming. Carol had been principal at St. Luke's for 15 years. At barely five feet tall, thin, with short blond hair and small, rectangular glasses, she hardly seemed intimidating. But to those who worked with her, while Carol was kind, she also was no nonsense, and known for dealing in straightforward fashion with everyone, and appreciating when others did the same.

Father Burns pushed his large, horn-rimmed black glasses further up on his wrinkly face. "Well, yes, but," he started. Burns always spoke carefully and deliberately. He paused and ran his frail-looking right hand over the very few remaining black hairs on top of his 72-year-old head.

Burns looked at McDermott and then Fleming. "Well, we did have a very good year."

"Yes," said McDermott, urging on his superior.

Concern crossed Burns' face. "But I think we will need more than 'very good' years over the next few years to make sure our school does not get axed by the diocese."

"Have you heard anything specific, Father?" asked a now suspicious Mrs. Fleming.

"No, I have not, Carol. But I also have not gotten a straight answer about our long term status."

"That goes for me, too," said Fleming. "I've received great feedback on our trust for tuition scholarships. But the conversation always wanders around to general concerns about school populations, without specifically mentioning St. Luke's, of course. It's very frustrating. I don't like that kind of avoidance."

"I know you don't," said Burns, "and I can't blame you."

"So, what do we need to do to make sure this place does not get shut down some time in the near future?" asked Carol Fleming.

Father Burns replied, "That's what we need to start thinking about, right now. And since I'm retiring at the end of this year, it falls on you two."

"You both know Father Stone, right?" asked McDermott.

While Father Burns nodded, Carol said, "Of course. All of the Stone children have gone to St. Luke's."

Ron continued, "He has a parishioner who has made a fortune in video games, and is now looking to make his mark by boosting elementary and high school education. According to Father Stone, so far, he has been planning and talking about providing aid directly to certain public schools. But Father Stone also noted that he provided the bulk of the funding that St. Bartholomew's used to buy its property when it left the Episcopal Church, and he is very active in their church."

Father Burns asked, "What's your thinking, Father McDermott? Might this person be willing to contribute to our school?"

"I'm not sure, and neither is Father Stone. But if we're open to it, Father Stone offered to talk to this man on our behalf, and if there is interest, to set up a meeting."

Carol said, "Why not? What's the downside?"

"There is none," said McDermott.

"Well, there's your answer, Father McDermott. Please tell Father Stone we would appreciate any interest in helping to further build up St. Luke's and its mission. Can you tell us who this person is?"

"His name is Michael Vanacore."

Chapter 22

Part of Mike Vanacore's story seemed to be a replay of others' in the computer, digital, broadband economy.

The thirty-two-year-old billionaire fell in love with electronics and computers while growing up in Hawthorne, California, which happened to be the Beach Boys' hometown. Vanacore's hard-working parents supported his interests and talents as best they could, and rejoiced when his excellent grades in high school, particularly in math and science, earned him a full ride to the School of Engineering at Stanford University.

Since they were intense gamers, Vanacore and two college friends decided to do more than complain about the shortcomings of various video games. By their sophomore year, they were consumed by creating their own video games, and managed to generate some buzz. Vanacore's buddies, however, moved on under parental pressure when grades slipped badly.

But Vanacore had little trouble maintaining high marks, while at the same time creating a video game business.

He found a couple of angel investors to provide start-up capital, and by his senior year, Corevana Entertainment had grown to more than 100 employees, and $30 million in sales.

But rather than dropping out to focus exclusively on his firm, as other young tech turks had done, Vanacore finished his degree. After graduation, Corevana's growth only accelerated, and its initial public offering made Mike Vanacore a billionaire at the age of 26.

Along the way, Vanacore became known in various circles for maintaining his Christian faith taught to him growing up. Compared to some of his fellow tech nerds, who earned reputations for power trips and/or wild parties that came with newfound wealth, Vanacore was highlighted now and then in the business media for being, well, Christian.

As the U.S. Episcopal Church wandered away from the traditional Episcopal parish of his childhood, Vanacore actually spoke out. Some in the Episcopal Church took notice given his wealth and youth, but he was quickly discounted as just another "conservative" who refused to change with the culture. Some noted the irony of such criticisms given how he made his fortune.

When Vanacore decided to buy a home across the country on Long Island as an occasional escape from his California-based business, he stumbled upon St. Bart's one Sunday. He apparently fell in love with the beautiful, castle-like stone church set on four lakeside acres in Eastport, and most importantly, with what was being taught and preached in the building. When the parish decided to leave the Episcopal Church, eventually joining the Anglican Church in North America, it was Vanacore who ponied up a majority of the funds needed to purchase St. Bart's property from the local Episcopal diocese.

Vanacore was now expanding his charitable giving into primary and secondary education. His plan was to use his wealth to make substantive changes in individual local public schools, that is, in the kind of school he attended.

But his parish priest, Father Tom Stone, was about to ask Vanacore to listen to an alternative.

On the way out of Mass on Saturday night, Stone asked Vanacore if he had a little time to talk.

Ten minutes later, they were seated in Stone's office, talking across the priest's unique redwood, surfboard-shaped desk. A friend and parishioner had the desk specially made as a gift, given Stone's off-duty love of wearing Hawaiian shirts, and his high school and college years spent living and surfing in southern California.

In fact, though about 20 years apart, Stone and Vanacore shared more than a common faith, but also a southern California connection.

Vanacore ran his right hand along the front of the desk. "As I said before, you have the best desk ever. A surfboard. Love it."

"It was a gift from Clint Gullett. Handmade. It's a great reminder of my California days. I'm sure he'd be glad to let you know who makes them," replied Stone.

"I'll ask him. So, when was the last time you hit the surf?"

Stone laughed. "It's been at least, what, 25 years."

Vanacore slipped into a mock surfer voice, and declared, "Dude, we have to remedy that."

With his thin, tall frame, topped off by thick blond hair, and Clark Kent glasses, it was easy to see Vanacore moving comfortably in either the video gaming or surfing communities.

The young billionaire continued, "But I'm sure you didn't ask me to stop by to talk about surfing."

Stone replied, "No. Ever since you told me about the education foundation you're starting up, something has been nagging at me. But I was not sure if it was my place to say anything, and then I got a call this morning."

"Tom, you know I'm open to hearing your ideas and thoughts on anything, and considering that you're a priest, and therefore, you teach people, I'd love to hear what's on your mind."

"I appreciate that. I know your focus is on targeting and helping select public schools."

"Right."

"Have you thought about supporting parochial schools instead, or as well?"

Vanacore paused. "Well, not really. I went to public schools growing up, and that's kind of guided my thinking on this."

"I can understand that. But given what you've told me about your childhood and your parents, do you think they would have sent you to a Christian school if they could have afforded it?"

"Actually, I have no doubt about that. I remember overhearing them talking about it late into the night at the kitchen table, and regretting they couldn't afford it."

"Today, it's even tougher. Most families simply can't take on the added cost of a religious education for their kids."

"Like my parents. I understand that. But does it matter? I went to public school, and it was my parents, our priest and parish that kept me in the faith."

"I'd say you were very lucky then. Given the state of our culture, it's not easy to keep kids strong and active in the faith. Listen, Maggie and I have sent all our children to parochial school, and they obviously have gotten an up-close-and-personal church experience growing up as well. But when you consider the impact that schools have on children, just given the time spent in school and what's being taught, there is that possibility of what's being taught at home getting undermined in school. We only saw the upside in sending the kids to parochial school."

"Yeah, that used to drive my parents nuts. My father complained about having to undo what was being done in school at times."

"Now think about how many parents don't even know what's going on and being taught in school, or when they do know, not having the confidence to take it on, like your father did."

Vanacore took his glasses off, and chewed on one of its arms. After a few seconds, he put the glasses back on his face. "Okay, Tom, you make a good case. What more were you thinking? What was the call about that stirred you to set up this little meeting?"

"As you know, the school that Maggie and I sent the kids to, and still send one, is St. Luke's Catholic School. It's been a tremendous blessing. And by the way, make no mistake, you can send your children to what you think is a faithful, traditional Christian school, and even then it unfortunately can turn out to be something different. But that most certainly has not been the case with St. Luke's."

"Well, that's good."

"Absolutely. However, there is a lot of uncertainty about the school's future, given recent closings of Catholic schools. I'm not asking this because of my family's link, but because St. Luke's is a great place and it's in the midst of planning how to grow and secure its future. I thought it would be an ideal opportunity for you to talk to the people who run a quality parochial school, see what the school offers, and consider the challenges it faces." Stone paused. "I can set up a meeting or meetings with Father Burns and Father McDermott, the principal, Mrs. Fleming, staff, parents, whatever. What do you think?"

"I would love to meet with the people at St. Luke's."

"That's great. Shall I set it up?"

Vanacore smiled. "Yes, but on one condition."

"What's that?"

"Before the end of the year, you have to promise to come out to my place in California and go surfing. The entire family is invited, and you'll fly on my jet."

"Mike, that's really nice, but I ..."

"No 'buts,' Tom. Either you promise to get back on the board at my place, or no deal on meeting with St. Luke's."

It was Stone's turn to smile. "You drive a hard bargain, Mike. Take a free trip to surf in California, or else? What can I say, but yes, and thanks?"

"It'll be sick."

After Mike left, Tom called a friend for a little guidance on the economics of education.

Chapter 23

Jennifer and Stephen's flight from Long Island's MacArthur Airport was just over an hour long, touching down on the BWI runway at 4:15 on Sunday afternoon.

By the time they picked up two small pieces of luggage, grabbed a taxi, and checked in at their hotel in the Navy Yard section of Washington, D.C., it was nearly 6:30.

After arriving in the room, Stephen slipped off his sneakers and fell onto the king-size bed. "Well, what are we doing for dinner? Looks like the restaurant downstairs offers a pretty standard menu."

Jennifer unzipped her wardrobe bag. "No, I don't think so." She pulled out her two business suits and blouses to hang up in the closet.

"You have a better idea?"

"As a matter of fact, I do." She opened her computer bag, and pulled out two sheets of paper. "Tickets to the Nationals game tonight."

"You're a wonderful wife. Who are they playing?"

"Well, you might not like this…" She pulled out a Cardinals hat from the same bag and placed it atop her short auburn hair.

Stephen groaned. "If I must."

"Yes, I'm sure it will be sheer torture to get you to go to a ballgame."

"Can I root for the Nationals?"

"I would expect nothing else from a Reds fan. Be warned, though, if the Cardinals lose, you'll be in trouble."

"Oh, really." Stephen slipped his arms around Jennifer, and pulled her close "You know I cannot resist a beautiful woman in a baseball hat?"

"Even a Cardinals hat?"

"I'll make an exception for you."

"How generous." She smiled and they kissed.

Jennifer finally pulled away and said, "Okay, enough of that, or we'll never get to the game."

The ballpark was a short walk from the hotel, and their seats were several rows up from the visitors' dugout on the third base line.

Stephen loved that there was nothing pretentious about Jennifer. She smoothly adapted to all situations, from church dinners to policy conferences to formal affairs to ballgames. Since they were at the ballpark, each had a beer and hot dog, while sharing sweet potato fries for dinner.

He also found it endearing that his new wife kept score at games. As she dutifully wrote down each team's line up, Stephen watched with a smile on his face.

She broke her concentration, and glanced at him. "What?"

"Nothing."

"Go ahead, say it."

"Keeping score?"

"Of course," she replied.

"Why?"

"Why not?"

"Indeed."

"That's what we true fans do, you know. It also might have something to do with being an economist. I don't know. My mom always kept score when she took us to Cardinal games during our summers in St. Louis."

"I think it's great," Stephen reassured, and kissed her on the cheek. "Just don't keep score during our marriage."

"Wait a minute, that's not a bad idea."

A wave of gratitude swept over Stephen. *Thanks again, Lord.* He put his arm around Jennifer's shoulder, as they both looked out to the field as the Nationals starting pitcher tossed a strike to begin the game, much to the pleasure of the hometown crowd.

Stephen took a deep breath as he looked around at the blue seats, mostly filled as the Nationals were playing well, the green grass, and the large video screen looming over right-center field. He commented, "This is a nice ballpark."

Jennifer paused. "It is. Unfortunately, the taxpayers got stuck with the bill."

"Ah, my frustrated economist wife, try to enjoy the game anyway."

Chapter 24

If they had been able to see that far from their seats behind the third base dugout, Stephen and Jennifer would have been surprised by the four individuals sitting on the first base side. More specifically, seeing two of those individuals together would have generated some amazement.

Senator Trevor Tenace bought four season tickets each year since the Expos had abandoned Montreal to become the Nationals. His guests tonight were Ted Brees, Graham Foster, and Zyanon Lebedko.

The game served as the means for introducing Senator Brees to Pastor Foster and Lebedko, an investor and business leader from Belarus.

The contrast between the three Americans and this Belarusian would grab the attention of even a passing observer. Tenace, Brees and Foster ranged in age from mid-thirties to early forties, and were fit, handsome, in or approaching their prime career years, and gave off a casual, but firm self-confidence.

Meanwhile, Lebedko had about thirty years on the other three, but looked even older. He was thin, suffered from a limp, and what little hair he had left was gray. In words and action, Lebedko communicated being worn down, defiant, humble, hopeful, compassionate and tough, all at once. It was a mixed brew born of a hard life.

Tenace explained to Brees that Lebedko was in the U.S. to testify at the Senate hearing, and to talk with the media.

At the behest of Pastor Foster, Lebedko gave Brees a quick rundown on his past. In a heavy accent and with little emotion, he reported, "My parents and all four grandparents died at the hands of the Nazis, in one of the villages that were simply wiped from existence. My sister and I escaped, and we lived with our cousins. After the war, under the Soviets, my aunt and uncle taught us to be devout Christians in secret. Later, for the sake of my wife and children, I worked with the communists to make a living. They valued my managerial skills, but distrusted my independent streak. Under surveillance, our secret meetings with other Christians were discovered. All were executed, including my family, but for me."

"How horrible," commented Brees, who was seated in front of Lebedko and Foster, and next to Tenace.

"You cannot understand what it was like if you did not live through it. The Soviets kept me alive, and moved me around for some time to improve the operations of assorted factories. I considered suicide various times, including efforts that might take some local party leaders with me. But I knew that was not what God would want me to do. It truly was my faith that kept me going, knowing that I would see my family again, one day."

Foster gently placed a hand on Lebedko's shoulder.

Zyanon continued his reflections. "I thought the end of the Soviet Union was the answer to my prayers. And it was, in a sense, for a short time. I struck out on my own with a small furniture factory, hoping that I could finally help my neighbors with real jobs and improved lives. But the government soon reasserted heavy controls over business and other aspects of life. While many of my nation's neighbors were working to put their communist past behind them, we returned to it in certain ways."

"Terrible," added Brees.

"Yes," said Lebedko, staring at Ted Brees with what could be interpreted as a skeptical eye.

Tenace asked, "And what about now, Zyanon?"

"It is my hope that this new regime is being truthful when it talks of greater openness, more opportunity and a new respect for individual rights."

Foster looked at Brees. "Zyanon has been the director of the Entrepreneurship & Values in Action effort in Belarus. And I think it is safe to say that he has been surprised and pleased with this new government taking a more hands-off attitude on the group's efforts with various small businesses. Right, Zyanon?"

"So far, Snopkov has been far more accepting than his predecessor. In fact, his government has been somewhat helpful. I've had positive meetings with Mr. Slizhevskiy, the minister of trade, and our ambassador to the U.S., Oleg Rumas, wants to meet while I am here. That's all for the better. But that could change. It must be kept in mind that this President is not a president in the way Americans think. He remains a dictator, and his background included time with the KGB."

"Ah, like the leader of your big neighbor," said Brees.

"Yes, unfortunately."

Tenace chimed in, "It is our hope, Ted, that helping small businesses will boost the economy, further build a middle class, and, as has been the case in some other nations emerging from dictatorships, work to expand political freedoms."

"I can see that. It's my hope as well." Brees turned to Lebedko. "Zyanon, your story is a powerful and sad one. I am very sorry for all that you have been through. But I hope that my support for this aid project can make some kind of difference."

Lebedko's worn face seemed to be unable to shake off that hint of skepticism. But he did smile, and said, "Thank you, Senator Brees. It is much appreciated."

Senator Tenace smiled and in a voice dripping with southern hospitality, he declared, "Gentlemen, that is all good news. Now, how about I order some traditional American ballpark fare – hotdogs and beer – for each of us?"

Pastor Foster served up his bright smile and agreed. "That would be wonderful and much appreciated, Senator Tenace." He turned to Lebedko. "I did not ask before, Zyanon, but is this your first baseball game?"

"Actually, no. We have a bit of baseball in my country. The first game I ever saw, though, was in the 1960s. While my family was still alive, I was granted a special vacation to Cuba. Castro and baseball, of course. So, we were taken to a game."

"And what do you think?" replied Foster.

Lebedko drank in the scene before him at Nationals Park. After a long pause, he finally said, "Everything is better with freedom, including baseball."

"Amen to that, my brother," said Foster.

Brees leaned over to Tenace and whispered, "I'll skip the dog and beer, and go for a Tanqueray and tonic, with the Greek salad, if you don't mind."

"Of course not, that's fine, Ted," said Trevor Tenace, who rolled his eyes after turning away from his fellow Senate member.

Chapter 25

By the middle of the seventh inning, the Cardinals were up 7-2 to the delight of Jennifer Grant, along with a small smattering of fellow Red Bird fans around the ballpark.

After singing "Take Me Out to the Ballgame," Stephen asked, "How about some ice cream?"

Jennifer replied, "Tempting me, are you?"

"Yes."

"Okay. Want company?"

"Stay here, and enjoy your rout. Helmet sundae or waffle cone?"

"Surprise me. But it has to be ..."

"Chocolate. I know. Back shortly."

On the way back from the concession stand, with two small plastic helmets filled with ice cream, Stephen and Graham Foster nearly ran into each other.

"Stephen, what the heck are you doing here?"

"Watching baseball."

"And eating ice cream, I see. Twice within a month, after not seeing each other for years. How are you, Stephen?"

"Good, Graham. How are things?"

"Actually very exciting. I just had a meeting about that project I mentioned to you at the wedding."

"Sorry, project?"

"The project that Margo and I sent a donation to in lieu of a wedding gift. It's a group helping Christian entrepreneurs in other nations? There's a big push to shift U.S. foreign economic aid more in that direction."

"Interesting and ironic."

"Ironic? How so?"

* * *

Stephen sat down next to Jennifer. "Here's your ice cream. Sorry, it's melting."

"You took awhile. Was the line long?"

"Well, no. I bumped into Graham Foster."

"Really? It always amazes me how much D.C. can seem like a small town when things like that happen. How is he?"

"He's great." Stephen took a spoonful of ice cream.

"That's it. Nothing else?"

"Oh, no, there's more. I'm just not sure you're going to like it."

The right hand holding a plastic spoon stopped midway between the helmet cup and Jennifer's mouth. "What does that mean?"

"We don't have anything going on tomorrow night, do we? Graham invited us to his Monday night service and dinner afterward at his house."

"Fine with me. Why would I not like it? Based on what you heard, you're the one who will get agitated with the worship style and preaching."

"True. But remember when Graham mentioned making a donation to a different charity at the wedding?"

"Yes." Stephen could see the wheels turning in his wife's head.

"I believe that's the issue you're here to testify against."

"Oh, crap."

"I mentioned that to Graham, and I think part of the reason he wants us to come over is so that he can use his vast powers of persuasion, not to mention that new smile of his, to sway you to his side."

Jennifer thought for a moment, and then shrugged. "It won't be the first time that someone tried to do that. It'll make for an interesting night. But there's a question."

"And what is that?"

"Who will Graham be more annoyed with by the end of the night – you for taking on his prosperity preaching or me for trying to set him straight on the ills of government subsidies?"

Stephen laughed. "Tough call. If he wasn't a friend and I wasn't a pastor, we could make a wager."

Jennifer barely suppressed a smile. "Five bucks?"

Chapter 26

Many, if not most, young pastors would appreciate living in a three-level, three-bedroom, three-bath townhouse, with a large kitchen, spacious living room, a study and a deck providing a view of the Capitol dome in the distance. Toss in an annual salary that was well above church guidelines, and serving at New Jerusalem was one sweet pastoral gig.

But after two years at New Jerusalem as one of the assistant pastors, it was increasingly apparent that Leonard Schroeder was less than happy. The only real requirements for the pastors and staff at New Jerusalem were an unfailingly positive attitude and unbridled enthusiasm. Pastor Schroeder was coming up woefully short on that front. That drew the attention and concern of the senior pastor, Graham Foster. But the more Foster provided counsel and encouragement to Schroeder, the more Schroeder grew in his irritation and negativism.

After a night of youth basketball and closing up the church recreation center, Schroeder was now working on his second Beck's, leaning on the deck railing and staring out at the Washington Monument and lit up Capitol in the distance.

His Android phone buzzed. "Good evening, sir."

"Leonard, how are you tonight?"

"Fine, thank you. And yourself?"

"Well. Are you having any second thoughts?"

Schroeder took a deep breath, glanced again at the Capitol and then turned to his right, looking at the large red brick, colonial-style New Jerusalem Worship and Fulfillment Center. "None whatsoever."

"Good. Things are moving very fast, and I just wanted to confirm your readiness."

"I'm ready."

"Excellent. We will talk soon, Pastor Schroeder."

The call ended.

Schroeder smiled, and turned away from the Washington Monument and New Jerusalem's Worship Center to go inside.

Chapter 27

Mr. Audia decided against Marcel's on this Sunday night. His desire for a late-night dinner led him to Bistro Francais in Georgetown.

After finishing his Banana Royale dessert, Audia told the waiter, "Please let the chef know that the veal chop with porcini, shiitake & morel mushroom cream sauce was exquisite."

"I will be happy to do so, sir. Might I get you something else? Perhaps a nice espresso or cappuccino?"

Audia replied, "Yes, make it a Café Viennois."

"Very good."

Audia's iPhone rumbled in the pocket of his light tan blazer. It was a text message: "Number two is a go for tomorrow night."

His reply: "Good."

Audia then took note that it was nearly midnight.

The waiter arrived with his espresso and whipped cream.

Audia said, "I'm very sorry, but it turns out that I need my rest tonight, and that will only keep me up."

"Not a problem, sir. Is there something else you would like?"

"No. I'm sure this will cover my check and the tip for your service."

The thin, dark face of the waiter lit up at seeing the $100 bill on the table. "That is most generous, sir. Thank you."

Audia dropped his linen napkin on the white tablecloth, got up and started toward the door. "Have a nice night."

Chapter 28

Jennifer said, "This is one of the very best starts to a day in D.C. I've ever had."

She and Stephen had gotten up early in order to stroll among the monuments on the National Mall before Jennifer headed to her D.C. office.

The taxi dropped them at the Washington Monument. They walked past the 555-foot high obelisk, down the hill and across 17th Street, and then gradually descended further into the World War II Memorial. The oval memorial featured water and fountains surrounded by 56 pillars representing the states and territories at the time, and two 43-foot arches noting the war's two theaters – Atlantic and Pacific.

Jennifer observed, "It's hard to believe that this was so controversial when being constructed. I think it fits perfectly on the mall."

"I agree. The last time I was in D.C. was with the Boy Scout troop that the church sponsors, and it was about a year after this opened."

"You really haven't been here in a long time."

"No reason to be here, until now that I'm married to a famous, sought-after economist. At the time, though, I did offer a rather compelling history lessons for the Scouts."

"Right, how did that go over?"

"As you might expect. About half were interested, and we had to make sure the other half didn't wander off."

"Like your typical Sunday sermon then?"

"Amusing."

"Thank you."

As the morning stroll continued along the reflecting pool, Grant noticed someone in a tan trench coat heading in the same direction, though hanging back on the opposite side of the water. It was the second time the coat caught his attention, especially given the relatively clear skies and the fact that the infamous Washington heat and humidity had just started to climb.

Stephen stopped at the top of the stairs of the Lincoln Memorial, and turned back to look east. "Toward the end of my time with the agency, I used to come here a lot. I called them my 'Mr. Smith Goes to Washington' moments."

"And what were those moments about?"

"Well, the more I thought about leaving the CIA to become a pastor, I'd put it to the test. This mall and the monuments, along with The Wall at Langley, always provided the most powerful reminders of why I love this country and wanted to serve it. And I knew that if I had doubts about becoming a pastor, they'd come out here. Eventually, the last few times I came, the doubts were gone. And other than that time after the 9-11 attacks, I haven't doubted the decision."

"I'm kind of glad you made that choice, by the way," Jennifer said, as she pulled him close and they kissed.

After taking in President Lincoln, they moved back outside the massive columns. Stephen spotted the trench coat lingering to the south.

Jennifer looked at her watch. "I have to get to the office. What are you going to do with the rest of your day?"

"Not sure. I thought about checking out the Korean War and FDR memorials."

Jennifer's face crinkled like she had just eaten something sour. "FDR, ugh, now there was a president who was clueless on the economy. Made sure things were a complete mess until after the war."

"Sounds like an economics sermon is coming on. I might wander off."

"Cute."

"How about I come by to see the office around five thirty, and we can head to Graham's church from there?"

"Perfect." They exchanged kisses, and Jennifer said, "Love you, Stephen."

As she turned in the direction of the Vietnam War Memorial and Constitution Avenue, Stephen replied, "And I love you, Mrs. Grant."

Grant took delight that his wife's beauty was evident whether she was coming or going. He finally broke his revelry.

And now for my trench-coated friend.

He went down the steps, and over to the Korean War Veterans Memorial. Grant slowed his pace among the statues of the soldiers.

For so many, the Forgotten War, but these are pretty powerful reminders.

On a bench sat a man in a brown suit, yellow shirt, a dark brown tie, and the trench coat. The tie was askew, and the suit, shirt and coat were wrinkled.

Grant sat down next to him, still looking at the frozen soldiers. "I see your wardrobe hasn't been upgraded, Charlie."

"Screw you, Grant. Oh, I'm sorry, am I allowed to say that to a pastor?"

"Two things cross my mind, Charlie. Part of me is glad to see you, and I want to know how you are. The other part is wondering why you're following my wife and me on a Monday morning in D.C."

Charlie Driessen, a 25-year CIA veteran with little hair atop his head but a prominent gray mustache, declared, "She is a gorgeous woman. Why the hell did she marry you?"

"Charity on her part. Are you going to answer either of my questions?"

"I'm fine, thank you. Had to have my gall bladder out a couple of years ago. Never even got a card. What kind of pastor are you, anyway?"

"Sorry about that, but as you know, I didn't know."

"Yeah, maybe."

"And why are you tailing me?"

Driessen paused. After a few seconds, he answered, "It's Paige."

"Paige? What's up?"

"She's playing, or in Paige's case, as you know, maybe it's better to say, she's flirting with fire.'"

"Charlie, specifics?"

"I kind of keep an eye out for Paige. She still plays things fast and loose. She's periodically jumping into the sack with someone she shouldn't. I'm pretty sure that I'm the only one on the job who knows. But if it gets out, she could be in some serious shit at the agency."

"Whom is she sleeping with?"

"Do you remember Gerhardt Schmidt?"

"Schmidt? You mean the former East German Stasi operative?"

"The same."

"How long has she been doing this?"

"Not sure."

The two sat in silence for a minute.

Paige, what are you thinking? Or, are you thinking at all? Though, with Paige, it could be calculating. Never know.

Grant finally asked, "Okay, what do you want me to do?"

"You've reconnected with her recently, from what I understand."

"Yes, kind of. To the extent possible, given her situation and mine."

"Understood. But as much as I've tried, I don't think anyone ever got closer to Paige than you. She needs to be confronted on this, and quickly, without word circulating. I think you might be able to pull it off better than anyone else," advised Charlie. "Maybe you could wear your collar to offer her counsel," he added wryly.

"My collar and Paige still do not completely mix."

"Whatever. Are you willing to do it?"

A friend in need. Grant said, "Of course. I assume she's in D.C."

"Good. I knew I could still count on you, Grant."

"By the way, how did you know I was in town? Last time was six or seven years ago."

Driessen laughed and shook his head. "Are you kidding me?"

"Right, stupid question."

"Good to see you, Grant. You're actually missed, and thanks for talking to Paige."

"Take care, Charlie."

Charlie Driessen got up and walked away without a glance over his shoulder.

Chapter 29

Ryan Bates startled when the passenger door opened.

"You know, I shouldn't be able to sneak up on the FBI like this." Paige Caldwell took the seat next to Bates in the dark Chevy Impala, and handed him a cup of hot coffee. "Light and sweet, right?"

Bates seemed a bit bewildered. "Ah, yes. What are you doing here, Paige?"

She brushed back her black hair. "Just talking with a colleague over some coffee." She smiled and winked. "Don't you miss working together, Ryan?"

He regained his bearings. "To be honest, not really."

"I'm hurt. Is this a CIA-FBI thing, or is it personal?"

"Our lone inter-agency assignment did not work out too well in the end."

"Fair enough." She took a sip of her coffee, and looked down the street at the open-air restaurant that was the focus of Bates' attention. In feigned innocence, Caldwell said, "Hey, look over there. It's Senator Ted Brees, along with his top aide. What's her name? Kerri Bratton, right?"

"Yes, it is," said Bates with a mix of both irritation and resignation in his voice.

"When is Brees going to marry her, anyway? I assume they're still doing the nasty, since that was what broke up his marriage."

Bates did not reply.

Caldwell pushed ahead. "And who is that with them? Let's see. There's Carlos Luis, Mexican businessman, and Jose Mora, a Mexico economic development official. Oh, dear, isn't that Manny Rodriguez?"

"Yes. That's them."

"Pretty opportune for you that my old partner Grant happened to come across Manny."

Bates said, "Yes, and in California on his honeymoon nonetheless with Senator Brees's ex-wife." He eyed Caldwell closer, but she offered no reaction. "There's also the problem that the CIA apparently lost track of Rodriguez over the years."

"Not true."

Bates raised an eyebrow slightly. "What does that mean?"

"We found out that Mr. Luis was being extorted by Lydia Garcia."

"The Mexican drug lord?"

"The same. Old Manny there is presenting himself as a legit real estate investor, but he's working for Lydia. She chose the wrong target, though. Luis is a kick-ass entrepreneur, and wasn't ready to just play along. He was smart enough not to turn to the Mexican government for help, not being sure who could be trusted. So, he contacted us. And we've got his family covered."

"Nice of you to let us know."

"Ryan, I'm doing more than just giving you a heads up." She reached inside her white blazer, and pulled out a device that looked like a typical smartphone. "A little present for the FBI." She hit the touch screen, and the conversation between the U.S. Senator and the three men from Mexico came through with digital clarity.

Bates asked, "Luis agreed to wear a wire?"

"Yes, he did. Of course, once he arrived on our soil, it's all about the FBI. So, here you go." She handed Bates the smartphone. "We'll pass on recordings from the gathering the three Mexicans had with Senator Ellis as well. We knew about that gathering without Grant's heads up. But nothing interesting in terms of giving us anything that points to the beheading of Senator Farrell."

"Unfortunate, but Farrell's murder fits the profile for Mexican DTOs," Bates insisted.

"I tend to agree. And the fact that Manny Rodriguez is in the mix here raises suspicion even higher."

* * *

Ted Brees declared, "Gentleman, I appreciate your points about the impact this would have on the Mexican economy, and therefore, on the flow of illegal immigrants into the United States. I'm in full agreement. But the smart political move here, given what the President and many of my Republican colleagues in Congress want, is to make Belarus the initial step in shifting U.S. foreign aid to small businesses. That'll serve to smooth out the process, and I cannot imagine who would then oppose Mexico as being the next test case."

"What about your Congressional Black Caucus? Will they not push an African nation, if not the entire continent of Africa?" asked Jose Mora, with an unmistakable tone of frustration.

"Well, I certainly cannot speak for the Black Caucus," answered Brees in a cool tone. "But I think you have to understand that there is little opposition to this basic idea. It's just a matter of where Mexico is in line, and how quickly the line will move."

Mora interrupted, "Yes, Senator, that is our concern." He had already taken off the jacket of his tan suit, and now pulled at his collar as beads of sweat formed on his skin. "We do not know how long that line will be, or where our country will be positioned. And the American political system is not known for its speed."

Carlos Luis broke in with a calmer, more reassuring voice. "As a business owner, Jose, I would love to see all governments work faster and more efficiently. But that is rarely the case in our nation, in the U.S., or most anywhere else. Wouldn't you agree, Senator, despite the best efforts of individuals such as yourself?"

Brees smiled along with Luis, adding, "I wish I could disagree, Carlos, but I cannot. At the same time, I think the U.S. does better than most."

"Indeed, it does," replied Luis. "Do you mind if I bring up another issue related to Belarus and this effort of your government?"

"Please," said Brees.

They paused as their lunch plates were removed.

Luis resumed, "Well, I'm rather surprised that given your separation of church and state, that there is not greater discomfort about working with this Entrepreneurship & Values in Action group? After all, they make little secret of working with and focusing on Christian businesses."

Brees glanced across the table at Kerri Bratton, who indiscreetly nodded back. Brees said, "To be honest, my friends, I have similar concerns. But, again, this President is dedicated to working with faith-based groups. For good measure, when it comes to Republican voters, they're the heavy churchgoers in our country."

Luis, Mora and Rodriguez fell silent.

Bratton took the opportunity to fill the void. "Senator, I'm sorry, but we need to get you to the next meeting."

"Of course. Manuel, Carlos, Jose, I want to be clear. I am fully supportive of Mexico being next in line after Belarus when it comes to this pilot project. And I will do all I can to make sure that is the reality."

Bratton made sure Brees got a separate check, and the two left the three Mexicans behind.

The three men switched to Spanish.

Manuel Rodriguez looked grimly at Mora and Luis. "That is not how it was supposed to go. My employer will not be happy. And you both need to understand what such unhappiness means, such as for your respective families."

* * *

With Rodriguez's ominous words, Paige glanced sideways at Agent Bates. "That's my cue. Adios, Ryan."

Paige Caldwell got out of the sedan. As she started walking away, she removed another smartphone from a different blazer pocket. She flipped open the encrypted device, and hit a number.

"We can't wait any longer. Rodriguez is not pleased how the meeting with Brees went. He made a clear threat against both their families. We have the Luis family secure, right?"

The voice on the other end said, "You know that."

"Don't get pissy. Now it's time to move in and secure Mora's family, quietly."

"Will do."

Caldwell closed the phone, turned a corner, and hit "Unlock" on her keychain. The deep impact blue Mustang GT chirped. She slid into the leather-trimmed seat, started up the 5.0 V8 engine, and hit the roof retract button. She took a moment to tilt her head up to the sun, closed her eyes, and took a deep breath. Paige then put on her Fendi sunglasses, smiled, and pulled into traffic with more speed than was necessary.

Chapter 30

The cab dropped Jennifer and Stephen off just short of 6:30 in front of New Jerusalem. The church actually was a gated compound in northern Virginia on the Potomac River. It featured a large church, a building with a gym and pool, four townhouses, and finely manicured grounds. Each building was colonial in style, with the church building sporting clear, arched windows on each side, and large white columns in the front.

They stopped to read the sign just outside the church, which informed visitors that this was the "New Jerusalem Worship and Fulfillment Center."

Stephen mumbled, "Fulfillment Center? What exactly is that?"

"Steady, my love," whispered Jennifer.

They went up a few stairs, past the columns, and through two large glass doors. A few feet into the building, they stopped to take in their surroundings.

Jennifer started to giggle, but quickly caught herself. She leaned closer to Stephen, and whispered, "Are you okay?"

Stephen replied, "I'm not sure."

They were in an expansive lobby, spreading from one side of the building to the other, dominated by a shiny, oak floor, white walls, and two sets of double doors leading into another room. But it was three kiosks in the room, one on each side and the other in between the doors, that drew attention.

Jennifer and Stephen both looked left initially. Jennifer asked in a soft voice, "Is that a coffee and espresso bar?"

"Apparently," replied Stephen. They looked to the center kiosk. "But if you're looking for something decaf and healthier, I believe that's a juice and smoothie bar."

They continued to turn their heads in unison to the right. Jennifer added, "I don't know if you had lunch, but it looks like you can get a small sandwich or pastry over there. Hmmm, even a salad, apparently."

There were lines of four or five people at each booth. A person came away from the food stand with a sandwich in a box tray. Jennifer said, "Oh, and look, you can get your food in a convenient, disposable tray, just like at those nice movie theaters."

Normally, Stephen would enjoy these little exchanges of sarcastic, even sardonic, observations with his wife, but he couldn't muster any joy this time around. At best, their private banter only served to limit his irritation. He said, "It's 6:30, so unless you need a strawberry-mango smoothie to get you through whatever we are about to experience, shall we go through those doors?"

"Maybe there's another booth around offering something stronger. I think you might need a stiff drink."

"True."

After they walked into the next room, Jennifer said, "Honest, I was just kidding about the movie theater."

It was a massive theater with over a thousand seats, a stage with a podium, a huge screen behind the stage, and a mega-watt sound system that confronted the couple as they walked through the double doors. On the screen, a video of sweeping natural vistas, from beaches and rivers to fields, mountains and forests, was running.

The accompanying music – which seemed to be a strange cross between David Lee Roth and Michael Bublé – was not recorded. Instead, a full band on the right side of the stage was performing.

Jennifer and Stephen decided to take a seat in the back left of the theater. The seats were plush and roomy. Jennifer pointed to the backs of the row in front of them, "Look, cup holders. Very handy."

Stephen rolled his eyes and shook his head. "But if you notice, not a cross to be found anywhere," he whispered.

Jennifer looked around. "You're right. What's up with that?"

"I've read that some prosperity churches look at crosses as barriers, too much of a downer."

Grant noted that the room was about half full, which was rather remarkable for a Monday night, and almost everyone was well dressed, with many in business attire. Congregants seemed to be broken into three groups. The first paid close attention, swayed, tapped their feet, clapped and/or sang along with the band. The second chatted in small groups in their seats as they ate and drank. And the third moved about the room greeting people, talking in groups, and/or sipping flavored coffees.

When the band finished their Roth-Bublé hybrid, the room broke into applause, along with a few cheers. The lead singer, who was dressed in a light gray suit and an open collared black shirt while sporting long, wild blond hair, seemed to be soaking in the crowd. "Thank you, New Jerusalem. And thank you, Jesus!"

Massive shades then came down to cover the large, arched windows, and more serene music was piped in through the sound system. Most people found their way to seats, placing their espressos and smoothies in the cup holders. Newcomers were guided in the right direction.

Then out on stage came Pastor Graham Foster. The room erupted in applause.

Even given all he had just taken in, Grant was still taken off guard when his friend from seminary walked out dressed in a short sleeve, tan, button-down shirt, brown cargo pants, and hiking boots. It also was still hard adjusting to the gelled hair and big, white-toothed smiles.

Stephen whispered to Jennifer, "Graham looks ready to head out on safari."

She replied, "I think he looks like an exceedingly happy Indiana Jones."

"My friends, welcome," started Foster. "Let's thank New Jerusalem's worship band for their marvelous performance."

Foster led the applause, and then gave a thumbs up to the band members.

He continued, "So, you might be asking your neighbor, what's up with Graham sporting the Indiana Jones look?"

Jennifer smiled and whispered into Stephen's ear, "Never doubt me."

Stephen replied, "I'm learning not to doubt every day."

They refocused on Graham Foster, who said, "Well, first, I do love Indy and the movies, and yes, even *Kingdom of the Crystal Skull*."

That remark drew some laughs around the theater.

He continued, "Second, it's kind of fun dressing up this way on occasion. It gets one in the mood for an exciting adventure. Of course, here at New Jerusalem, we're always focused on the adventure that is life when we believe and allow God to invest in us, in our families, in our careers and finances, in our health, in our lives."

This garnered a wave of applause from around the theater.

Graham asked, "What did our Lord promise?"

Jennifer and Stephen jumped when nearly everyone in the room replied, "'I came that they may have life and have it abundantly.' John 10:10." That was followed by more applause.

Pastor Foster said, "To start our conversation tonight, let's first look at a clip from, yes, an Indiana Jones movie."

Jennifer whispered to her husband, "Being a movie buff, maybe you'll enjoy this."

Stephen just raised his eyebrows.

Foster continued, "You'll probably recall that this was at a critical moment in *Indiana Jones and the Last Crusade*. After Indiana's father is shot by an American working with the Nazis, Jones must work his way through various deadly traps in order to get to the Holy Grail and save his father."

The lights dimmed on cue, and on the big screen behind Graham Foster came Indiana Jones walking through a narrow passage to emerge at a precipice, with seemingly no way to get across.

Jones reads from the book providing the clues needed to reach his goal, "Only in the leap from the lion's head will he prove his worth." He looks ahead and observes, "Impossible. Nobody can jump this." He then reluctantly concludes, "It's a leap of faith."

The scene cuts to Indiana's father, who, in pain, says, "You must believe, boy. You must believe."

Indiana then puts a hand over his chest and takes a step forward. He does not fall, but instead, walks on a bridge that was camouflaged. Jones is relieved and elated, and proceeds to walk forward.

The clip ended, and the lights came up to the applause of those in attendance.

"Isn't that an amazing scene for something coming out of Hollywood?" asked Graham Foster, which was followed with still more applause. "Indiana Jones saw an impossibility before him. After all, how could anyone jump across that chasm? It sure looked impossible. But then he chose to believe. He chose faith. And the impossible turned out not to be impossible at all. Instead, he found that a way had been provided. Indy takes steps, tentative and unsure at first, but then confidently, crossing the rest of the bridge in order to find what he is seeking. And in the case of this movie, it was the cup of Christ. Or, as Indy puts it in the movie, 'That's the cup of a carpenter.' I just love that line. And finding that cup, that is, finding Jesus Christ, means Indiana's father is healed from his gunshot wound. That's a powerful message about what God can do in all our lives if we choose faith, open the door and allow Him to invest in us."

The applause was at its loudest.

Stephen was completely deflated. *Graham, how did you wind up here?* He settled back in the chair, and cradled his right cheek in his right hand as he listened to another forty-five minutes of prosperity preaching that focused on being positive, making sure one's faith was forceful, and reaping rewards. Grant tried to figure out what he would say at dinner with his friend.

After the service, Jennifer and Stephen waited, uncomfortably, next to the espresso bar while Graham and Margo shook hands and hugged those leaving the service.

Two other men were doing the same as people left the front doors of the building. Stephen overheard them being called "Pastor Billy" and "Pastor Lenny."

After everyone attending the service was gone, Graham and Margo greeted Stephen and Jennifer warmly. Graham said, "Stephen, you have to meet Bill and Leonard, they're assistant pastors here at New Jerusalem."

Leonard Schroeder was in his early thirties, thin, and sported short black hair, and a tightly cut beard and mustache. Judging by his body language, Grant immediately thought that Leonard had missed New Jerusalem's "be positive" memo.

In contrast, Bill Johnson shook both Jennifer and Stephen's hands with significant enthusiasm. Grant noted that Johnson's smile was not nearly as polished as Graham's.

Or, not nearly as phony? Stop it. Don't go there, Grant.

Though just 29, Johnson looked about a decade older due to the fact that little of his light brown hair remained, and he carried a notable potbelly.

After a brief, amiable conversation, Graham said to Bill and Leonard, "We're taking the Grants back to our house for dinner, so I'll see you guys tomorrow. Thanks, again, for all you do."

Foster then hugged each man. Grant noted that Johnson responded happily, and Schroeder rather coldly.

Chapter 31

A flower garden separated the Worship Center from the four townhouses. The two couples strolled along the garden's brick path.

Graham Foster said, "Since you're staying in D.C., we'll have dinner at our place here, rather than heading out to the house in Waterford."

Stephen replied, "That sounds great, Graham." As they approached the four, three-story townhouses, he asked, "Who lives here?"

Graham said, "Leonard and Bill each have one, as do Margo and I, and the other is used on an as-needed basis, including by staff and guests."

After entering the townhouse, Margo announced, "We're going to have dinner on the third floor deck. Since it's such a beautiful night, we'll have an ideal view of the Washington Monument and the Capitol Building, if that sounds nice?"

Jennifer said, "Wonderful. Can I help at all?"

Margo replied, "Thank you, but everything should be nearly ready. I texted Terrance, and we should be all set."

Stephen asked, "Terrance?"

Graham answered, "He's our household manager, chef and chauffer. Given our schedules, it just isn't realistic that we could keep up with the townhouse, our home, or much else."

Margo added, "I'd be lost without him. He is a marvelous blessing. We're so thankful that the Lord sent him our way."

Stephen noted that Margo had changed some since the day she and Graham had gotten married nearly a decade earlier, though far from the massive transformation Graham had undergone. Margo had the same thick brunette hair and fair complexion. She just seemed more refined, as well as a bit more restrained or buttoned up.

The fried catfish, coleslaw, hush puppies, potato salad, corn with green and red peppers, and sweet southern iced tea was enjoyed in a light breeze, with the lit up Capitol viewable in the distance. Stephen and Graham dominated much of the conversation reminiscing about seminary days.

But when Terrance served lemon bars for dessert, Graham broached the subject that Stephen was partially hoping would go unmentioned. "So, Stephen, what do you think of New Jerusalem and the service tonight?"

Stephen took a sip of his iced tea. *How shall I put this?* "Well, I think you probably know, Graham. Not exactly my thing."

Graham smiled. "Really?"

"Ah, yes."

That was followed by silence.

Graham resumed, "Stephen, we've known each other a long time. You can speak freely."

"Since you're an old friend and gracious host, I'm trying to be diplomatic."

"Stephen Grant, diplomatic?" Graham laughed. "Neither one of us was very diplomatic at seminary. Come on."

Okay. "I'm concerned that you've left behind Holy Scripture and the Lutheran Confessions for prosperity preaching. And what's up with 'Fulfillment Center' and not a cross to be found? And you've replaced the liturgy with, what, smoothies?" Stephen didn't take direct note of the narrowing stare he was getting from Jennifer, but he could feel it.

Graham said, "That's disappointing, and a bit surprising."

"Surprising? What did you expect, Graham?"

"I thought you might be a bit more expansive or open in your thinking than some of our colleagues from seminary. After all, the best man at your wedding was an Anglican priest, and a Catholic priest also was in the wedding party, right? And then there was that whole thing – what, nearly two years ago? – with the Pope."

"Correct, but what does any of that have to do with this?"

Graham said, "I assumed that you were ecumenical."

"Actually, Graham, I favor ecumenism, as do my friends, Father Stone and Father McDermott. But not the stale, old ecumenical movement focused on anything but the faith; instead, it's an ecumenism among traditional Christians. We recognize our differences, pray that we grow closer, and celebrate and publicly affirm so much that we have in common."

"So, what's the problem with what we're doing?" Graham pressed on. "Everything we do at New Jerusalem is rooted in Scripture. I think that phrase you used – 'prosperity preaching' – is merely a way to attack our efforts and others trying to tell people about the great rewards to be found in Jesus. Doesn't Jesus fulfill each of us?" He answered his own question. "Of course, He does. And while the Lutheran Confessions were emphasized at seminary, I've come to realize that they're not terribly relevant to the twenty-first century. Along the same lines, things like crosses, along with words like 'church,' simply don't appeal to many people today. They create obstacles to spreading the Good News. And as for our food and beverage booths, isn't it better to make people feel at home in God's house? It's all in service of our common goal."

Jennifer and Margo were stuck in the position of spectators at a theological tennis match.

Stephen replied, "I'm not sure where to start. First, I'm not sure where ecumenism comes into play here, since New Jerusalem is a Lutheran church and you're a Lutheran pastor. Or, at least, that's still my assumption, which leads to my second point: You seem intent on abandoning what Lutheranism brings to the Christian table. For example, the Lutheran Confessions remain critical, not just in terms of keeping we pastors properly anchored in Scripture, but as a teaching tool that clarifies and anchors those in the pews."

Graham shook his head, and started to say something, but Stephen did not give him the chance. Instead, he added, "Of course, as you say, we are fulfilled in Christ. But calling your church a 'fulfillment center' does two things. It shifts the focus onto the person, the self, and away from our complete dependence on Jesus. And the same goes for the lack of crosses. Rather than going by focus group responses about how people feel about or react to crosses, why not explain how the cross shows what Jesus sacrificed for us and how through His death on a cross and His resurrection, we are forgiven, redeemed and saved? That's the pure joy of the cross. In addition, there's the fact that Christians can speak to suffering like no other religion specifically because of what Jesus – God incarnate – went through leading up to and on the cross. There is a great deal of suffering in this world, including, of course, for the faithful among us. Unfortunately, this leads to the big question: Are you truly teaching what Holy Scripture tells us?"

Graham lost his omnipresent smile for a brief moment, and asked, "What do you mean by that?"

I'm knee deep in it, so might as well forge on. Stephen answered, "You're misinterpreting Scripture."

Graham regained his smile and soothing voice, asking, "Stephen, how could you come to that conclusion?"

"Take John 10:10, which apparently has become a favorite here. When Jesus says, 'I came that they may have life and have it abundantly,' it's not about wealth and riches in this life. It's about eternal life through faith in Jesus Christ."

"You limit the Lord, Stephen. Look at what Jesus did for His faithful disciples at the start of the fifth chapter in Luke, for example, blessing them with so many fish that one boat could not hold it all."

"I don't limit the Lord at all, Graham. Instead, I simply recognize that, while God bestows all kinds of blessings, there also are challenges and suffering, including for the faithful. Jesus redeems and restores, but the consequences of man's fall into sin remain in this world. Faith itself is a gift from God. It's not a human work, or something that when we perform it at the right level or in the right way, God necessarily responds with material blessings."

Stephen paused to take a sip of iced tea, and finally glanced at Jennifer, who actually gave him a slight smile. He continued, "You pointed to the opening of Luke 5. While Jesus bestows blessings on Simon Peter and his fellow fishermen, notice that it was Jesus telling them to lower their nets and filling them with fish, even while they doubted, in order to get their attention. Remember that after that huge catch, Jesus then says that 'from now on you will be catching men,' and they left everything behind. And for most of the apostles, their lives on earth generally did not end well. They experienced spiritual abundance, and an unimaginable heavenly reward. But as Dietrich Bonheoffer made clear in his life and book, there is a cost of discipleship."

Graham sighed, but maintained his smile, which now carried a hint of sympathy. "Indeed, God has different plans for each of us. But people don't realize the force of faith, and how powerful God can be in their lives."

It was Stephen's turn to smile sympathetically. "And what about the faithful Christian who does not reap the rewards of this world, Graham? How many Christians struggle or fail in their careers or businesses? Might you actually be undermining or shaking their faith? What do you tell them? That they need to believe harder?"

Graham said, "I tell them to have faith, Stephen." Graham glanced at Margo, and said, "Listen, it's getting late, and we're not going to settle this tonight. But we need to keep this conversation going." He got up from the table, went inside for a few seconds, and returned. "Here is my new book. I think I mentioned it was coming out soon. It's actually being released tomorrow. Please, read it, and then let's talk some more."

Graham handed the book to Stephen, who looked at the cover dominated by Graham Foster's smile, and a title declaring *Let God Maximize Your Returns*.

Jake warned that I wouldn't like the title. He was right. Stephen politely replied, "Thanks, Graham. Congratulations on the book. I will read it, but you need to sign it."

Graham said, "Of course." He pulled a pen out of his pocket, and wrote on the first page.

Stephen looked at Jennifer, and said, "Graham is right. It is late, and we need to get back to the hotel, so you can get ready for tomorrow, right, Jen?"

Before she could answer beyond a nod, Graham interrupted, "Yes, at the ballgame, Stephen mentioned that you were testifying tomorrow before the Senate Foreign Relations Committee on foreign aid going directly to small businesses, rather than to governments."

"That's right, Graham," replied Jennifer.

"But I understand you're testifying against the idea?"

"Yes, I will be."

"You know, this is tied in with the group that I'm very active with, the Entrepreneurship & Values in Action nonprofit. We gave to them in your name for a wedding gift, and..."

After barely saying a word all night, it was Margo's turn to interrupt. She cleared her throat gently, and said, "Now Graham, you need to let our nice friends here get to their hotel for a good night's rest. You'll be at the hearing tomorrow, so why not chat about this with Jennifer then?"

"Where are my manners?" asked Graham. "Naturally, you are quite right, my dear."

Stephen said, "We need to call a cab to take us back."

Graham replied, "Nonsense. Terrance will be glad to drop you at your hotel."

Jennifer said, "Oh, no, we could not impose like that."

Margo responded, "It is in no way an imposition, and we insist."

Stephen and Jennifer demurred. Margo instructed Terrance, and the short, thin 30-year-old seemed more than happy to undertake the drive.

As they approached the front door, Graham said to Jennifer, "I hope some time tomorrow, if we have the chance, you'll let me try to convince you otherwise on this foreign-aid matter, Jennifer? I am very enthused about the possibilities, and the opportunities that the Lord might create in other nations."

"I'd be more than happy to discuss it with you, Graham. At the same time, though, you know how hard it's going to be to get Stephen onboard with what you're doing here at New Jerusalem? When it comes to economics and doling out taxpayer subsidies, I'm an even tougher nut to crack."

Graham declared, "I take that as a challenge," and smiled broadly.

Chapter 32

Mr. Audia positioned himself in the shadows of New Jerusalem's Worship Center. He could see those entering and exiting the four townhouses, but at the same time, no one could see him.

Audia watched via the screen of a portable night vision camera. He took photos of the first person leaving the Foster's townhouse, a short, thin male who climbed into and started up a church van.

He was followed a few minutes later by a couple. Audia took more photos. The driver of the van opened a sliding door so the man and woman could get in, and the white vehicle left the grounds, disappearing down the darkened road.

Audia slipped the camera into a small pouch on his belt. He pulled the hood up on his black jacket, and zipped it up so that his face would not be recognizable by any of the security cameras. He quickly checked the weapon strapped to his waist, and the other on his back.

He moved quietly and quickly across the garden to the Foster's townhouse, and tested the front door. It was unlocked. Audia pulled out a Glock 37 with a suppressor attached, slipped inside without a sound, and stood perfectly still, breathing quietly.

The Fosters had gone upstairs to their bedroom suite after the Grants left. Graham already was changed into pajamas, and Margo was in the bathroom readying for bed.

Graham said, "Margo, honey, I'm going to run upstairs and get the last of the dessert, plates and cups off the deck so Terrance won't have much to do tomorrow. It'll just take a few minutes, and then we can pray."

Margo replied, "Thanks, Graham. That would be nice."

Graham left the spacious bedroom, with its four-poster bed, and went up a flight of stairs. He failed to notice the figure in black listening and waiting a flight down.

Audia moved up the stairs, again with little sound.

But just as he entered the bedroom, Margo Foster was emerging from the bathroom.

At the sight of Audia and his gun, she let out a partial shriek, before being silenced with a bullet to the chest.

She toppled back into the bathroom. Audia walked over and put one more bullet in her head, and another in her chest.

Graham Foster had just come in from the third floor deck when he heard his wife's cutoff scream. He dropped a plate of the remaining lemon bars on a table, and moved quickly to the stairs.

He called out, "Margo, are you alright?"

As Graham moved down a few steps, he saw the gun, and then, too late, the rest of the man holding the weapon emerging from his bedroom. "Oh, God, no," he whispered.

Foster's pause before moving down the stairs made it easier for Audia, who smiled, holstered the gun, and reached his right hand over his head to grab the hilt of a second weapon.

As Audia unveiled the sword, with a short, single-edged, slightly curved blade, Graham Foster pulled up short from his charge, and froze. That allowed Audia to swing the medieval weapon with power and accuracy. The result was that Graham Foster's head separated from his body. The head tumbled to the left, as the body fell to the right.

Audia admired the blade, and then the results of his work on the floor. He whispered to the dead Foster, "It's a Medieval French Falchion sword. They said it was crude, but I kind of like the results."

Audia moved up to the third floor, making sure the rest of the townhouse was clear. After finding no one else, he headed back to the stairs. But he spotted a large stack of books on a table next to some lemon bars. He slipped the sword back into its sheath, selected the smallest lemon bar, and shoved the entire cake into his mouth.

He quietly uttered, "Mmmm," as he picked up one of the books. He looked at the picture of a smiling Graham Foster, and descended the stairs, stepping around Graham's body and head.

Audia swallowed the remaining lemon bar, and read aloud, "*Let God Maximize Your Returns.* Ha, now that's ironic, Pastor Foster, isn't it? I'm guessing your sales will jump after tonight, but you won't be around to reap the returns. Too bad. But now you're no doubt going to be very upset with me because I have to go get your wife's head." He unsheathed the Falchion sword once more. "The French are, or at least were, so civilized regarding instruments of death, don't you think?"

When he was finished, Audia left the decapitated heads of Graham and Margo Foster on the downstairs couch. He spotted the television remote, laughed, hit the power button, and arranged the couple's heads as if they were watching.

He took Foster's book, and left the New Jerusalem grounds without revealing himself to the security cameras.

Chapter 33

Stephen grabbed the hotel telephone after just one ring.

Whenever awoken unexpectedly, he noted the time. It was an old habit. The clock said 3:11 AM.

"Yes, hello?"

A deep, emotionless voice on the other end asked, "Is this Pastor Stephen Grant?"

"Yes, and who is this?"

"Harmon Shore. I'm a homicide detective with the Arlington County Police Department."

"Homicide? What's happened?"

Detective Shore said, "Pastor Grant, I have some very bad news. Pastor Graham Foster and Mrs. Margo Foster have been murdered."

"Murdered? No, we just saw them a few hours ago."

Stephen's raised voice and tone woke Jennifer. She placed her hand on his shoulder.

"I'm sorry, Pastor Grant."

Grant calmed himself, and lowered his voice. "Thank you, Detective Shore. Can you tell me what happened?"

"At this point, all I can say is that it's a very ugly scene. I understand that you and your wife were dinner guests of the Fosters last night."

My God, Graham and Margo are dead. Ugly scene? "Yes, we were. What do you mean that it's an ugly scene?"

Detective Shore continued, "I'd like to come by and ask a few questions, if you don't mind?"

"Of course. We're staying at ..."

"Yeah, I have that information. My partner and I will be there in about an hour or so."

"That'll be fine. Goodbye." Grant hung up the phone.

Jennifer's voice radiated concern, "What happened?"

His voice was unsteady and barely audible. "Graham and Margo, they're dead."

"Oh, my God, no."

When Stephen turned and Jennifer saw the tears, her own eyes welled up. She wrapped her arms around him, and pulled him close.

"The homicide detective said it was an ugly scene," he reported.

She hugged him tighter.

He eventually added, "I've been around death a lot. I know how to deal with it. Or, at least, I'm supposed to know how to deal with it based on my SEAL, CIA and church training. But when it hits home – my parents, Hans and Flo, and now Graham and Margo – I'm not sure what to do."

"I know, Stephen, no one knows what to do." They were quiet for a time. Then Jennifer added, "But as I've heard you tell people who were grieving, we have the hope – no, the confidence – that this is not the end, including for your parents, Hans and Flo, and now, Margo and Graham." She sighed. "He 'abolished death and brought life.'"

They held onto each other for what seemed like hours to Stephen, but actually was less than 20 minutes.

He stirred, picking his head up from his wife's shoulder, kissing her gently.

Stephen willed himself out of bed when every fiber of his being did not want to do so. "Unfortunately, two homicide detectives are on their way to ask us some questions."

Jennifer merely replied, "Okay."

Stephen looked out the hotel room window into the dark, early morning. "After not really talking with Graham for so long, we end on a disagreement."

"Stephen, I don't think Graham took it as any kind of attack. You obviously differed on something important to both of you. But I didn't come away last night with the impression that he took it as some deep rift."

"You're probably right. I hope so."

"Did you read what he wrote in his book?"

"Actually, no." Stephen walked over to the desk, picked up the book, and opened it. He read, and then smiled sadly.

Jennifer asked, "What does it say?"

He read:

Stephen,

I pray that you find at least a few things of merit here, and despite our disagreements, that we can stay united in friendship and in our commitment to spread the Good News.

>   *Yours in Christ,*
>   *Graham*
>   *John 15:12-17*

Jennifer asked, "John 15:12-17? Refresh my memory."

Stephen replied, "Jesus speaks to His disciples about friendship." He paused, with another tear or two forming. "It actually includes Jesus saying, 'Greater love has no one than this, that someone lay down his life for his friends.'"

Chapter 34

The questions from the homicide detectives were perfunctory.

It was Stephen who wound up gathering more information. He worked to keep his rage under control as the police told him that the "ugly scene" meant both Margo and Graham had been decapitated, and their heads then mockingly deposited on the living room sofa. He wished Jennifer had not been there to hear the description.

For good measure, while the security cameras captured the assailant entering – just moments after Jennifer and Stephen had left – and exiting the townhouse, his face could not be seen. This stirred Stephen's anger still more.

Though they obviously did not say so, Stephen picked up that the police had nothing, and were very concerned that they'd be getting nothing, at least from the crime scene. Stephen knew the detectives had to be hoping that this assailant had done something stupid afterward.

The detectives were gone just before six. Jennifer was showering, leaving Stephen lying on the bed thinking.

A professional hit on Graham with a gruesome message. How does that make any sense? Who the heck would hire someone to kill a pastor? Did you just ask yourself that question? Idiot.

Grant's mind wandered to the very real possibility that there still might be a person or two out there interested in killing him. It was just a short time ago, after all, that two people tried to do just that: one because of what he had done as a pastor, and the other because of what he had done in his old line of work. He caught himself, and decided to push back into the recesses of his mind the discomforting possibilities from his CIA days, and resume his concentration on Graham and Margo.

Jennifer emerged from the bathroom wrapped in a towel, but with her hair and makeup done. She walked over, gave him a gentle kiss, and then proceeded to get dressed. "I know the original plan was for you to come up to the Hill for my testimony. Unfortunately, I still have to testify. But what are you going to do?"

Stephen answered, "I don't know."

"Are you okay?"

"I don't know the answer to that either."

"Were you possibly going over to New Jerusalem?"

Stephen pulled his mind away from the murder conundrum, and tried to focus on the legitimate questions Jen was asking. "Well, ..."

But as he started to speak, his cell phone rang. Stephen looked at the screen. The caller's name was blocked. He answered, "Hello."

"Pastor Grant. This is Special Agent Rich Noack from the FBI."

Grant said, "Agent Noack, how are you?"

"I'm fine, Pastor Grant, but I'm sure you are not doing so well. My sympathies on Pastor and Mrs. Foster."

"Is this call related to their murders?" *What else could it be?*

"It is, and it might go back to the call you gave us recently about Manuel Rodriguez."

"Really?"

"Yes, could you come to a meeting in my office at eight this morning? If not, given the situation, I completely understand. But I'd like to pick your brain."

"Count me in."

"Good, see you shortly."

Stephen hung up, and said to Jennifer, "I know what I'm doing this morning."

Stephen Grant hoped that helping the FBI's Noack might ease his anger, and get him focused on something more constructive, like perhaps helping those left behind at New Jerusalem, as his wise wife hinted.

Chapter 35

It was official. With this visit, it was twice within two years. Stephen Grant now had been in FBI offices more often as a pastor than when he was with the CIA.

After his security checks, Grant was led into the elevator and up to Rich Noack's office by Ryan Bates. Along the way, Bates said, "My sympathies on the Fosters."

"Yes, thanks," said Stephen. "How are you, Agent Bates?"

"Me? I guess I'm fine."

Bates then remained quiet until saying, "Here we are."

The two men turned into Noack's office. Judging by his hesitation, Bates was just as surprised as Grant to see the person for whom Noack was pouring coffee at the small, round conference table.

Stephen smiled and said, "Paige, what are you doing here, in an FBI office of all places?" They gave each other a quick kiss and hug.

"I'm slumming it," she replied. Paige looked in his eyes. "Stephen, I'm sorry. Rich just told me that you were friends with Graham Foster and his wife."

Grant cleared his throat. "Yes, thanks, we went to seminary together."

And then there's Charlie Driessen's heads up on Paige and Schmidt.

Grant continued, "Hopefully, we can catch up later?"

"Yes, right," Paige replied.

Grant turned, "Special Agent Noack, thanks for calling me in." They shook hands, as did Bates and Caldwell. "But I'm not sure how I can help."

After allocating coffee as needed, the four sat down at the table.

Grant had a twinge of feeling out of place, given the summer-weight suits, crisp white shirts, and ties worn by both Noack and Bates; and the light gray, pin-stripped pants and white shirt sported by Paige. Grant was in a red polo shirt, khakis and dock siders, not exactly law enforcement or intelligence attire. But he quickly refocused on what mattered.

Noack began, "As I said, I wanted to pick your brains. It's clear that the murders of the Fosters and Senator Jimmy Farrell are related."

The light went on for Grant. "That's right. Farrell was decapitated as well. But what links him with the Fosters?"

"It doesn't look like they knew each other, at least not well. Their link seems to be on a political issue. An effort to shift U.S. foreign economic aid from governments..."

Grant interrupted, "... to entrepreneurs and small businesses."

Noack said, "You're following this?"

"Not only did Graham try to sell Jennifer and me on this, but Jennifer actually is testifying on the issue today in the Senate. I think Graham was going to try to change her position." He looked at both Noack and Bates. "I assume you guys know that I'm married now, and who I married?"

They both nodded.

Noack said, "Farrell was the Senate's leading opponent of this program, while Foster was a leader in favor of the effort."

Grant replied, "So, who has a motive to murder people on both sides of the issue?"

Noack reviewed the politics, noting that Belarus was in the lead to be the pilot project, with Mexico running second and left hoping to be next in line if the program expanded.

Caldwell then chimed in. "That's where our old friend Manny Rodriguez comes into play," she looked at Grant, "the man you happened to spot while in California."

She then served up the information the CIA uncovered on Rodriguez and his boss, Lydia Garcia, as well as the threats against and roles played by Carlos Luis and Jose Mora.

Bates tied things up. He concluded, "So, it's pretty clear that the Mexican drug gangs are at work here."

Grant asked, "But why kill Farrell?"

Bates responded, "What do you mean?"

"Well, perhaps there's a certain logic to killing Graham, given his leadership for Belarus. But based on Agent Noack's assessment and, much to her chagrin, my wife's as well, Farrell had very little support. He didn't have a real chance to kill this. It's one of those rare overwhelmingly bipartisan efforts. Farrell didn't favor Belarus over Mexico, or vice versa. He was taking a stand that very few others in Congress supported."

Caldwell said, "That's a good point, Stephen. It doesn't make any sense to kill Farrell, given that the opposition to this effort is so weak. He wasn't going to make any real difference."

Bates said, "You don't know that for sure. And I doubt the Mexican drug gangs have an up-to-the-minute assessment of U.S. congressional politics and legislative odds. They're not that astute."

Caldwell replied, "I disagree, Ryan. When you get to the levels of Garcia and Rodriguez, yes, they're evil thugs, but they're not stupid thugs. There has to be another reason why Senator Farrell in particular is dead."

Bates licked his lips. "I think you're giving them way too much credit."

It was Noack's turn. "No, there's something to this. Maybe Farrell was more than just opposed to this. Perhaps he knew something. Maybe he was on to the Mexican link to the drug gangs."

Grant said, "To take it a step further, does it make any political sense to so publicly and gruesomely eliminate their targets? Doesn't that risk a political backlash against Mexico?"

Caldwell responded, "I think that's more understandable. After all, that's how they've been doing business in Mexico for a long time. Beheadings are used to send a message, exhibiting power and reach, and intimidating both the public and politicians as a result."

They kicked around additional possibilities and scenarios for another twenty minutes without getting anywhere.

Noack looked at the clock on his office wall. "Okay, I have to wrap this up. I've got another meeting. We're going to further investigate the Farrell angle. Thanks, again, for coming."

Paige and Stephen left the building together.

They stopped under a tree on Pennsylvania Avenue. Paige asked, "Are you sure you're alright, Stephen?"

"I'm having a tough time getting past the viciousness of the murders." He took a deep breath. "Frankly, I'm frustrated. Don't know what I can do with my anger."

"You should be angry, and rest assured," she leaned in close and lowered her voice, "I'm working another angle or two to get more information. I'll keep you in the loop as best I can. But right now, I've really got to go." She kissed him on the cheek, and started to walk away. But she paused, turned and asked, "By the way, how's Jennifer dealing with all of this?"

"She's strong."

"Good. Being married to you, she'll need to be." Paige smiled, gave a flirty wave, and turned away.

Before his mind could wander to his intimate past with Paige Caldwell, Grant's phone rang. He was glad for the distraction. "Yes, hello."

"Pastor Grant, this is Pastor Johnson at New Jerusalem. I need some help."

"Of course, Pastor, anything I can do..."

Chapter 36

The Senate Dirksen Office Building was named for Everett McKinley Dirksen, an Illinois Republican who not only served as Senate Minority Leader from 1959 until his death in 1969, but also had a cameo in the sci-fi invasion film *The Monitors*.

In Room 419, four witnesses were sworn in and then sat down at a long table ready to testify.

In the wood-paneled, high-ceiling chamber, they looked up at senators on the Foreign Relations Committee, whose seats were arranged in a large horseshoe. Nearly half of the committee's 19 members actually were in attendance, a rather rare occurrence, with various staff members sitting behind the senators.

Behind the witnesses, the room was nearly filled with lobbyists, media, and other interested spectators. And in front of the panel on the floor were a handful of photographers and cameramen, in addition to a stenographer at a small desk.

Each witness speaking to the committee already had submitted their written testimony, and now had up to ten minutes to summarize those remarks.

Two of the witnesses were economists – including Jennifer Grant – another was the vice president for international trade with one of the nation's largest business groups, and the third was an analyst from a policy foundation funded by labor unions.

Senator Duane Ellis, the committee chairman, opened the hearing by noting the tragic murders of Graham and Margo Foster, pointing out that Graham was a leader on this issue, not to mention an active caregiver in the Virginia and D.C. communities. Ellis then offered his opening statement in favor of the proposal, though partial to Mexico as the starting point, and commending both sides of the aisle for their bipartisanship on the general topic.

The ranking member, Trevor Tenace, also commended the Fosters, called for justice to be served regarding their horrible murders, and offered his support for this first step in shifting foreign economic aid from governments to "actual job creators," while also praising this "rare and most welcome case of bipartisanship." He preferred Belarus, however, as the initial pilot.

Three more Democrats and two more Republicans echoed similar sentiments.

But Senator Kristen Madsen offered a different take. In her opening statement, she was critical of foreign economic aid in general, and declared that things would not improve by the shift being proposed. She concluded, "Foreign aid as an engine for lifting other nations out of poverty has been a longtime failure. I don't see how this will change in any substantive way. After all, the U.S. federal government has a miserable track record in doling out subsidies in our own country, never mind in other nations."

Ellis thanked the members, and then turned to the witnesses.

The thirty-something, fit, dark-haired VP for the business group, dressed in a tailored, charcoal gray suit, positively gushed his approval for the program. He summed up, "This is the type of innovative thinking we need in order to make foreign aid far more effective, to the benefit of those in other nations, and to U.S. firms and workers doing business internationally. It's a win-win."

The other economist – a bespectacled, short, gray-haired professor in his late sixties from a small college in Idaho – seemed annoyed to be there. He lectured about the failure of foreign aid in the past, but went on to note that he long advocated a shift in aid away from foreign governments to foreign businesses. The professor failed to hide his exasperation at politicians taking so long to catch up to his own brilliance.

The representative from the labor union group served up a passionate list of ills and evils emanating from the business community in the U.S. The more he spoke, his fat, fleshy cheeks turned a deeper red, contrasting ever more sharply with his light brown mustache and hair. He argued, "If it's this bad in the U.S. – and it is – then just imagine what greedy businesses in developing nations are doing to workers. Those workers need protection by governments supported by U.S. aid, not more dollars handed over courtesy of U.S. taxpayers to businesses that carelessly exploit workers."

Jennifer was next, the last in line. After thanking the chairman, ranking member and other members of the committee, she proceeded:

> In reviewing the issue of foreign aid and economic development, I looked back to the late economist Lord Peter Bauer. Starting in the 1960s, Bauer challenged the global political establishment, not to mention many fellow economists, when he criticized foreign aid.
>
> He was a trailblazer in making clear that foreign aid failed to spur economic development and growth, but instead tended to perpetuate poverty and create dependency on such government-to-government aid. One of the

problems was that aid expanded the size of government, and its control over the economy. He defined such aid as 'a transfer of resources from the taxpayer of a donor country to the government of a recipient country.'

On dependency, he once put it: 'A pauper is one who relies on unearned public assistance, and "pauperization" accordingly denotes the promotion and acceptance of the idea that unearned doles are a main ingredient in the livelihood of nations.'

The empirical work overwhelmingly confirms what Bauer recognized and observed on the failure of foreign aid. I have referenced some of that work in my written testimony.

Nonetheless, this failure of foreign aid rarely was acknowledged in political circles, where it's very easy to spend other people's money and justify such spending by claiming that others are being helped. Investigating whether people are being helped or not is a much larger task, and since the results might not line up with the political assumptions and rhetoric, why bother?

Given that unfortunate, longtime political reality, I think Lord Bauer would be as surprised and pleased as I am to see this, at least tacit, recognition of the failure of traditional aid on both sides of the political aisle. If it holds, this would mark a dramatic and productive shift in attitude.

Supporters of the proposal we are discussing today, that is, shifting aid from governments to small businesses in targeted countries, might turn to Bauer for support. Perhaps they would note that he once wrote: 'When foreign aid is given by one country to another, it is received not by the people, but by the government: it does not go to individuals or firms in the private sector, but to the central government. This necessarily increases the weight of the government in the economy, which in turn must increase the concentration of power, even if the recipient government does not intend this result.'

But why then am I opposing this measure? Well, I seriously doubt that Lord Bauer would have supported government handouts to businesses either. And that is what this is.

Resources taken from the private sector to be spent by government means that those resources will be allocated according to political concerns and decisions, rather than being done so according to the disciplines of prices, profits and losses in the marketplace, which ultimately are determined by consumers. Nor are such resources allocated by the incentives of private ownership, which are completely different from the incentives at work in government. Even with the best intentions, and no matter which nation is chosen and which not-for-profit go-betweens are selected, there is no getting around that these dollars are being redistributed according to political preferences.

For good measure, what is being communicated to the entrepreneurs and small businesses in the targeted nation? The message is that you still must rely on government in some way. Rather than coming up with a business plan that makes sense to private investors, and offering a product or service appealing to consumers, the purpose of the firm is shifted to trying to appeal to those doling out resources being supplied by government.

For a time, foreign economic aid was pushed as a means for increasing investment in a nation, thereby presumably generating development and reducing poverty. But it turned out that government-led investment simply turned out to be wasteful and all about the political class, rather than helping people. Poverty persisted and even got worse.

Then there was a push to provide such aid only to nations that were getting their fiscal, monetary and trade policies right. That appealed to many former critics of aid. But it turns out that such aid either made no difference to the recipient nations, or as was the case with the original foreign aid model, actually made matters worse. Why? Because these were still resources being distributed according to politics, and therefore, the effort actually worked against whatever positive reforms were occurring.

And now we have the current idea to try to eliminate foreign governments from the aid equation, and use not-for-profits to distribute aid to small businesses. No doubt, this sounds very appealing. But in the end, such aid still amounts to resources being allocated according to politics, albeit supposedly limited to the politics of the United States. So, U.S. taxpayers, both individuals and businesses, will have their earnings taken in order to subsidize businesses in other nations. And rather than promoting true entrepreneurship, we will be expanding dependency on government.

Lord Bauer wrote: "Building up resources ... both requires and advances social and economic processes that serve to develop qualities, attitudes, arrangements, and institutions, the presence of which promotes the effective use of the resources generated. When, however, the increase in the resources takes the form of the inflow of free or subsidized aid from abroad, the essential process of generating them is lost."

This program would not change this reality of foreign aid.

Despite claims made to the contrary, we know what nations need to do to grow, create jobs and reduce poverty. They must establish and enforce private property rights, allow for free movement of capital and labor, provide sound money, limit the size of government, impose light tax and regulatory burdens, open up to international trade and investment, limit government corruption, establish the rule of law, and provide for a fair, independent judiciary.

Quite simply, freedom is the foundation needed for real economic opportunity and growth.

I appreciate this opportunity to speak before the Committee, and look forward to answering your questions.

Other than Senator Madsen, no other senator had a question for Jennifer Grant.

After the hearing, Senator Madsen waved Jennifer behind the senators' seats on the dais. In a low voice, she said to Jennifer, "Thanks so much for bringing some reality to these proceedings."

"Apparently, I was not a hit with others on the committee."

"Don't think of it that way. They needed to hear this, and some of my Republican colleagues get it, but see this as a popular proposal that they can support as an improvement over the old foreign aid model. They challenged the union guy because he doesn't really have a clue. But they didn't go after you because you actually know what you're talking about, and they don't want to look bad or strengthen the case against what they're supporting."

Jennifer gave her a look of doubt.

Madsen continued, "Trust me." She then softened a bit, putting aside her senatorial edge, and guiding Jennifer further away from those who remained on dais. "Before I run, I heard that you not only knew the Fosters but had dinner with them last night?"

"Yes, Stephen and Graham were friends from their seminary days."

Senator Madsen said, "Jennifer, I'm so sorry, and please pass on my condolences to Stephen as well."

"Thanks, Krissy ... I mean, Senator."

"We'll talk soon. Take care."

A quick hug, and Senator Madsen was off to her next meeting.

When Jennifer returned to the table to retrieve her belongings, one person remained in the seats for visitors. The blond, blue-eyed man stood and buttoned the jacket of his dark suit as Jennifer was picking up her computer attaché. He said, "Dr. Grant, I enjoyed your testimony, and your Q&A with Senator Madsen."

Jennifer replied, "Thank you. I think you might have been the only other person in the room, other than Senator Madsen, who agreed with what I had to say."

"You seem to be fearless. But be careful, Dr. Grant, this town can be dangerous." Audia smiled and nodded at Jennifer Grant, and then left the room.

Chapter 37

While Jennifer was talking development economics in the U.S. Senate, her husband was on his cell phone in a taxi talking to St. Mary's new assistant pastor, Zack Charmichael.

Stephen relayed what had happened to the Fosters, and told Zack that they would not be getting back home later today, as originally planned.

"I'm heading over to New Jerusalem now. Pastor Johnson is looking for me to help out with the viewing and funeral."

"Take as much time as needed, Stephen. I can handle things here."

"I appreciate that. Sorry about this baptism of fire, Zack."

"Absolutely no worries. It's not exactly your fault."

"Still, thank you."

"You're welcome."

"One more thing, can you have Barbara shoot out an email to the prayer list, letting parishioners know what happened and asking them to keep the family and friends of the Fosters, along with the members of New Jerusalem, in their prayers?"

Barbara Tunney was the longtime church secretary at St. Mary's, and was the force keeping things organized and running smoothly.

Zack answered, "Of course, will do."

"Again, thanks. I'm pulling up to New Jerusalem, so I have to run. I'll keep you up to date as I know things."

"My prayers are with you and Jennifer."

"Blessings, my friend." *I'll need those prayers, Zack.*

After he hung up, Grant paid the cabbie, got out of the car and started walking up to the New Jerusalem Worship and Fulfillment Center. Grant noted that there probably were a couple dozen cars in the parking lot. While heading around to the back of the building, he saw that the Fosters' townhouse was still sealed off as a crime scene, with a couple of police talking outside. He felt a pull in that direction, but stayed on track.

Grant entered the church via the door to the administrative offices, as Pastor Johnson instructed.

After being pointed in the direction of a conference room by a sniffling receptionist, he was surprised by the number of offices and the staff size at New Jerusalem. He was not surprised, however, by the solemnity of the place, broken here and there by someone crying quietly and a couple of groups praying.

The conference room had large windows looking out on the manicured grounds, and was dominated by a huge, shiny, black conference table with 14 seats around it. Another ten chairs were along the walls.

Grant was struck by the fact that Pastor Johnson was seated at one end of the table, with Pastor Schroeder completely at the other. Johnson was reading a Bible. Schroeder simply stared out the window. Neither noticed Grant in the doorway.

"Gentlemen," Grant said.

They both turned to look at him. Johnson's eyes were wet and red. Schroeder's were distant.

After a second or two of hang time, recognition kicked in, and Pastor Bill Johnson got up to greet Grant. "Pastor Grant, thanks so much for coming."

Johnson took Grant briefly off guard with a bear hug. But Stephen understood, and returned the greeting.

Leonard Schroeder, though, did not get up. He merely turned his seat around, and folded his hands on the table in front of him. "Yes, thanks for coming, Pastor Grant." Schroeder failed to make eye contact with Grant, or for that matter, with Johnson.

Johnson offered Grant a seat, and expressly added appreciation for Grant being willing to help out over the coming days. While Schroeder sat silently, Johnson explained what had been done so far. "We prayed and read the Bible with staff, opened the Worship Center for anyone needing to pray or just rest and think, with music and video running constantly, and we've sent word out via email and social media to let people know what ... happened."

Grant simply replied, "Okay." He looked at Schroeder, expecting something, but getting nothing.

Johnson asked, "Unfortunately, I can't get my head or heart around what exactly did happen." He looked at Grant as if seeking some new insight that would clarify things.

"I know. I'm frustrated and angry."

Johnson said, "I'm just at a loss as to why Margo and Graham were targeted for such an atrocity."

Grant looked to Schroeder, who had now shifted to stroking his beard and looking up at the ceiling. He decided it was best to get focused on how the next few days were going to play out. "Pastor Johnson, you..."

Johnson interrupted, "Please, how about Bill?"

"Okay, and it's Stephen." Still nothing from Schroeder. "You mentioned on the phone, Bill, that the idea was to have viewings on Thursday and Friday, and the funeral on Saturday?"

"Yes, I don't see how we could start it all tomorrow, with the size of our church and given the ongoing police work."

"That makes sense," replied Stephen. "How have you done this before at New Jerusalem?"

"Actually, we don't have much experience at this location."

Grant said, "I'm not sure what you mean."

Johnson seemed a bit uncomfortable. "Pastor Foster never liked to do funerals here at the Worship and Fulfillment Center. Since I've been here, we've never had one."

"How long have you been here?"

"Almost three years."

"In a church this size, how could you have no deaths in three years?"

"Actually, a few members have passed away since I've been here. The viewings and funeral services are always done offsite, at a funeral home."

Pastor Schroeder finally spoke up in a tone tinged with annoyance, "Pastor Foster did not like funerals. Since I've been here, he never did a funeral. Always left it to me."

"Okay." *That's really weird.* "Well, nonetheless, from what you said on the phone, Bill, the plan is to have the viewings and funeral here."

"Yes, right, Leonard?"

"That makes sense, Bill, given how many mourners are expected to come. I'm going to leave the plans to you two, if you don't mind. I have to go."

As both Grant and Johnson looked on in amazement, Schroeder got up and left the room.

Grant commented, "That was odd."

Johnson sighed. "He hasn't been himself lately. He's changed. Less and less engaged at New Jerusalem. And other than the few words you just heard, he hasn't said much more since Terrance found the ... um ... bodies."

"I've seen people react to death in much stranger ways over the years. Withdrawal is not unusual."

"I suppose."

Grant observed, "Unfortunately, Bill, we have to get back to planning the next few days."

Chapter 38

"Well, how was your day, honey?" Stephen asked sarcastically, greeting Jennifer as she arrived at Clyde's of Georgetown.

They exchanged a kiss, and sat down at a small table with a red-checkered tablecloth, just across from the long oak bar.

"Nothing compared to yours, I'm guessing. By the way, after you called earlier, I contacted the hotel, and they extended our room into Saturday. What about St. Mary's?"

"I keep apologizing to Zack, but it sounds like he'll be fine. I also talked to Barbara, and she seems very impressed by our new pastor. But she did promise to babysit him if any problems cropped up."

Jennifer smiled. "I'm sure she did." She picked up a menu. "So, what was your day actually like?"

Stephen started with the meetings at New Jerusalem. He recapped the funeral plans for the coming days, and then noted the complete disengagement of Pastor Schroeder. Before getting to his meeting at the FBI, he asked, "How did the testimony go?"

Jennifer paused as if still trying to figure that out. "It went fine, I guess. Krissy was the only senator who asked me questions. Afterwards, she assured me that no one else asked questions because they basically did not want to be derailed from their intent to spend more on this bipartisan initiative."

"You don't sound convinced of her assessment."

"Well, I guess it makes sense. It's just that I would have liked to have engaged the other senators directly, and help them understand that handouts to businesses are not the route to economic growth and lifting people out of poverty."

"Didn't your exchange with Senator Madsen drive home that point?"

"Yes, it did. But who knows if anyone else on the committee was even listening?"

"From what you told me, and other assessments I've heard, you knew this was an uphill battle going in, that it was going to happen with the only questions really being which nation to start with and how much would be spent. Right?"

"Yes," Jennifer replied shortly.

"Hey, don't get mad at me. I'm on your side, remember?"

"I'm not mad at you. It's just very frustrating for this economist, at least, to watch politicians throw around other people's money in such a careless manner. At the same time, though, this economist should understand that this is what politicians largely do, no matter which party they happen to be members of in the end."

"And then there is what some will do to get their hands on that money from other people."

Jennifer looked at Stephen quizzically. "Yes, and do you have something to add to this economist's ranting?"

"I love when you refer to yourself with the third person title of 'this economist' whenever you get passionate about something work related."

"Stephen," she replied in mock sternness.

"Okay. My first meeting today at the FBI with Agent Noack also included Ryan Bates and Paige."

The waiter arrived and stopped their conversation. They gave him the drink and food orders all at once. Stephen chose the jumbo lump crab cake sandwich with coleslaw and fries, while Jennifer selected the roasted Portobello and fried mushroom sandwich with roasted red pepper and tomatoes, red onions, arugula and basil aioli. They both chose to drink Coke.

After the waiter left, Jennifer asked, "How did Paige get in on this?"

Is that just an innocent question, or annoyance? She's signaling neither. "Noack decided to call her in to pick each of our brains." He paused briefly for another comment, but getting none, he plowed forward. "It turns out that the murders of Margo and Graham are tied to the murder of Senator Jimmy Farrell."

Jennifer's mouth dropped open. "Oh, my." She then started to put the political angle together far more quickly than Stephen had. "Farrell and Graham were both involved with the foreign aid issue."

"Correct."

"But they were on opposite sides. Why kill the two of them?"

Stephen shared the theories that had been kicked around at his meeting earlier regarding the Mexican drug gangs.

She said, "So, your catching sight of Manuel Rodriguez while we were in Napa helped."

"Perhaps, but I think Paige and the CIA probably were already on top of that. They didn't share everything with me. After all, I'm still ex-CIA."

Their Cokes arrived, and each took a sip.

They sat silently for a few moments, lost in their own thoughts. Jennifer resumed, "Trying to step back from this to look at it dispassionately, I just realized something."

"What is it?"

"Consider what's going to happen once the full story breaks in the media. Mexican drug gangs murdering a U.S. senator, a pastor and his wife, all to get their hands on dollars from U.S. taxpayers. That's a big scandal, and it will affect both parties, and generate more distrust of politicians. What does Paul write to Timothy about money being the root of all evil?"

"Actually, it's: 'For the love of money is a root of all kinds of evils.'"

"And that is more accurate in terms of the realities of money in the world. Money can be used for great good or for evil. But as this economist" – she smiled and nodded at her husband – "tells all who will listen, under free enterprise, success only comes when you serve others, by meeting or creating a need or demand. But when it comes to government, all you need to do is take something from others, and you suddenly have huge amounts of money at your disposal to spend. That provides dark soil in which all kinds of evils may take root."

"That almost sounded like a sermon."

Jennifer smirked, and took another sip of her soda.

Stephen added, "But I see what you mean. It turns out that I not only love you for your general hotness, but because you teach economics to this theologian and quasi-historian."

"Thank you."

Their food arrived. Stephen didn't realize how hungry he was, not having eaten lunch, until the aroma of his sandwich and fries hit his nostrils.

After they gave each other positive assessments on their respective meals, Stephen said, "I'm glad you're done with the testimony. I've been worried about you since I heard that the foreign aid issue was what seems to have tied together these murders."

Jennifer smiled at her husband. "Oh, so that explains your seemingly innocent texts and calls throughout the day?"

Stephen felt his cheeks actually flush a bit. "Yes, of course, that was part of it. Apparently, these people are willing to kill just about anyone to make their point. And yes, I'm grossly overreacting. But I plan to keep you close until we leave on Saturday. D.C. has become a dangerous place right now."

Jennifer slowly allowed her smile to fade. "What did you just say?"

Stephen replied, "What's the matter?"

"It's probably nothing."

"Tell me."

"It's just that when I was done talking with Krissy after my testimony today, a man remained in the chamber. He said that he agreed with what I had to say."

"But..."

"But he added that I should be careful. He commented that this town can be dangerous."

They were silent.

Jennifer added, "Stephen, I just took it as a comment on the politics of Washington, and I'm sure that's how it was meant."

"You're probably right, Jen. But we are not taking any chances."

He pulled out his cellphone and called the FBI's Noack.

Within ten minutes, the meal was done, the bill paid, and Jennifer and Stephen were in the back seat of a dark SUV on the way to the J. Edgar Hoover Building so Jennifer could provide a description of the man who warned that D.C. could be a dangerous town.

Chapter 39

Each spoke on an encrypted phone.

"I reached out on what you asked, liebling, and I have valuable information," said Gerhardt Schmidt.

"Well, spill it," demanded Paige Caldwell.

"You Americans are so impatient."

"As I remember, it was you who was, shall we say, 'impatient' the other night."

"That hurts."

"Gerry, I unfortunately do not have time to play right now."

"Fair enough. The man you are after, that killed Senator Farrell and the pastor, is a longtime, shadowy killer for hire. I believe you Americans know him as Mr. Audia."

"Actually, we've never been quite sure if Audia was more than one person."

"Oh, yes, he is but one man. My contacts tell me that he has been employed in recent years by various Middle Eastern, African and Latin American regimes, a group or two that you might label terrorists, along with assorted business interests in Russia and Southeast Asia. He's known for his ability as an assassin who can use a variety of techniques."

"And now he's working for a Mexican drug cartel?"

"Yes, that is what I've been told. And if it interests you, I know where he is, or at least where his base of operations currently is."

"How the hell do you know that?"

"I am sorry, liebling, that I cannot tell you who gave me this information. But I was told that he was spotted in the U.S. Senate today. He actually stopped to speak to the wife of your old partner, Grant."

"Are you sure?"

"I can assure you that the parties that relayed this information to me know Audia, and would have knowledge of his location. He had been in their employ recently."

Caldwell said, "I probably don't want to know more about your sources."

"You are both beautiful and wise."

"Thank you, lover. I owe you."

"And I will demand payment."

"Promises, promises," replied Caldwell, and then hung up.

She thought for a moment, and then dialed another number.

At the same time, Schmidt also made a call. "I've placed the information."

"Excellent. Audia has done good work, but he clearly is a liability now."

"Agreed."

"Will they act?"

"That is a safe bet. If I know the CIA, they want him all for themselves. And you and I understand that he will never go. Rather, he will fight and take others with him."

"Most certainly. But what if he survives?"

"Trust me," assured Schmidt, "that is unlikely. But if my CIA friend does not eliminate him, I will."

"And if you need to take down all of them, are you prepared and willing to do so?"

"Of course."

Schmidt ended the call. He looked at his phone and said out loud to himself, "But I would rather not have to eliminate Ms. Caldwell."

Chapter 40

Stephen and Jennifer decided to order a pay-per-view movie on the hotel television in order to get their minds off of things, and try to relax. This was not an unusual ritual for Stephen over the years, though he spent far fewer late nights watching films since getting married.

However, he could not turn off his brain tonight. His concerns and anger over the deaths of the Fosters had only been amped up by Jennifer's incident in the Senate.

Keep trying to tell myself it's nothing, an innocent coincidence. But I'm unconvincing.

Grant was taught long ago not to believe in coincidences under circumstances like these. He felt a little better that the FBI had someone at street level keeping an eye out.

But all of his senses were heightened when the knock at the hotel room door came. He looked at the clock: 10:11 PM.

Jennifer said, "Who could that be?"

In a whisper, Stephen said, "Stay here."

He lowered the sound on the television, slipped out of bed, and headed to the door.

I really wish I had my Glock.

Stephen was not ready for what he saw when peering through the door's peephole. Paige Caldwell and Charlie Driessen stood patiently, each dressed in black.

He opened the door, and said, "Come in."

Jennifer pulled the covers up.

Okay, this is kind of awkward. "Jennifer, you know Paige."

They both nodded and said their hellos.

Stephen continued, "This is Charlie Driessen. We also worked together at the CIA."

Driessen said, "Mrs. Grant. Very nice to meet you."

"Yes, and you, Mr. Driessen." She then looked at Stephen in bewilderment.

Stephen sympathized. *This room feels cramped all of a sudden.* "Okay, what can I do for you two?"

Driessen said, "This is her idea." He looked at Paige, and actually took a step back toward the door.

Paige glanced at Jennifer, and then looked back to Stephen. "Can we talk?"

This just gets better by the second. Stephen noted that Jennifer made no effort to speak, or to move. She just watched.

Stephen looked at Paige. "Yes. Whatever you have to say, we can say in front of Jennifer."

Paige clearly was reluctant, but relented. "Charlie and I have an off-the-books, unofficial assignment, and I wanted to give you a chance to get in."

"Me? Why?"

She hesitated again. "I've been provided with the location of the person who murdered Senator Farrell and the Fosters."

Stephen could feel the old surge of adrenaline.

Jennifer stiffened her back.

Paige continued, "I don't want to scare you, Jennifer, but it's someone who spoke to you in the Senate Dirksen Building today."

"Son of a ...." Grant cut off what he wanted to say. He looked at Jennifer. "It was him." He turned back to Paige. "Jennifer gave a description to the FBI tonight."

Paige replied, "So that's why Agent Bates is sitting outside the building."

"It's Bates? Did you talk to him?"

"Absolutely not. Remember what I said, Stephen, off the books, unofficial?"

"Are you two sure he didn't see you?"

It was Driessen's turn to insert a comment, "Shit, don't insult us, Grant."

Paige looked at Jennifer and then at Stephen. "Given that this guy killed your friend and his wife, and approached Jennifer, I'm giving you an opportunity to come, Stephen. You might say, for old time's sake." She smiled.

Jennifer cut in, "Stephen, you're not really..." But she came up short when seeing the look on her husband's face.

Stephen moved to the bed and sat on the edge next to his wife, while both Paige and Charlie further retreated toward the door. "Jen, I'm going to go with Paige and Charlie. I want to see this guy caught and shipped off to whatever hole the CIA chooses to put him in."

She opened her mouth, but stopped. Jennifer then put her arms around her husband and pulled him close. She whispered, "This is not what I signed up for, Stephen. But I understand. I love you, and you better come back safe and sound, or you'll have to deal with a very pissed off wife."

He whispered, "I got it. I love you, too."

Stephen got up and turned to his old co-workers.

"I have nothing in terms of clothes and other, well, necessities." He was dressed in a t-shirt and shorts.

Paige said, "Throw on a pair of sneakers. I have everything else you'll need."

He slipped his sneakers on, and said, "Let's go." He turned and waved at Jennifer. "Back soon."

She said nothing. Instead, she bit her lower lip.

As Paige and Stephen moved to the door, Driessen stepped back across the room, and leaned down to Jennifer. He took her hand, and whispered in her ear. She squeezed his hand tight.

The three left, and Jennifer was alone. Tears slowly journeyed down her cheeks, as she stared blankly at the flickering lights of the television screen.

Chapter 41

Driessen drove the dark van, with Caldwell in the front passenger seat and Grant suiting up in the back.

"What did you say to my wife, Charlie?"

"Not your concern, Grant."

"I see you're still very forthcoming."

"I am what I am."

Grant turned his attention to Caldwell. "Why are you breaking the law tonight operating on domestic soil? Why not hand it off to the FBI?"

"This shadowy piece of crap we're going to apprehend, only known as Mr. Audia, is not just wanted for these murders, but also has been linked to a variety of assassinations and terrorist actions. Langley does not want him lost in the domestic justice system. They want Audia for everything he's done, and they want the information he has in his head. His lawyers would only get in the way."

Can't really argue with that.

"Agent Noack will be very angry," said Grant.

Caldwell replied, "If he finds out, you're damn right he will be."

Grant secured the body armor. "You know, something just occurred to me."

"What's that?" asked Caldwell.

"Is my being here more than just personal involvement and for old time's sake? If anything goes wrong, I could serve as a convenient dupe. You know, you have no authority, just helping an old colleague bent on getting revenge. Maybe you were even trying to stop me."

Driessen laughed. "You're still one paranoid son of a bitch, Grant."

Caldwell ignored the comment, and said, "Open the metal case, Stephen."

He snapped open the case and found a 10 mm Glock 20 and magazines with 15 rounds each. He slipped a magazine into the gun, and put three more in the pouches on his belt.

Driessen said, "Finish up getting ready. We're just about there."

Chapter 42

Driessen parked the van on the side of the road, just short of the house where Audia reportedly was.

Caldwell said, "Okay, it's a wooded, long front lawn and driveway. Let's spread out, and move quickly and quietly to the house. Charlie, you take the back, let me know when in position, and on my mark we go in. Stephen, you stay several steps behind me."

"All good," said Driessen. "Watch for security measures, like motion detectors, and if lights go on, I assume we just move our asses with even greater speed."

"Yes," said Caldwell.

"Right," acknowledged Grant.

Under the cloak of darkness, they moved out of the van, drew their weapons, spread out and moved forward.

Nothing else moved, not even a breeze to rustle the leaves.

Grant worked to stay focused, to push back the memories of similar situations he was in while with the CIA. Suddenly, his CIA days weren't so many years ago. They felt like yesterday, including working with Paige. *Strange how years can just be wiped away sometimes.*

Caldwell was a couple of yards in front of him, with Driessen about 20 yards to their right moving along the driveway.

With one step by Driessen, spotlights from the otherwise nondescript high ranch snapped on, temporarily blinding Grant.

Each fought to regain their vision, while moving forward at a faster pace.

Grant recognized the sound of a tranquillizer gun. Driessen fell.

The same sound, and Paige struggled and then crumpled in front of him.

Grant should have moved for cover. He realized that after taking two steps in the direction of Paige. Before he could move, a tranquillizer dart hit, though it bounced off his vest.

With the additional time, Grant moved left in the direction of a line of trees. But the second dart lodged in the side of his neck. He managed another two steps, and then fell to the ground.

Hell of a shot given our vests. Odd thought. Then he started to pray. *Jesus, help ...*

Chapter 43

Grant vaguely felt something hit his cheek. He struggled to wake up, to shake off the disorientation. Finally, he got control of his eyes, and saw a man with blue eyes and blond hair staring intently.

Audia smiled and said, "There we go. Now, you're awake. I'm hoping that you can answer a few questions for me. Your partner was not cooperative. I have to admit, I could tell from the start that he's a hard bastard." He glanced at Driessen, who was on the floor unmoving, battered and bruised. Both of his knees were bloody messes.

Grant looked at Driessen, and it all came back as to what he had been doing. *Is he dead?* He looked around, and spotted Paige on the other side of him, also unconscious on the floor, hands tied behind her back, but apparently untouched, so far.

When he tried to move, Grant found his arms, torso and legs tied tightly to a chair. *God, if you could help me bring back all that training the government gave me years ago, I'd really appreciate it.*

Audia was sitting a few feet away. He continued, "These two, I assume, are government. But what about you? I had to laugh when I recognized you. You and your wife, Dr.

Grant, who by the way is quite a looker, were with the Fosters before I had to eliminate them."

"You son of a bitch."

"Tut, tut. Not so nice from a pastor." Audia was twirling a black nightstick in his right hand.

Grant's eyes narrowed.

Audia continued, "Yes, Pastor Grant, I did a quick check online, and apparently you're a 'Pistol Packin' Pastor,' according to a *New York Post* headline from a little more than a year-and-a-half ago. Isn't the Internet handy? Apparently, you're quite a good shot."

Grant did not respond.

"I bet you have a fascinating life story, but that's neither here nor there. What I need is information. Specifically, how did you find me, and how much do you know about my work? If you or your friends do not tell me, I will kill you all."

"I'm pretty sure you're going to kill us anyway."

"Alas, that is a reasonable assumption on your part. Actually, I will test you, and see if you break. If not, then I will test the woman. Like your wife, she's quite beautiful as well, but in a different way, don't you agree? What's with all of these hot women around you, Pastor Grant?"

Grant struggled to keep his emotions in check. "What is it that you want to know, Mr. Audia? That's what you're known as, right?"

Audia smiled. "Very good. Your friend here would not give me that much, even after I shot both his kneecaps. I like you, Pastor."

"That's nice. Why don't you let us all go then?"

"You know that's not going to happen."

Audia sprang to his feet, twirled the nightstick a few times, and then swung it full force into Grant's left bicep. He toppled to the floor, pain surging up and down his arm and into his chest. While on the floor, Audia delivered two more blows to Grant's side, and then grabbed Grant's hair and shirt to pull him up, with the chair back on all four legs.

Grant struggled to clear away the pain. When he looked down, he saw Paige open an eye and close it. He turned and became fixated on Audia's face.

"Not even a scream or curse. Just a couple of grunts. Impressive Pastor Grant. Maybe the Lord is on your side." Audia laughed robustly. "Now, before I start on the other side, then get to your face, probably your kneecaps as well, and, if I have to, your pretty partner, would you like to tell me how you found me?"

"I have no idea. I just went along for the ride when I heard they were after such a sick, twisted son of a bitch. To be perfectly honest, I was kind of hoping that I'd be able to see you shipped off to hell tonight."

"Sorry, not tonight, Pastor. And now I think I'll jump right to the face." He flipped the nightstick into his left hand. As he started to wind up, Paige rolled toward Audia and shoved her right boot into his genitals.

Audia lost his balance, falling into and then onto Grant. But Grant remained firmly tied to the chair. He couldn't find his way free. Paige got to her feet, and tried to land a kick into Audia's face as he rose up. But he swiped aside her effort with a strong left arm.

Grant then knew it was over. Audia was just too strong and experienced, while Paige still had her hands tied behind her back.

Grant's fury raged as he watched Audia crash a fist into Paige's left cheek. She went down to the floor.

Audia picked up the nightstick and grabbed Paige by the hair. He paused to sneer at Grant.

"Don't do it," said Grant in a low, tight voice.

"Ha, are you serious, Pastor Grant?" Audia smiled.

But suddenly Audia's expression went blank as a hole appeared in his forehead. Blood emerged. He released

Paige and fell to the floor. Audia's brutality was brought to an end by a suppressed gunshot.

Grant felt relief come over him like a cool, soothing wave on a hot day. *Off to hell you go, Mr. Audia. Thank you, Lord.*

The relief was short-lived as the shooter emerged from the shadows behind him. Grant was taken off guard by the mask covering the shooter's entire head.

The mystery man holstered his gun, and pulled out a knife as he approached Paige. But the masked shooter simply cut the ties on her hands, closed the blade, handed it to her, turned and left.

Paige looked at the knife, and watched him leave.

Once their rescuer was gone, she sprang into action. She cut Grant loose, and they both moved to Driessen. He was still alive, but they could not tell for how long.

Caldwell found a sweatshirt, slashed it with the knife, and tied off the wounds to Driessen's legs. Grant moved when she ordered him to the van for first aid.

Chapter 44

As Grant emerged from the van with the first aid kit, along with a new phone, he heard a familiar voice.

"Stop! FBI."

Grant turned. "Is that you, Noack?"

"Grant?"

"Quick, follow me. An agent's beaten and shot. He needs medical assistance." Grant was having a tough time moving his left arm, and the throbbing in his side was growing more painful with each move. But he sprinted back to the house where Charlie Driessen lay bleeding, with FBI agents in tow.

After Driessen was stabilized and moved, Grant and Caldwell were treated at the back of a large FBI van. Noack came over after they were patched up. Caldwell held an icepack to her cheek. Bandages were wrapped around Grant's chest a few inches below his armpits, with a cracked rib suspected. He also had an icepack strapped to his left arm above the elbow.

Noack nodded and two FBI agents moved away. He stared at Grant, and then Caldwell. "You stupid asses. I'm not sure who's a bigger idiot. You, Grant, a pastor who no longer works for Uncle Sam. Or you, Caldwell, for operating on domestic soil, and I'm guessing, dragging Grant into this."

Caldwell responded, "I got information on Audia, and decided to act on my own, not under orders. I knew I could count on Driessen and Grant for help."

"Right. Thanks for the company line. But I'm guessing there's a lot more to this." He turned to look at Grant. "Right, Pastor?"

Grant chose to remain silent.

Noack shook his head at their duplicity. "I'm guessing the CIA wanted their hands on Audia to extract all he knew. You're lucky that Bates got a tip on where you were."

"Who called?" asked Caldwell.

"Don't know, yet. But they told Bates where, and that you were in trouble."

Caldwell continued, "Apparently, you weren't the only people contacted. It sure wasn't a masked FBI agent that saved the day by shooting Audia, and cutting me free."

Noack said, "No, it wasn't. Do you know who it might have been?"

"At this point, no clue."

Noack maintained his look of skepticism.

Grant had doubts about Paige's response as well.

Bates arrived with two large evidence bags, as well as a smaller one. "You two okay?"

Grant said, "Fine, thanks." Stephen thought Bates was the one who looked a bit shaky.

Caldwell skipped over the question. "What do you have?"

Bates looked at Noack to see if it was alright to respond.

Noack said, "Sure, go ahead. They don't share, but we might as well."

Bates reported, "We've got two laptops, and a smartphone. We can't get in right now, but when we get back to the FBI, it shouldn't take long."

Noack said to Bates, "Go now, and get it done." He turned to Caldwell, "I'm keeping this with my team, for now."

"Thanks."

Noack added, "As far as anyone is concerned, Audia murdered Farrell and the Fosters; he was shot dead here; and we're investigating to find his killer. It's the truth, as far as it goes." He looked at Grant, then back at Caldwell. "Get the hell out of here, both of you."

Chapter 45

Jennifer heard the key card click. She rolled on her side, with her back to the door.

Stephen came in and closed the door quietly.

The clock said 6:15 AM.

He whispered, "Are you awake, Jen?"

"Of course I am." She still didn't turn to look at her husband.

Uh-oh. Not happy?

"Stephen, are you ... alright?"

"A little beaten up, but in one piece."

She spun around and got out of bed. "Beaten up? What did you do, you ... idiot?"

"Idiot? And I thought you cared."

She guided him to sit on the bed, and removed his shirt.

He cringed. "Easy, Jen. Pretty sure I have a cracked rib."

She looked at the bandages around his midsection, but let out a gasp at the black bruising on his arm.

Jennifer helped him remove the rest of his clothes, and slowly eased him down on the bed.

Stephen closed his eyes, as Jennifer gently stroked parts of his body that were not painful to the touch.

Jennifer said, "I stayed up all night, praying that you would come back to me unhurt. Now I'm just thankful that you're back, even with these injuries."

"I'm sorry, Jen. But now the man who killed Graham, Margo and Senator Farrell – the same man who spoke to you at the hearing – is no longer a concern. He's unable to murder or terrorize innocent people any more."

"Stephen," Jennifer hesitated, "did you...?"

"No, it wasn't me." *But have to admit that I wish it had been me. Oh God, so tired.* "In fact, we're not sure yet who it was, but..."

Stephen never finished his sentence, slipping into a deep sleep.

Jennifer sat and watched him. "Being married to you is never going to be boring, is it? Not exactly the quiet life of a pastor's wife. Till death do us part, my love. But I'd prefer natural causes."

Chapter 46

While dozing off briefly, for most of the seven hours since Stephen had fallen asleep, Jennifer read, and watched a little news on television. But all the while she essentially sat watch.

She heard an unfamiliar cell phone buzz come from Stephen's pants that had been tossed over a chair. Jennifer looked at the thick black phone as it rumbled, and then opened it. "Hello."

The person on the other end did not answer. Jennifer repeated, "Hello."

"Jennifer? It's Paige Caldwell."

"Paige. Are you as bad off as my husband today?"

"No, and I'm very sorry. But Stephen played an important role in stopping a murderer and terrorist."

"I'm sure." Jennifer exhaled, and allowed her body to sag a little. "Hold on, Paige, I'll wake him."

Jennifer gently prodded Stephen. When his eyes were open and focused, she handed him the cell phone. She raised an eyebrow, and said, "New phone? It's Paige for you."

"Ah, thanks." He spoke into the phone, "Paige, how's Charlie?"

"He'll live. But it's going to take a couple of surgeries, and it sounds like a long period of time before he gets back to being fully mobile again."

Lord, thank you for Charlie's life. Please help his healing. "That's relatively good news, I suppose. Will the agency treat him right, given the circumstances?"

"No worries there."

"You know, he's concerned. Asked me to talk to you."

"Charlie is a good guy. But he worries too much. No time now for idle chat about me."

But we will talk when this is over. "Any word from the FBI on the laptops or phone?"

"I talked to Noack, and he says that Bates is working on it and frustrated. Bates managed to get into one computer, which had been Senator Farrell's, but it was wiped clean. Nothing salvageable. The hope is that whatever Farrell had was transferred onto Audia's own computer. The house Audia was in is being picked over, but nothing of value, at least not yet."

"Nothing else?"

"No."

"What about the masked avenger?"

"Nothing there, either. Listen, given that Audia is dead, it's time for you to go back to being a pastor. I'll let you know if there's anything else I can pass on." And Paige hung up.

Grant flipped the phone closed. He held it up to Jennifer, who was watching from a chair across the room, and said, "Encrypted."

"Of course," she replied. "What every pastor needs, an encrypted phone from the CIA."

He asked, "Are you mad?"

"Stephen, I know who you were, and who you are. And just based on how we came together, I understand that you're not the typical Lutheran church pastor. I didn't marry the typical pastor. I married you. Yes, a little part of me, to be honest, has had some fun tweaking you about Paige and the phone. But most of me is just worried about you."

"Thank you. And you know that I would never hurt you, betray you, in any way, especially the way Ted did."

Jennifer smiled, came across the room and sat next to Stephen. "I know that, without any doubts. What I'm trying to get straight is just how often your old life is going to pop up in our new life."

Good question. I wish I knew the answer.

She kissed him, and rested her head on the arm and shoulder that were untouched by the pain that had been dealt out the night before.

Stephen said, "By the way, what did Charlie whisper to you before we left last night?"

"He promised to do all he could to make sure you came back to me."

Chapter 47

"What do you think of our school community here at St. Luke's, Mr. Vanacore?" asked Carol Fleming, the principal.

Mike Vanacore, Fleming, and Fathers McDermott, Burns and Stone sat down in the conference room, just off the principal's office.

Vanacore smiled broadly. "It's been great, Mrs. Fleming. The parents that we spoke with seem dedicated and passionate. And how did you get that many students to come into school during summer vacation? You never would have gotten me to enter any school building during the summer when I was growing up."

That drew a few laughs around the table.

Father McDermott commented, "Our parents, families and students are committed to our mission. Most become involved in the school enthusiastically."

Vanacore asked, "I'm a big believer in making the mission clear in my business, and establishing a culture that supports our mission and goals. There certainly are parents and students involved at public schools just as committed to a solid education. What makes a place like St. Luke's so different?"

Father McDermott answered, "When getting that question, I always point out that we can offer a complete education, when the public schools cannot."

"What do you mean?" asked Vanacore.

"We pull it together under the banner of 'Excellence, Love and Values Rooted in the Faith.' First, we obviously place a major emphasis on educational excellence. Public schools say the same thing, but since we're a parochial school, we don't have to play by the politically designed curriculum imposed on public schools these days. Instead, we emphasize an education rooted in the classics, rich in history, a great emphasis on writing, and strong in math and science. Second and third are love and values. Again, other schools can say similar things, but the critical point is that we can explain why. We can teach about the ultimate, sacrificial and salvific love of Jesus Christ, and what that means in each of our lives and what it says about how we should treat others. And when it comes to values, we can teach students why something is right or wrong going back to Holy Scripture and Church tradition, not being left to struggle with the latest whims in our society. Finally, we make clear at St. Luke's that educating children in the faith is a central mission of our church. As Father Burns always notes, there's nothing more important than passing on the faith to our children."

Vanacore said, "I agree with pretty much everything you've said, Father McDermott. But why would St. Luke's and other parochial schools need resources from my foundation more so than local public schools? Aren't public schools facing tough times, especially during a down economy? And given what you can do, and what they can't, don't those schools need added help?"

Father Stone decided to weigh in, "Actually, no, Mike, they don't."

Vanacore smiled at his priest and friend. "Sorry, you'll have to make that case."

"I'm more than happy to do so. Even during the depths of the last recession, per pupil spending in public schools across the nation averaged about $11,000. And New York was tops at roughly $18,000. It's typical for school districts around here to go well above $20,000 per student." He turned to Mrs. Fleming. "How much does St. Luke's spend per student?"

"As is the case with the public schools, costs are lower for primary as opposed to secondary schools. But we come in at about $5,800, with tuition covering 60 percent on average."

Vanacore said, "That's an impressive discount on the full cost."

Stone continued, "But it's still an enormous burden on most families to come up with the additional money for tuition at St. Luke's, or any other parochial school, especially since they pay some of the highest property taxes in the country to support local public schools. St. Luke's works hard to hold tuition down through other means, including our educational trust, but it's a simple reality that many families cannot afford to choose a parochial school, even if they desperately wanted their children to go there."

Stone was looking Vanacore in the eyes.

Given his family's background, Vanacore could understand that dilemma all too well. He nodded knowingly. "But what about those in public schools needing the added resources because public schools can't do what St. Luke's can do?"

Father Stanley finally spoke up. "How would your additional dollars change any of that, Mr. Vanacore? Unfortunately, essential aspects of education would still be off base, and your money would simply be lopped on top of an already-breathtaking level of spending."

Stone said, "As a businessman, Mike, you see the benefits of competition. In the video-gaming marketplace, what would happen if you slacked off on quality, stopped innovating and jacked up prices?"

"We'd be out of business."

"But in the case of public schools, what happens?" Stone answered his own question. "They get rewarded with bigger budgets. Allowing more families to send their children to parochial schools not only is good for those students, but it would seem to me that losing students just might provide a little kick in the pants for some public schools."

Vanacore smiled at Stone, "Right." He turned to the others, and said, "Okay, Mrs. Fleming, gentlemen, you've provided a lot for me to consider. Do you have additional materials about St. Luke's that I can take home and review?"

"Absolutely," replied Fleming. She handed Vanacore the folder she'd been carrying throughout his tour.

"Thank you for the visit, and I'll get back to you soon."

They all shook hands, and Vanacore left with Father Stone. As they walked out to the parking lot, Vanacore stopped Stone and said, "Okay, Tom, what's the deal with you knowing the per pupil spending numbers, and serving up that little economics lesson on competition? As long as I've known you, I never thought numbers or economics were areas of expertise."

Stone said, "Well, I have a friend, Jennifer Grant. She's an economist, and she gave me some basics on the economics of education."

"Jennifer Grant? Formerly Jennifer Brees?"

"Yes. Do you know her?"

"I'm one of her firm's clients. They do great work."

"She just married my good friend, Stephen Grant, the pastor at St. Mary's Lutheran Church. I was the best man."

"Small world. Do they surf, too?"

"You know, Mike, when it comes to Stephen Grant, I would not be surprised."

Chapter 48

With Pastor Grant out of town, it was clear that Drew Frazier, the church council secretary, was doing an end run to the new guy, Pastor Charmichael.

Zack looked like he had just been run over by a freight train. Drew had pushed his way by the church secretary, Barbara Tunney, which was no easy feat, and landed in a chair at Zack's desk in the pastor's new office. And for more than half an hour, Drew had laid out the family and business background of Jennifer Grant in a conspiratorial tone.

Drew spoke of Jennifer's father, who owned casinos in Las Vegas. He told Zack, "It seems to me that this guy is tied to the mob."

He went on to note that Jennifer's firm had a large number of clients in banking and investment businesses. Drew paused for some kind of dramatic effect, when adding, "And those include hedge funds and private equity firms." He nodded his head, as if just revealing some grave evidence.

Obviously bewildered after taking in this long rant from Drew Frazier, Zack said, "Ah, okay, Mr. Frazier, what am I supposed to take away from this?"

"Well, it's the mob and Wall Street, and this woman is married to Pastor Grant. And now he wants to stop taking a salary from our church in order to live on dirty money."

Zack regained his footing. "Wow, those are pretty strong assertions, Mr. Frazier. And quite frankly, you're coming across as ..." He paused apparently to choose the right words. "You're coming across as rather extreme and angry. Is there something more behind all of this that I can help with?"

Drew grew more agitated. "You're damn right I'm angry. But 'extreme'? I can see that you're not going to be any help."

Zack said, "I'm sorry, but..."

"Oh, please, don't 'sorry' me." He slammed his hand down on the rather bulky file resting on his lap. "I would like this file copied and distributed to council members for discussion and potential action at our next council meeting."

"I don't think that's appropriate, Mr. Frazier. But hold on one minute, I'm going to talk to Barbara to see how something like this has been handled before." He got up, opened the door to his office, and went to Mrs. Tunney's office. Zack quietly filled Barbara in on what Drew had been saying, as well as his request.

Her voice rang out, "Oh, he does, does he?"

The 71-year-old, gray-haired widow pushed her glasses up, rose from her chair, straightened her dress full of small pink and purple flowers, and marched directly into Zack's office. Pastor Charmichael followed.

She looked at Frazier in disgust. "Starting trouble again, Drew."

"Don't start with me, Barbara."

She nearly shouted, "I've always known that you're a crackpot. Heck, I would guess that most people at St. Mary's think you're a conspiracy nut, but they're just too nice to say so. Well, I'm done being nice. By making baseless and just plain nasty insinuations against Mrs. Grant, not to mention Pastor Grant, you've gone way too far this time."

While she was talking, Frazier had gotten out of his chair to stand just a couple of feet from Barbara. He matched Tunney in volume. "I want these files copied and handed out to the council."

Barbara laughed in his face. "You know what you can do with those files, don't you?"

Frazier clenched his teeth, stared her in the eye, and then, finally, looked away at Zack. Getting no response, he stormed out of the office, cursing under his breath.

Zack, who had been watching the exchange in stunned silence, said, "Well, that was interesting. Are you alright, Barbara?"

She took a deep breath. "Yes, Pastor, I'm fine. Do you mind if I sit down?"

Zack jumped forward, and while guiding her to a seat, said, "Please, sit down here." He went out to her desk, and brought back the iced tea she was drinking.

Barbara said, "Thanks," and took a sip. "That man has been a pain in the ass at this church for decades." Looking startled by her own choice of words, she looked at Zack, and added, "Excuse me, I'm sorry."

"No need," said Zack. "You handled it all pretty well, I think."

She smiled in a grandmotherly way. "I can get away with that, with someone like Drew. As a pastor, especially a new arrival, you really can't."

"Yeah, I appreciate that. If you have a few minutes, why don't you fill me in on Drew and his history? I'd like to understand what I'm dealing with here."

Barbara relayed that Drew Frazier had some three decades of irritability under his belt, but that it had reached an entirely new level about seven years ago. That's when his wife divorced him. "After two years of retired life with Drew, she'd had enough." Barbara saw the slight frown on Zack's face, but continued. The rest was about a few attempts at new careers and businesses, with each failing. She also had heard that this put him in a deep financial hole. "All of that, unfortunately, seemed to transform his crankiness into bitterness."

After giving the rundown on Drew Frazier, Barbara went back to her desk to complete the week's service bulletin.

Zack picked up the phone and called Stephen's cell.

Grant answered, "Hello, Zack, how are you?"

"Hi, Stephen. I just survived an encounter with Drew Frazier."

"What's he done now?"

Zack gave Stephen the complete rundown on Frazier's accusations and request, and Barbara's response.

Stephen observed, "Crap. He's such a crackpot."

"Funny, that's what Barbara called him."

"To his face?"

"Yes."

Stephen laughed. "I owe her a dinner. And I owe you one as well, if that's enough to make up for leaving you to Drew Frazier during your first week at St. Mary's?"

"Don't worry about it. As I said before, it's not like you're off playing."

Stephen felt another shot of pain in his chest as he moved. "Hardly."

"But I'll take that dinner, anyway. So, when you get back, can we talk about Drew Frazier some more? On a certain level, I kind of feel bad for the guy."

"You're feeling more generous toward Drew than I am right now. I've been around the block with him a few times. But you're right. I'm going to talk to Jen about this. And I'll make time when I get back to New York. Thanks, again."

After the call ended, Stephen turned to Jennifer, who was working on her laptop at the hotel room desk. "I have more bad news. This time it has to do with Drew Frazier."

She rolled her eyes. "What is he up to now?"

"Remember that I mentioned his protest at church council on the salary issue?"

"Certainly."

"He's apparently pursued this further. He ambushed Zack, and us, this afternoon with accusations about your father and the mob, not to mention your firm being linked to Wall Street, which, in Drew's view, is a bad thing."

"What! That little shit."

A rare curse from my wife.

"Jen, don't worry. It's from Drew, and therefore amounts to nothing. I'll just…"

Jennifer interrupted, "No, Stephen, you'll do nothing. I will go to the church council about Frazier, directly, in front of all." She paused, and calmed her voice. "If that's alright with you?"

What am I going to say, "No"? "Well, can I suggest that you first sit down with him face to face, and see how far you get?"

Jennifer took a deep breath. "There you go being all pastor-like. You're right. That makes sense. Are there any more curves that can be thrown at us this week?"

Stephen answered, "I hope not. I've had my fill."

Jennifer looked back at her work on the computer screen, but Stephen could tell that she was not concentrating. Her thoughts were elsewhere.

She looked up, and said, "Since we're in for the rest of this afternoon and tonight, why don't you call room service, and have them send up some champagne and strawberries? I could use a little self-indulgent change of pace."

"Right. By the way, how are we paying for this, with mob money or those dirty Wall Street dollars?"

"That's not amusing."

"I'll get right on those strawberries and champagne. Will there be anything else?"

Chapter 49

Stephen's original plan was to head to New Jerusalem early on Thursday to assist Pastor Johnson, and perhaps even Pastor Schroeder, if he was interested, in making sure that all was ready for the afternoon and evening viewings.

With Audia dead, the FBI had pulled their guard on the Grants, and Stephen felt better about Jennifer heading over to her D.C. office earlier in the morning. They'd meet up again at the church.

Stephen took his time getting ready. He carved out some overdue time for devotions, for a little light exercise and for touching base with both Zack and Barbara. As he was dressing in the clerical clothes Barbara sent him in an overnight box, the television, which had been on for a while, finally earned his attention. It was Ted Brees, the new senator from New York, and Jennifer's sleazy ex-husband, on the screen next to Senator Duane Ellis.

No one on the face of the planet created an odder mix of thoughts and emotions in Stephen than did Ted Brees.

First, a vague annoyance emerged that this man had been Jennifer's first spouse. As much as he understood it intellectually, when Brees's name came up, or he popped up on television, as politicians often did, Stephen, quite simply, experienced a knee-jerk reaction of jealousy.

Fortunately, it quickly passed as Stephen recalled that Jennifer was his for the rest of their lives.

Second in the Ted Brees emotional line up was anger. Stephen would feel angry toward Brees for the way he mistreated and hurt Jennifer.

The third emotion was always a bit perplexing. He'd ask himself, *How did Jennifer ever marry an idiot politician?* They actually discussed this a few times, and Stephen was left with Jennifer concluding, "He changed tremendously, or more likely, he never was the person I thought he was when we got married." Again, Stephen could understand this. He had heard it several times while working with couples having marital troubles at St. Mary's.

Fourth, there was the question of divorce. Stephen did not take divorce lightly. Even in his relatively short time as a pastor, he saw several marriages that ended for superficial and selfish reasons. Often, one spouse had no regard for marriage being created by God, as well as little or no serious thought given to how ending a marriage in such a way would affect others around the couple, particularly children. It too often was about how one person felt at a particular moment in time. That's not what marriage was about, but Stephen knew that was what popular culture said marriage was. Of course, this was another example of mankind's fallen, sinful nature. Given this reality, on the one or two occasions when he allowed his mind to raise a question about his own marriage, Stephen quickly pulled back, recalling that it was Ted who committed adultery, was unrepentant, and destroyed his marriage to Jennifer.

In the end, though, Stephen would arrive at a feeling of thanks when Ted Brees intruded into their lives. Stephen would conclude, *Thank you, Ted Brees, for being such an asshole that you apparently had no real idea as to what a joyous, beautiful, caring and wise woman you were married to, and for allowing her to come into my life in a way that I could never have imagined.* That thought would be followed by Stephen offering up a half-hearted prayer that the Lord forgive his less-than-generous thoughts toward Ted, a fuller prayer that Ted Brees find his way to Christ, and a deeper prayer of thanks for Jennifer.

Stephen had just finished his Ted Brees emotional journey when he focused on what Brees and Ellis were saying.

It was an unusually bipartisan moment for television. Brees and Ellis embraced the idea of shifting foreign economic aid to small businesses, and they praised the work that Pastor Foster had done in the area. They also seemed to agree that it was likely that the pilot program would be approved for Belarus, and if all went as expected, Mexico would be next. The two appeared pleased to say that the Senate majority leader had pushed up the vote to today on the matter, as a kind of appreciation of Graham Foster.

When asked specifically about the murders, Brees and Ellis tried to top each other's outrage, as well as satisfaction that the FBI had killed the assailant, who apparently also had murdered Senator Farrell.

As for questions regarding motive and the link between Farrell and Foster, each said that they had not been briefed on such matters, but were confident that the FBI would soon come out with all of the details.

Stephen's cell phone rang, which gave him the small pleasure of pointing the remote at Ted Brees and clicking the power button off.

Stephen did not recognize the number, but given the 703 area code, assumed it was Pastor Johnson from New Jerusalem. "Hello."

"Pastor Grant?"

"Yes, who is this?"

It turned out not to be the pastor that Grant expected. "This is Pastor Schroeder at New Jerusalem."

"Hello, Pastor. How are things going this morning?"

"Actually, things are moving along fine. I spoke to Pastor Johnson, and while we appreciate all of the help you've provided in planning the viewings and funeral, we do not want to intrude any further. So, we decided that it's appropriate that he and I should handle the services."

"It's really no intrusion. I'm willing to help out however I..."

Schroeder cut him off. "Again, we appreciate that, but it's too much. I assume that we'll see you later today or tomorrow?"

"Of course, but..."

Again, Schroeder interrupted. "Thank you, Pastor Grant, but I have to get back to matters here. I'm sure you understand."

"Yes..."

"Goodbye, Pastor Grant." Schroeder then ended the call.

Okay, what the heck was that all about?

Stephen thought about calling Pastor Johnson directly, but decided against it. *I'll make a point to check in with him later.*

Stephen paused to think about what to do with the few hours he had planned on dedicating to New Jerusalem. The answer was obvious, and Stephen was ashamed that he had not planned on it earlier.

Chapter 50

"Son of a bitch, look at you, Grant. You really are a man of the cloth," proclaimed Charlie Driessen from his hospital bed, as Stephen Grant entered the room.

"The nurse said I could come in. They don't ask many questions with the collar."

"I bet. Shut the door, will you?"

Ever careful. "How are you feeling, Charlie?"

Driessen grunted. "At least I'm better off than that dirt bag Audia."

"True enough. But what's the plan of action, especially with the knees?" Grant glanced at the immobilized legs.

"Ah, crap. Basically, I'm getting new knees made of metal and plastic. It's supposed to hurt like hell for a time. Probably a few months of rehab. And then, no guarantees about how well I'll get around."

"I have little doubt about you recovering."

"Yeah? You get some kind of message from above?"

"No, you're just too pigheaded to do otherwise. But would you like to pray anyway?"

Charlie laughed a little, and said, "No."

Grant added, "How about I add you to my prayer list?"

Driessen paused and looked Grant in the eyes. "I guess I can live with that."

"Good."

"How are the ribs? Heard one's cracked."

"You know the deal. It'll be fine."

The two men went on to catch up on key points of their lives since Grant left the CIA more than a decade-and-a-half earlier. While Driessen shook his head at how different things had become for Grant since his CIA days, Grant was struck by how little Driessen's life had changed. *But then again, the guy's clearly doing what he was meant for.*

Grant decided to switch gears to their botched raid.

"How do you read what happened on Tuesday night? Did Audia know we were coming? And who was the masked guy that saved our butts?"

"He couldn't have known we were coming. But he obviously was on guard in case somebody showed up uninvited."

"I guess you're right."

"Trust me on that one. By the way, he was some freakin' shot to take each of us down wearing vests. That required pinpoint accuracy in an incredibly short period of time."

"I was thinking the same thing."

"I'm sure you were, given that you were probably the best shot I'd ever seen, and I'm not sure you could have pulled it off."

"What about our masked avenger?" asked Grant.

"That's one for the books. I don't have a fucking clue. Oh, sorry about the f-bomb."

"The collar getting to you? Don't worry about it. I'd be worried if Charlie Driessen started apologizing because of me."

"I'm wondering if Paige has some ideas. So far, she hasn't shared with me. I assume you haven't spoken to her about Schmidt yet?"

"No chance."

"Well, now you have another issue to quiz her about."

"Thanks, I appreciate it."

The hospital door opened, and in came a nurse. "I'm sorry to interrupt, but it's time to get some updates on how you're doing, Mr. Driessen."

Grant smiled at her, and said, "Hello."

Driessen grumbled a bit, and then told Stephen, "Get the hell out of here, Grant."

Stephen said, "No problem, Charlie. We'll talk soon." He took a couple of steps toward the door.

Driessen said, "Hey, Grant."

"Yes?"

"Thanks for coming ... and for the prayers."

"You're welcome, Charlie. God bless."

As Grant was leaving, he heard the nurse ask, "He seems very nice. Is that your pastor?"

Driessen's response began, "Not exactly..."

Grant would have liked to linger to hear how the rest of that conversation went. But he smiled to himself, and headed to the elevator.

* * *

Grant grabbed a quick lunch, and then spent the rest of the day at New Jerusalem.

Pastor Schroeder offered Grant nothing more than basic pleasantries.

In a private moment, Pastor Johnson explained that Schroeder suddenly engaged on, and then took over, running the death proceedings for the Fosters. In the end, he apologized to Grant, and shrugged his shoulders.

So, Grant wound up adopting the unofficial role of greeting and talking with various Lutheran clergy and administrators who showed up, most still shocked by what had occurred.

Chapter 51

Early Thursday evening, FBI Special Agent Ryan Bates completed his presentation to Rich Noack and other colleagues.

Bates reported that, while nothing could be retrieved from Senator Farrell's laptop, it didn't matter. All of it had been transferred onto Audia's computer, and it confirmed their expectations that Audia was working for the Mexican drug lord Lydia Garcia.

Another techie confirmed Bates' assessment. "Ryan passed the machines on to my team, and we came up with the same results."

After several more inquiries, Noack gave a heads up to the field leader of the team watching Carlos Luis and Jose Mora, as well as Garcia's right hand man, Manny Rodriguez, that they would be moving in shortly.

Noack also made a call to Paige Caldwell at the CIA.

* * *

The 39-year-old FBI Special Agent Trent Nguyen, born in Saigon to an American nurse and a Vietnamese businessman, had received the FBI Star for being injured by an IED in Baghdad, and the FBI Shield of Bravery after he kept several al Qaeda terrorists at bay outside a school in Kabul while aiding an investigation by Afghanistan authorities.

Nguyen seemed universally liked. His unwavering commitment to protecting his nation and fellow citizens, combined with a smart, alert mind, were recognized by his superiors. But he fended off any promotions that would have had the effect of reducing his time in the field.

Colleagues appreciated his professionalism and leadership skills, while love for his small family was apparent during down time and outside the office. That all translated into his earning the trust of fellow agents.

Now, he was directing a team in Washington, D.C., just before 1:00 AM. The objectives were simple enough. Three hotel rooms. In one was Carlos Luis, and in the second, Jose Mora. The two men were friendlies to be secured and protected. The third was a suite occupied by Manny Rodriguez, an unfriendly, who was to be secured and arrested. Rodriguez, of course, might not come quietly.

Stealth was the choice for entry. Three teams of four, each person in a vest and weapon drawn, waited quietly in the hall outside the rooms. The hotel supplied key cards.

Nguyen led the squad at the suite door. He signaled the others, and the cards were slipped into and out of each door. Clicks followed, and with a sudden burst of silent speed, each room was entered with eyes and weapons scanning.

Carlos Luis responded with a smile, while showing his hands for the agents to see.

Jose Mora bolted upright in bed. He responded to a near-whispered order to put his hands up. Then he asked, "My family? Please tell me my family is safe."

He was assured.

Nguyen and three fellow agents entered the two-bedroom suite. The room was drenched in silence and darkness. Nguyen pointed two to one bedroom, and indicated for the other to follow him to the second bedroom.

Each duo moved quickly. Nguyen opened the door, and found no one. Before he could check more thoroughly, a woman's scream annihilated the silence, followed by an exchange of gunshots and shouts that transformed the suite into a cacophony of noise and flashes of light.

By the time Nguyen and his number two reached the room, the other two agents were on the floor. One groaning and moving slightly, shot in the chest but kept alive by his vest. The other was dead, with half of his face torn away.

Nguyen looked to the bed. A naked woman was crying and rocking, her legs bent up against her chest.

Trent Nguyen looked at the rest of the room. The window had been shattered open, curtains pushed away, and a thick cord ran from under the bed out the window.

Nguyen leaped to the window, and looked down to see a naked man slowly repelling down the four floors, holding on with a handlebar attached to a descender to brake his decline. Pointing his gun at Rodriguez, Nguyen shouted, "Stop, FBI!"

Rodriguez paused, and looked up. Then he laughed, and resumed his descent.

Nguyen holstered his gun, grabbed the line, and went out the window in what appeared to be one fluid motion.

As Nguyen approached the second floor, he looked down. Rodriguez was just about on the ground.

When Manny Rodriguez let go of the line, he looked up with a smile of satisfaction and expectation.

That smile was crushed and Rodriguez was brutally thrust into unconsciousness by the right boot and then full weight of a rapidly descending Trent Nguyen.

* * *

Two Black Hawk helicopters sat on a secluded stretch of concrete just outside of Laredo, Texas. While waiting, the four CIA aviation specialists in each copter checked and rechecked systems, including the 20mm turret gun cannons and laser-guided rockets.

Outside, Dennis Morrow reviewed mission details with a dozen paramilitary personnel, all dressed in black body armor.

With a beep in his ear, Morrow stopped and clicked the button on the side of his helmet. "Sir?"

"The FBI has Rodriguez. Luis and Mora are fine, and our teams have their families in safe houses. The Mexicans have given tacit approval. Execute Operation: Monterrey."

"Yes, sir. We'll be going video live in the air." Morrow clicked off the communication link via his helmet, and announced, "Okay, we're a go."

The two Black Hawks were in the air and streaking south in the dark sky within ten minutes. Ten of the CIA paramilitary personnel were on the mission's Black Hawk 1, with two marksmen in Black Hawk 2. Given the limited landing space, Black Hawk 2 would stay in the air, taking down hostiles, with Black Hawk 1 touching down to achieve the objective of extracting Lydia Garcia.

Just over a half hour later, the Black Hawks approached the Garcia compound positioned in the mountains just south of Monterrey. Morrow kissed a small crucifix on a chain, and then slipped it back against his chest.

The noise of the choppers brought heavily armed men out of three buildings – the main house, a barrack, and a garage. They started firing into the air at the copters.

The crew positioned Black Hawk 2 according to plan, firing a laser-guided rocket at the garage, which immediately erupted in a loud, bright inferno, charring two men beyond recognition and knocking down two more of Garcia's men who were in the open. A crewman turned the 20mm cannon, and mowed down four men firing from the ground. And a marksman from the open side door made sure that the two Garcia guards on the ground did not get up.

As a hail of bullets emerged from the barrack building, the pilot pivoted Black Hawk 2 in order to unleash two more laser-guided rockets that burned and demolished the two-story structure. Suddenly, half of Lydia Garcia's drug army was dead.

Black Hawk 1 touched down, and the ten men fanned out and moved toward the two-story house, responding to fire emerging from five windows.

Black Hawk 2 rotated again, and the two marksmen were able to silence the shots coming from two of the upstairs windows.

But one officer on the ground fell when a bullet ripped into his left leg. Morrow ordered two men to pull their colleague back to the chopper, while leading the other six closer to the house.

The firing from the third second-floor window also was ended by several shots from Black Hawk 2.

However, the drug gangster in the north, first floor window managed to shoot a crewman from Black Hawk 1 who was reaching out to help his injured team member get aboard. The crewman dropped to the floor of the copter, and then tumbled out of the aircraft, dead before he hit the ground.

Another shot from the same window struck one of the paramilitary personnel in the arm as he was moving to the fallen Black Hawk 1 crewmember.

Morrow saw where the shots hitting his men were coming from, and pointed the remaining six men to the front door and the south window serving up additional fire. As Morrow closed quickly on the north window, he grabbed an M-67 grenade off his belt, pulled the pin, and tossed it into the window, pushing himself against the wall until the fragmentation grenade exploded.

Morrow quickly went to the window, and saw a dark figure on the other side of the room rolling over on the floor, then sitting up and moving to aim the rifle still in hand. Morrow squeezed off two bursts from his Colt M4 Carbine assault rifle, and the person fell back.

He went through the window, and moved to the body. When he saw it was a woman, he said, "Shit."

Morrow felt for a pulse on Lydia Garcia, and found none, which was not surprising given the five bloody entry holes in her chest and stomach.

Morrow clicked a button on his helmet. "Garcia was firing from the north window. She's dead. Time to pull out."

With Garcia confirmed dead, once the six CIA personnel were out and moving back from the house, Black Hawk 2 was free to lay down fierce cover fire on the house with its 20mm cannon.

After all personnel, including the dead crewman, were onboard, Black Hawk 1 rose from the ground, and started turning toward the south. When sporadic fire re-emerged from the house, Black Hawk 2, still hovering slightly to the north, launched two laser-guided rockets that left the compound devoid of any more gunfire. In fact, as the sound of helicopter engines turned north and faded in the distance, all that was left to hear in the onetime fortress of Lydia Garcia was the crackling of fire and wood.

Chapter 52

The U.S. Senate was scheduled to vote on the Foreign-aid Reaching Entrepreneurs and Employment Act, or the FREE Act, early Friday afternoon.

Just three hours before the scheduled vote, at a joint FBI and CIA press conference, two spokesmen reported what the agencies had found out about Lydia Garcia, a Mexican drug lord, who hired a contract killer for a murder spree in Washington, D.C., resulting in the deaths of U.S. Senator Jimmy Farrell, Larry Payton, Pastor Graham Foster, and his wife, Margo Foster.

While declaring that they could not go into detail, it was announced that the contract murderer was killed during an FBI raid, one of Garcia's lieutenants was captured in the U.S. and was in custody, and Garcia was a casualty at her compound in Mexico when she fired upon U.S. law enforcement personnel.

When the spokesmen stepped aside, Donny Ryder, the U.S. attorney general, stepped to the microphones. He said, "This is an important victory for the U.S. These thugs reached into our nation's capital and murdered a U.S. senator, a congressional aide, and two good people whose only mission in life was to help others. It was critical that we resolved this and dispensed justice. And again, while we cannot release the full details on this case as yet, I feel compelled to point out that Senator Farrell was murdered because he suspected that the Mexican drug gang was trying to manipulate legislation being considered in the United States Congress. Senator Farrell's efforts to protect this nation resulted in his life being lost, but when the FBI acquired his information, it led to the plot being put to a stop, and led to the very people behind his murder. Senator Farrell made the ultimate sacrifice for his nation."

Ryder and the spokesmen left the room, ignoring the questions shouted by reporters.

Just a few hours later, after a short debate sprinkled with praise for Senator Farrell, for Larry Payton, and for the Fosters, the Senate passed the FREE Act, but by a smaller margin than had been expected earlier that same day. Some additional conservative Republicans switched from "yea" to "nay" in honor of Jimmy Farrell.

Chapter 53

The encrypted phone rumbled in his pocket just as the California Riesling was being poured to accompany flounder stuffed with crabmeat. Grant had been looking for this call, but was hoping to get it earlier while at New Jerusalem.

He quickly pulled the phone out of his pocket, and gave Jennifer an apologetic shrug.

Stephen looked at his hosts – Jennifer's business partner Yvonne Hudson and her husband, Dale – and said, "I'm sorry, do you mind if I take this call outside? It's important."

Dale responded, "Of course, Stephen. If you head out the glass doors off the living room, you can sit on the patio and have privacy."

Stephen said, "Thanks," while also offering an "excuse me" to the other dinner guests: Senator Kristin Madsen and her husband, Secretary of Commerce Cal Madsen.

Grant noted that no one looked all that bothered, as he had contributed nothing to the discussion about who should be appointed as the next chairman of the Federal Reserve.

He answered the call while heading to the doors. "Paige?"

"Yes. How's dinner going at the Hudson place?"

What the... When outside, he said with some annoyance, "Do you have a tracker in this phone?"

"What do you think?"

Let it go. "I shouldn't be surprised. What's going on?"

"Sorry about the tracker, and for interrupting your dinner."

Paige's tone changed and registered with Stephen. *Something's bugging her.* "Don't worry about it."

Paige gave Stephen a quick rundown on getting Rodriguez, and how the operation played out with Garcia.

When she was done, Stephen said, "I'm sorry to hear about the lost crewman." He made a mental note to keep the man's family and friends in prayers later. "As much as it would have been ideal to grab Garcia, all in all, I suppose it gets listed as a mission accomplished for the agency."

"I suppose."

"Okay, Paige, what's bothering you?"

"It just doesn't fit, or maybe it all fits too neatly."

"Assuming your instincts are still as good as when we were partners..."

"Assuming?"

"Yes, assuming that, what's specifically giving you doubts?"

"I don't have clear answers to the questions we raised in Noack's office the other day, and now I actually have more questions. I watched the interrogations of Rodriguez. He's really scared. I think someone dropped Gitmo into the conversation, and that got his attention big time."

"So, Rodriguez is scared."

"He denies having any info on Audia, and I believe him. That means either Garcia kept him out of the loop or..."

"That wouldn't be all that surprising, right? Compartmentalizing of cells. This way Rodriguez would be clueless if he wound up in the position that he is in right now."

Paige said, "Maybe. You're attending the funeral at New Jerusalem tomorrow, right?"

"Yes. I was there much of today as well. But then again, you already knew that, didn't you?"

She ignored the jab. "In addition to your pastoral duties, can I hire you to keep your old radar up, just for anything unusual or out of place?"

"What do I get paid?"

"Well, obviously, you don't get the fringe benefits you used to when we were partners."

"Paige, as a very happily married man, I understand that."

"That remains your loss. But I will buy you dinner at some point."

"Deal. Is there anything in particular that you would like to share, to perhaps give me an idea of what I should be looking out for?"

"No, I've just got suspicions at this point. Thanks, Stephen, I appreciate it. Bye."

Paige hung up, leaving Stephen to wonder.

I never let her tell me what the other option was if Garcia in fact did not keep Rodriguez out of the loop, and Audia wasn't working for them. Are we thinking the same thing, Paige?

Chapter 54

Amazingly and regrettably, this was Stephen's second joint funeral for a husband and wife within two years.

The first time, it was a husband and wife team – Hans and Flo Gunderson – who were like family, making him feel at home at St. Mary's from the time he arrived. Stephen knew they were now at peace in Christ, but he still missed them.

Now, a friend from seminary and his wife were struck down. Again, Stephen was confident in their after-this-life status, but the sense of loss was fresh, and given how they perished, raw.

Though disinvited from being involved in conducting the funeral, Stephen and Jennifer still continued to fulfill the quasi-greeter role for his fellow Lutheran clergy.

In the lobby of the New Jerusalem Worship and Fulfillment Center, Stephen spotted various politicians arriving and filing through into the auditorium.

Among the senators were Duane Ellis and Trevor Tenace, as well as Kristin Madsen. And from back home in New York came Governor Robert Shimansky and Senator Ted Brees.

Jennifer and Stephen made sure to greet Senator Madsen, and to avoid Senator Brees. In unspoken maneuvers, Jennifer and Ted managed to avoid each other without making eye contact, and without drawing attention to their mutual avoidance.

Just before the funeral was scheduled to begin, Stephen spotted two men speaking with Pastor Schroeder, whose body language indicated a significant degree of discomfort. The three were far off to the side at a door leading backstage of the auditorium. Schroeder spoke little, and while listening his eyes darted from the two men to the room in general.

When positions shifted slightly, Stephen thought one of them – the slim man with round glasses – looked familiar. He leaned in to Jennifer's ear, "Do you know those two speaking with Pastor Schroeder?"

"Sure, they're from Belarus. The overweight guy with the crazy gray hair and beard is the trade minister, Vadim Slizhevskiy, and the thin one with black hair is their ambassador to the U.S., Oleg Rumas."

As he started accessing the old CIA database in his mind, Stephen looked for Jennifer to confirm his thinking. "They're here because of Graham being with Entrepreneurship & Values in Action and their work in Belarus?"

"Right. Since they're at work with small businesses in Belarus, they're expected to be the group used to carry out the U.S. aid project there."

Then it clicked in his mind. *Coz mentioned an Oleg Rumas.*

Coz was Tony Cozzilino, Grant's mentor when he first joined the CIA. Coz, as Grant called him, was a tough veteran of Cold War espionage, from before the Vietnam War until the fall of the Soviet Union. He died at the hands of two former KGB in Barcelona. Minutes later, Grant had killed one of the murderers, and eventually came face to face with the other in a life-and-death struggle.

During various sessions with his mentor those many years ago, Cozzilino would provide a rundown on former

KGB that he thought still needed watching. Oleg Rumas, as Grant now recalled, was among a group that worried Coz because those men and women were not Russian KGB, but instead came from other nations captured behind the Iron Curtain by the Soviets.

If Grant was recalling things correctly, Coz had said that Rumas was dangerous because he managed to stay largely anonymous, with no clear evidence linking him to KGB actions. Yet, he was suspected of having a hand in some of the darkest moves against individuals who were less than faithful to the state.

Stephen then noticed the FBI's Ryan Bates just inside the front entrance doors of the Worship Center. Bates had his eyes trained on the same conversation that Grant had been watching.

When the conversation with the two Belarusian officials ended, Schroeder wasted no time in slipping through the backstage door.

Jennifer prodded Stephen from his observations. "Shall we go inside, Stephen?"

"Yes, of course, Jen. Let's go."

Chapter 55

After the funeral, there was no long procession of vehicles to a cemetery. Instead, the bodies of Graham and Margo Foster were to be interred in the garden between the worship building and the townhouses on the grounds of New Jerusalem.

A long procession of mourners, however, did walk by the two coffins, with each person depositing a red rose.

As the thorny flowers piled up on top of and spilled off the sides of the coffins, Stephen whispered to Jennifer, "I'll be right back."

He moved slowly out of sight of the burial proceedings, pulled out the encrypted phone, and called Paige.

"Hello, Stephen. Is the funeral over?"

"Just about. People are placing roses on the coffins. It gave me a quick opportunity to call. Do you know Oleg Rumas?

"Ambassador from Belarus."

"He was talking with Pastor Schroeder."

"It's no secret that Belarus supports the effort to get small business aid for their country. And it would make sense that Schroeder would step in after the death of Foster."

"Yes, but Schroeder looked extremely uncomfortable, like he didn't want to be seen with Rumas. For good measure, and I'm not sure if this means anything, Coz had warned me about Rumas."

"Cozzilino? Your memory still amazes me. What did he tell you some twenty years ago?

"That Rumas was one of those non-Russian KGB suspects worth keeping an eye on in the post-Soviet world. According to Coz, no hard evidence existed, but there were suspicions that Rumas played a role in silencing individuals not aligned with the state."

"Interesting. I've heard nothing on that."

Stephen added, "Obviously, the FBI has some concerns as well, since Bates is here and appears to be watching Rumas."

"Bates. Hmmm. When are you heading back to Long Island?"

"Our plan was to head back tomorrow, probably in the afternoon. But there's another question..."

Paige interrupted, "We need to talk tonight then. How about I buy you that dinner for the work you just supplied?"

Stephen wondered how Jennifer would react to his heading off for dinner with Paige on what they assumed would be the last night in an unimaginably eventful visit to the nation's capital. But it was unavoidable.

"Yes, but let's make it early. Where?"

"How about our old haunt in an hour and a half?"

"That works."

After hanging up, Grant noticed Bates still lingering at the outer edges of the burial. He approached and stood at Bates' side. "Hello, Agent Bates."

While keeping his gaze forward, Bates said, "Pastor Grant."

"Can I ask why you're here?"

"You can ask."

"I'm guessing it has to do with Oleg Rumas."

That got Bates' attention, and he turned to Grant to ask, "Why do you say that?"

Grant provided Bates with a similar rundown on Rumas as he gave Paige.

Grant thought Bates reacted a bit oddly. The FBI agent shoved his hands in his pockets, looked down at the ground, and did not say anything.

Grant filled the silence by adding, "I'm meeting Paige Caldwell in a while. If there's more, I'll make sure she gives you and Noack a heads up. Sound good?"

Bates then took Grant a bit off guard. He looked Grant in the eyes, and placed his left hand on Stephen's shoulder. "Pastor Grant, that would be much appreciated. Tell Paige we'll offer her the same courtesy." He then quickly removed his eyes from Grant's, and walked off into the part-milling and part-exiting crowd.

Stephen returned to Jennifer's side. It took about an hour for the remaining roses to be placed, and for the Grants to finish speaking with various people, pledging to get together soon, as people usually do at funerals.

Time to meet Paige. Stephen said, "Jen, I'm sorry, but I have to leave to meet Paige and hopefully tie up a few things on what's happened to the Fosters." He continued, not giving her a chance to reply. "Do you mind?"

Jennifer smiled. "Stephen, go finish what needs finishing."

"I don't deserve you."

She kissed him on the cheek, and said, "You're right."

Ten minutes later, Jennifer Grant and Stephen Grant were in separate taxis.

Ryan Bates followed the one that Stephen had entered.

Chapter 56

The Saturday 5:30 PM service at St. Mary's Lutheran Church had 35 people in the pews.

Before the service, during announcements, Pastor Zack Charmichael mentioned that Pastor Grant was still away in Washington, D.C., with the funeral for Pastor and Mrs. Foster.

During the service, Zack noted the Grants, and other family and friends of the Fosters, in the Prayer of the Church.

After the service, on the way out of church, a few members who had not yet met Zack introduced themselves. Most of the others who said anything beyond "Good evening, Pastor" or "Hello, Pastor" referenced that they were praying for the Grants and that the murders were horrible.

However, three people had something very different to say.

The first was Drew Frazier. "Pastor Charmichael, I'm glad you're here at least, otherwise we probably wouldn't have had a pastor or a service tonight."

"Now, Mr. Frazier, you know that's not true."

"Really? Do I now? It seems to me that someone around here needs to be focused on this type of stuff. I think it's going to happen more often, especially given all the money that Pastor Grant and his new wife have."

Zack stiffened, and clenched his teeth. Then he lowered his voice and said, "That was uncalled for, Mr. Frazier."

Frazier failed to lower his voice. "Uncalled for, eh? Well, I don't think so."

Zack leaned in closer to Frazier to whisper, "Mr. Frazier, I'd like you to come by the office this coming week. We can sit down and talk about what's really bothering you, and maybe we could partake in some confession and absolution."

Frazier grumbled, and stomped down the steps of St. Mary's.

A middle-aged couple – each tall, thin and wearing glasses – came next in line. Doris and Evan Bradcock were both public school teachers. The husband spoke up, "You know, Pastor Charmichael, the same kind of thing crossed our minds when Drew gave us some information on Mrs. Grant's income and background. We're not sure it's such a great idea to have a pastor who has greater wealth than the members of the congregation."

As Evan spoke, Doris nodded in agreement.

It was apparent that Zack's patience was being tested. He sighed a bit. "I'm sorry Mr. and Mrs. Bradcock, but I'm not really sure how to respond. Shouldn't we be supporting each other as a Christian family, rather than getting distracted by how much money some people have versus others?"

"Well, yes, but doesn't this have the potential to make some people feel uncomfortable?" responded Doris.

"I'm not really understanding why that should be the case. In addition, as a Christian family, we shouldn't really be talking behind people's backs. As Jesus teaches in Matthew 18, if we have a problem with one of our brothers, then we should take it directly to him."

The Bradcocks walked away, not looking very convinced. And they met Drew Frazier, who was still lingering, forming an unholy trinity in a place well known for creating and stoking trouble – the church parking lot.

Chapter 57

Grant and Caldwell grabbed a table in the dark corner of an uninspired restaurant in a borderline hotel in a marginal part of the nation's capital.

It was a place to drink and eat when two people didn't want anyone else to know that they were sharing a meal, and probably one of the rooms as well. That was the case years earlier, the last time Paige and Stephen ate there, when they were still partners at the CIA and in bed.

The waitress brought over two Buds and then left.

"This place still has the same shabby charm," Stephen observed with an uneasy sarcasm.

"It sure does."

Stephen was uncomfortable being in this place, with the history between he and Paige, while his wife was back in another hotel alone. He wasn't sure why, but he said, "I don't know if Jennifer would understand if she saw us here."

"Stephen, that's horse shit. Your lovely bride is a damn smart woman. She knows you, perhaps even better than I do – excuse me – better than I did. And that means she knows to trust you. So, stop feeling guilty about nothing."

Stephen felt his tight stomach muscles loosen. "Fair enough. But what about you and Herr Schmidt? Is this a stop for the two of you?"

"Charlie is a pain in the ass."

"Maybe, but he's looking out for you, and apparently, you need some watching out for. Screwing around with Schmidt is stupid."

"I thought it was harmless. I checked and rechecked, and his post-Stasi years have been filled with legit government and private-sector jobs, the latest being work with a trade association covering parts of Eastern Europe."

"Do you trust him?"

Paige laughed and took a sip of her beer. "There's no one outside the CIA that I trust, except for you."

That's sad.

She continued, "So, no, I don't trust him. He's been a great lay. Now it seems that Charlie, and you, might be right, which makes my stupidity even worse."

"Schmidt is the one that gave you Audia's location, right? And now you're seeing a possible link between Oleg Rumas, the Belarus ambassador, and Schmidt from their old commie days. And chances that the Mexicans were being set up are on the rise."

"You're so fucking smart."

Grant knew that lashing out actually was directed inward, at her own decisions.

Paige went on, "Obviously, Lydia Garcia and her cronies were anything but innocents. Just ask Carlos Luis and Jose Mora. But if they were set up in this case, that means I've been set up, and you know that does not sit well."

Grant said, "Right." *If so, I don't want to think about what she'll do to Schmidt.* It was his turn to take a swig of beer. "And I assume that our masked avenger was Schmidt?"

"Seems likely, but I haven't confirmed that yet. Unfortunately, this actually could get worse."

"How?"

"Snopkov, the president of Belarus, has been close to Rumas for more than four decades."

Stephen let the possibilities sink in, and said, "Crap." He took a bigger drink of beer. "But what about the evidence the FBI came up with, that Senator Farrell's laptop confirmed the link between Audia and the Mexican DTO?"

"There are only two possibilities that I can see. First, Rumas and Snopkov, along with Schmidt, simply had an opportunity handed to them by Lydia Garcia. Audia was working for her. She kept that from Rodriguez, and Schmidt simply took advantage of the situation by passing on the information he or Rumas or Snopkov dug up on Audia and his location."

Grant knew that this was not the scenario on which Paige was placing her bets. "Seems neat and tidy."

"Yes, it does."

"The second possibility then?"

"That's the one I don't really want to think about, but have to. It's the most troubling, and unfortunately, the most likely in my mind."

She finished her beer, and asked the waitress for another as their plates were deposited on the table. Each kept it simple and safe with well-done hamburgers and fries.

After a few bites of food and the arrival of Paige's second beer, Stephen said, "Okay, that second possibility you don't like, but believe most likely?"

"Obviously, Rumas and Snopkov hired Schmidt and Audia. Audia executes Farrell, his aide, and the Fosters in a manner reminiscent of how the drug gangs work in Mexico. Mexico gets a nasty black eye, Belarus gets the U.S. aid money, and I assume, Snopkov and Rumas manage to get control of the U.S. dollars that are supposed to flow to small businesses in Belarus. Seems like something you started to allude to back in Noack's office."

Grant shrugged a little. "But how do they get their hands on those dollars? The whole idea is that this new type of foreign aid bypasses the governments and goes directly to entrepreneurs and small businesses? I know Graham would not..."

Grant stopped mid-sentence.

Paige looked at him. "Go ahead, you're thinking the same thing that I am."

"No, come on?"

"It fits, especially based on what you relayed."

"So, you believe Pastor Schroeder is in on this with Rumas? That Schroeder will work himself into Foster's old position with the Entrepreneurship & Values group, doling out the dollars in Belarus? And the dollars, therefore, wind up with businesses or shell entities that Snopkov and Rumas control?"

"See, you put it together as well."

Grant really did not like the next step along this line because it led to FBI Special Agent Ryan Bates. "But that could point to Bates at FBI, right?"

Paige nodded ever so slightly. "It's hard to figure anything else to explain the report that Farrell's laptop – actually Audia's laptop – provided a smoking gun that Audia was employed by Lydia Garcia. Based on the orders from Noack that night, Bates had first crack at the PC. Farrell's machine was either already wiped clean or Bates did it. And Bates planted files on Audia's computer."

"This is getting hard to swallow. A pastor and an FBI agent in on a series of murders and assorted other deceptions in order to steer U.S. federal aid dollars to old-time communists in Belarus? Is this believable?"

"You've been away from this for too long. Think about what you saw with the agency, and how little it seemed to take to corrupt people who were probably viewed as non-corruptible by those who thought they knew them best. I don't want to believe this about Bates – I was kind of fond of him in a nerdy FBI kind of way – and I'm sure you don't want to believe this about a fellow pastor. But think. Just go to the Ames and Hanssen cases, and what about all of those Catholic priests who preyed on unsuspecting youth?"

Grant didn't like it, but Paige was absolutely right. "Why?"

"I can't explain those perverted priests, but there's a lot of dollars in play here. Why did Ames and Hanssen do what they did?"

"The love of money."

Chapter 58

Ryan Bates heard his name emanate from the speaker on the smartphone receiving the signal from the tiny listening device he stuck on the back of Stephen Grant's right shoulder. He dropped the cup in his hand, turned and vomited most of the coffee he had been drinking onto the Impala's passenger seat.

"Shit, I knew it!"

Pores over his entire body started excreting sweat as he listened to more of the conversation between Grant and Caldwell. Bates punched the steering wheel over and over again. Snot began leaking from his nose and onto his upper lip.

As the secure smartphone relayed more and more of what Grant and Caldwell were saying about him, his eyes darted around the interior of the car, apparently seeking some escape.

He started the vehicle, slammed it into drive, but then failed to take his foot off the brake. He screamed, "I can't fucking run." And then Bates began crying, "Jackie, Jackie, what will you think? Jackie, oh God. What have I done? You'll hate me forever."

The conversation between Grant and Caldwell continued, unaware of the intrusion by Bates and his wailing.

Grant said, "Listen, before we go to Noack on this, let's get more input just to make sure. I don't want to leave anything to chance on this, given what we're about to accuse Bates of doing."

Paige replied, "Okay, but I've used up my avenues. Does a church pastor have anything?"

"As a matter of fact, this pastor might. Remember Sean McEnany?"

"The member of your congregation that you asked me to do a background check on? Corporate and government security work, good Pentagon contacts, and former Army Ranger, right?"

"Yes, but I don't think you managed to get the full take on him. He remains something of a mystery. I've got a feeling that he might be able to give us more on Snopkov, Rumas, and Schmidt, and we can see if he serves up anything on Bates."

"Why not? Can he turn it around quickly?"

"I'll contact him when I get back to the hotel, and make clear that we need whatever he has by noon tomorrow. Does that work?"

"It does for me. If we're done, let's pay the check, and I'll drop you at your hotel."

Bates bit his right fist, and looked down the street at a slim alley next to the hotel where Grant and Caldwell were. It was between the hotel exit and Caldwell's car.

He reached under his seat for an unregistered gun and a suppressor. Bates looked to see who was around as he screwed the suppressor on to the pistol.

He removed his FBI gun, shoved it into the glove compartment, and then slipped the unregistered weapon into the same shoulder holster. Bates got out of the car, trotted across and up the street, and waited just inside the alley, peeking around the corner.

When Caldwell and Grant emerged from the hotel, Bates pulled back, grasped the gun inside his jacket, and resumed sweating and leaking snot. His breathing quickened.

After just a few steps, Stephen felt a tightening in his head and ears, like pressure building up. He stopped short to carefully look around. *A red alert?*

While with the CIA, Grant called them "red alerts." He would get this kind of feeling just before something was about to happen, like being shot at or otherwise ambushed. He never questioned them, but instead was thankful. He hadn't had too many since becoming a pastor – in fact, only one. But here was another.

Paige looked at him, and actually asked, "A red alert?"

With the passage of so many years, Stephen forgot just how much Paige knew about him. He nodded, and they proceeded far more cautiously.

Paige was looking left into the street when Stephen spotted the tip of a suppressor sticking ever so slightly out from around the edge of the hotel building. He decided on action. Moving low and quick, Grant came around the corner at a level he hoped the gunman would not expect. Grant plunged into the man's legs just below the groin, and kept accelerating until the target fell back, hitting the concrete ground hard. Pain screamed from Grant's cracked rib.

But the gun was not dislodged, and Bates came down with the butt of it onto the back of Grant's head.

As Caldwell followed around the corner, she was pulling her Glock from its resting place in the small of her back, under her blue blazer.

Bates pointed his gun at her. But before he pulled the trigger, Grant rolled onto Bates' arm, with the bullet then moving past Paige's black hair and lodging harmlessly in a brick just above the second floor in a building across the street.

Grant continued to roll, pinning Bates' arm to the ground. Caldwell was on top of the FBI agent. She drove her spiked right heel down into Bates' wrist, which resulted in his yelling and dropping the gun.

Her Glock was pointed at his head.

Paige's voice dripped with venom. "Do you know how much I want to shoot you right now, Bates, you little fucking prick?"

The soon-to-be-former FBI agent gave up, laid flat on the ground, unmoving, looking at the sky. He whispered, "Please, Caldwell, shoot me, shoot me." Bates started to convulse in tears.

Grant had rolled off Bates, and was lying on the ground as well, trying to focus his vision after the rap to the head.

Paige's tone shifted dramatically. "You alright, Stephen?"

"Getting there, I think," he replied.

"You still get those red alerts, huh?"

"Guess so, thank God."

"And this time, I'll agree with your thanking the Lord."

As Grant listened to Bates' weeping, he knew the man was broken, and that he would soon tell all to the FBI.

Chapter 59

As a pastor, Stephen Grant occasionally found himself in situations with people who were suffering emotionally. He had seen anger, sadness, depression, feelings of betrayal and abandonment, or a seeming vacuum of loneliness.

But very little of it came close to what he had seen and heard while with the CIA. People broken beyond anything most could conceive. Either everything they ever knew was gone, or the threat of pain, suffering and death took them to a depth of fear previously unimagined. Some became shells of what they had been.

When he entered the seminary, Grant pushed those recollections into a part of his mind rarely visited, except for dreams, or more accurately, nightmares. If he didn't almost repress those memories, on purpose, Pastor Grant was at risk of losing his compassion for the still very real, and often formidable, problems faced by his parishioners.

But watching and listening to Ryan Bates through the one-way mirror grabbed those memories from the past, from that secluded place in his brain, and thrust them front and center in the present.

Bates had become the shell – physically, mentally and emotionally. He answered all of the questions presented by the FBI interrogator without any resistance.

Bates said, "I was approached about six months ago by an old college friend – well, an acquaintance – at the State Department. His name is Josh Ludwick. He asked if I was interested in making some easy money. A contact from the Belarus embassy liked getting analysis on political developments from Washington insiders. Ludwick had been doing it himself, but was leaving D.C. Nothing sensitive or specific to his job, not even non-public information. He was just repackaging political developments and analysis that were available on the Internet, or provided by various consulting firms, into his own weekly memos. We shared an interest in politics, and he knew that I could use the extra cash. He was talking monthly payments of $5,000."

Bates paused, as if considering his next words. "I knew it was a violation of my FBI responsibilities. But I saw no harm in repackaging public information, and knew that if I handled it all properly, $5,000 a month would go unnoticed by the Bureau. It would provide the boost I needed to make sure that Jackie would have what she needed."

The interrogator said, "Tell me about Jackie."

Grant understood that the interrogator knew who Jackie was, but they needed it all from Bates.

Bates repeated a question he'd asked earlier, "She is safe, right?"

"Yes," again was the reply.

Bates also asked for a second time, "Can I see her?"

"No," was the repeated answer. "Jackie?"

"Jackie Moss is my fiancée. We dated in high school. But after our senior year, there was an accident. I was driving when two men were fleeing the police after knocking over a convenience store. The driver lost control of their van, and crossed into oncoming traffic. I tried to avoid the vehicle, but the direction I turned only made it worse when the van hit us. The front passenger side of the car got pushed into Jackie. She was lucky to survive. But she was 18, and she'd never walk again. It was my fault, at least partially, but she tried to reassure me that it wasn't. That's the way she is. We supported each other through college, and she was my foundation during FBI training. I joined the FBI because of Jackie. But it took her a long time to agree to marry me. She'd periodically say that I'd be better off with someone else."

Bates paused, and took a deep breath. Then he repeated the importance of the extra money. "The money, It would allow us to get a house after getting married that would give Jackie everything she'd need to be comfortable, to be at home."

Apparently, there was a bit left in the shell, as the story of Jackie generated a few more tears from his eyes. He wiped them away.

The interrogator said, "And what about the foreign aid issue?"

Bates said, "I knew there was trouble when I got a rare call from someone at the Belarus embassy. I was told to meet the Belarus ambassador, Oleg Rumas. The meeting took place outside the city, in a remote house on a bunch of acres in Virginia, late on a Saturday night. Rumas brought along an aide, who looked more like muscle. Rumas told me that I would now have, as he put it, a much more important job to do. I was to be paid far more handsomely. I was warned that there would be no questions or protests on my part. Rumas also said that Jackie and I would be welcome to come to Belarus when all was done."

"And what did you say?"

"I immediately protested, that I would do no such thing. But then Rumas made clear what he had been doing for decades to people who crossed him, and specifically, what happened to their loved ones. He asked me, 'You would not want anything to happen to your lovely Jackie, correct my friend?' He also made clear that there would be no place she would be able to hide."

Bates paused. "I believed him. I didn't doubt that threat in any way, and I could not let Jackie be hurt any more. So, I went along."

The interrogator asked, "And what exactly were you supposed to go along with?"

Bates replied, "I was told that I might be involved with an investigation or two, and that my sole objective was to point everything at Lydia Garcia and her Mexican drug gang."

"Anything else?"

"I was given an external hard drive, and simply told to keep it safe, at that point in time."

The interrogator ramped up the intensity in his voice when asking, "Were you told that Senator Farrell, his aide and the Fosters were targets for murder?"

A touch of indignation found its way into Bates' response, "Absolutely not." But then his body and voice sagged. "It was when I arrived on the scene and saw Senator Farrell's head in the bag, that's when I realized how bad this was, and how bad it was going to get."

"Yet, you did nothing. In fact, you just let things go on, and you continued to follow your orders from a foreign government in the face of a U.S. senator being murdered. Oh, wait, I'm sorry, in the face of Senator Farrell and Larry Payton being murdered. Isn't that right, Bates?"

Bates stared blankly at his questioner. "Yes, that's what I did," he said in a barely audible voice.

"What? Please speak up."

Bates continued his stare, and repeated a bit louder, "That's what I did."

"Then, Graham Foster, a pastor, and his spouse, Margo Foster, were murdered. Did you know they were targeted, Bates?"

"No, I didn't."

"But they perished, in part, due to your inaction, or more accurately, due to your traitorous actions. That's right, isn't it?"

"Yes."

"And after they were murdered, still you did nothing?"

Bates confirmed, "I did nothing."

"But today, you finally took action, didn't you? You heard that Paige Caldwell and Stephen Grant, through a listening device you planted on Pastor Grant, were on to you. They had put together the pieces. So, you panicked, waited in hiding, and then tried to murder these two people, didn't you?"

Bates was now staring at the metal tabletop resting between himself and his interrogator.

The FBI special agent slammed his hand on the table and yelled, "Didn't you?"

Bates slowly looked up and confirmed, "Yes, I tried to kill them."

The interrogator closed the file in front of him. He said, "And what would Jackie think about all of these things you've done?"

Ryan Bates winced. "She would be ashamed of me, so very deeply ashamed and disappointed."

"And she would be right."

Bates agreed. "Yes, she would be right."

"Do you think when she finds out what you've done that you will have hurt her far more than even Oleg Rumas could have hurt her in the end?"

Bates closed his eyes, and dropped his head.

Chapter 60

Paige was standing next to Stephen watching the entire interrogation of Bates, along with FBI Assistant Director Mort Steinberg and two others from the FBI.

When the interrogator left Bates alone, Paige said, "That guy needs to be put on suicide watch."

Steinberg stood with his arms folded and brow furrowed. It didn't look like his hairstyle, with a part down the middle and covering half of his ears, had changed since the late 1970s. The thick frames of his eyeglasses seemed like they came from the same era. The only differences now were gray streaks in the dark hair, and a much stronger prescription.

Unlike his dated style, Steinberg was on the cutting edge of law enforcement strategy, and his will was unbending in its pursuit of justice. He had been the New York assistant district attorney that none of the bad guys wanted to face, and the same went for his reputation with the FBI over the past 17 years.

Steinberg answered Paige's observation at first with a grunt. "Yeah, you're right. He's a mess. And he should be a fucking mess. I hope he doesn't go too far off the deep end. We're probably still going to need something from him."

Grant heard Steinberg in the background, but was focused on watching Bates, who now had his face hidden inside folded arms on the table. Bates didn't move.

Steinberg turned to Stephen. "By the way Grant, Noack has filled me in on you a bit. I understand that you served well in both the SEALs and the CIA, not to mention a couple of times now as a pastor." Steinberg smiled and shook his head.

Grant said, "Thanks. How is Agent Noack, in light of Bates being a key member of his team?"

Steinberg's small smile disappeared. "Noack and the rest of that team are being questioned and looked at just to make sure no one was working with Bates. I know Rich, and even in the midst of this mess, the one thing I know is that Rich Noack can be counted on. He'll be fine."

Grant continued, "Yes, but how is he handling what Bates has done? I got the impression that Noack was something of a mentor to Bates."

Steinberg said, "You're right, Noack was a mentor to Bates. I would imagine that he's none too pleased. I know I'd be pissed off."

Okay, I got the message. If you're concerned about Noack's psyche, then talk to Noack yourself after this is over. Grant turned and looked at the still unmoving Bates.

Paige asked Steinberg, "What did you mean that you might still need Bates?"

Steinberg started to answer, "Well, we still ..."

But Grant interrupted, "Assistant Director Steinberg, I'd like to speak with Ryan Bates, alone, if I might?"

Paige looked surprised. "Why, Stephen? What do you think you can get out of him?"

Stephen looked at Paige, and replied, "This has nothing to do with getting something out of him, Paige." He turned to Steinberg. "I'd like to talk to him, not as former CIA, but as a pastor. Ryan Bates needs to hear something very different right now."

Paige said, "Are you kidding me? This guy just tried to kill the two of us, and you want to go in there and, what, forgive him and tell him Jesus loves him?"

"Yes, that's exactly what I want to do."

Paige just stared at him with an incredulous look on her face. Her mouth was open, but nothing came out.

Grant turned to Steinberg. "Well, Assistant Director Steinberg?"

Steinberg stared Grant in the eyes for probably a half-minute, once again with brow furrowed and his arms folded, further rumpling his blue tie and white shirt. Then he grabbed Bates' file off the table, and took a quick look inside. Steinberg finally said, "Alright, Grant. Go ahead in. I'll make sure this room is clear, and the cameras and mikes will be off in there."

"Thank you, sir." Grant knew why Steinberg allowed him to go in and talk. If the FBI needed Bates to get more information, Bates was in no shape to do so. Grant thought that Steinberg was gambling to see if Grant could bring part of Bates back by offering some hope.

Steinberg, Grant and Caldwell left the observation room. Steinberg ordered the cameras and microphones off, and the observation room off limits. Before Stephen turned to go into the interrogation room, he looked at Paige. She stood with hands on her waist, head tilted slightly, and wearing a disapproving smirk.

Grant turned the knob and entered the room with Bates. He closed the door.

Paige asked Steinberg, "Why did you let him in there?"

Steinberg replied, "I checked his file. Bates is a Christian – according to his file, a Roman Catholic – so why not let the pastor go in and maybe bring him back from the brink? If Grant succeeds, we might be able to use Bates. You know, seeking redemption or forgiveness or whatever. Actually, I'd like to see a little good old Catholic penance in this case. And based on what Noack told me,

Grant's not going to screw anything up. So, why not roll the dice? There's no downside."

"Nice play, Assistant Director Steinberg," nodded Paige.

He said, "I know."

Bates did not pick his head up from the table even with the noise of someone entering the room.

Stephen said, "Ryan."

Bates looked up at Grant standing inside the door. "Oh, God. What are you doing in here?" He put the palms of his hands over his eyes, and rubbed hard. He then grabbed his hair, rested his elbows on the table, and looked down. "You're here to tell me how angry and disappointed you are, not to mention what you did to people like me, a traitor and an accomplice to murder, when you were with the CIA."

"No, Ryan, I'm not here to talk about any of that. I'm not ex-CIA right now. I want to talk to you as a pastor."

Bates spread his arms out on the table, palms turned up. He said, "Oh, even better. So, you're here to tell me about my soul entering eternal damnation. I'm going to hell, Pastor Grant. We both know that, and there's not a damn thing you can do about it. I'd prefer that you were Stephen Grant, CIA, and you could put me down with one shot, right here." He pointed to the middle of his forehead.

Grant sat down across from Bates. "Do you really believe that, Ryan?"

"What the hell else am I supposed to believe?"

Stephen said, "'And if he has committed sins, he will be forgiven. Therefore, confess your sins to one another and pray for one another, that you may be healed.' That's from James."

Ryan looked at Grant. "I just tried to kill you, Grant. Are you going to forgive me? I don't think so."

"I'm not going to bullshit you, Ryan. After what you pulled, I'm not in a forgiving mood. Quite frankly, there's a part of me that would like to kick your teeth out right now, especially because you tried to kill my friend." *Jesus, help me, please.* "But that's the same sinful nature that led to you doing what you did. So, yes, Ryan, not through anything in me, but with the help of God, I forgive you. And more importantly, God is willing to forgive you, as James tells us."

"Not this, Pastor Grant, God will not forgive this."

"Ryan, take a moment and think about what God has forgiven. How about St. Paul? When known as Saul, he actively persecuted Christians. He entered houses and had people dragged off to prison. And he gave thumbs up on the execution of Christians, like Stephen. But Jesus took this great persecutor, and turned him into a great Apostle to the Gentiles. His job was to open their eyes, to turn away from the darkness and to the light, and receive forgiveness of sins."

Bates was now silent, just sitting, unmoving, looking at his hands open on the table in front of him. Grant could not tell if anything was getting through.

They sat in silence for a few more minutes. Stephen said, "Do you want to pray, Ryan?"

Bates remained silent, but he did close his eyes.

Finally, Stephen declared, "Well, I'm going to say a brief prayer." He paraphrased from Martin Luther's Evening Prayer. "My heavenly Father, through Jesus Christ, Your dear Son, I pray that You would forgive all our sins. Lord, into Your hands we commend ourselves, our bodies and our souls, and all things."

They sat in silence a while longer. Grant looking for anything from Bates, while Bates kept his eyes closed.

Stephen said, "Ryan, I hope we can talk some more. I'm not whitewashing what you did, and the consequences. You're going to have to pay a dear price, no doubt. To some extent, I suppose you've already started that process. All I am saying is that if you truly repent and ask forgiveness – and remember you can't fool the Lord – then in God's eyes, your sins will be forgiven and washed away. That's an amazing miracle. It is hope."

Stephen got up from the table. After waiting briefly, and hearing nothing from Ryan, Stephen turned to go. He was about to touch the doorknob, when Ryan said, "Don't you get it? I don't deserve it."

"None of us do, Ryan, none of us."

Chapter 61

After the few necessary introductions were made, Steinberg leaned back in his chair behind a cluttered desk. In fact, as he looked around, Grant was amazed at how much clutter there was everywhere.

Steinberg's office had no style to speak of, and there was nothing in it that offered a glimpse into the FBI Assistant Director's outside life. Instead, there were just large piles of precariously stacked papers, files and books everywhere – on the floor, on his desk, and on the conference table.

Four people – Grant, Caldwell, Trent Nguyen, and Maxine Granger – wound their way to chairs positioned in front of Steinberg's desk.

Maxine Granger was a ten-year FBI veteran. She was a striking six feet, two inches tall, with her dark skin just a shade lighter than her hair, which was pulled back tightly in a bun. Her expertise was in all kinds of surveillance.

Steinberg said, "I don't know what you said to him Grant, but Bates is willing to help us find out how high up this Belarusian thing goes. He seems a bit more stable, or at least, as stable as any guy could be facing life in prison. But there looks like real remorse there. What did you give him, the 'God forgives' spiel or some fire and brimstone?"

Grant just looked at Steinberg.

Steinberg said, "Okay, okay, I get it. In confidence." The last two words he emphasized by making quote marks in the air. "Anyway, here's why I brought you four into my office before you head out of here after a wild day, to say the least. We need to act quickly. Rumas should have no reason to suspect that we have Bates and his information. So, I want to have Bates contact Rumas in the morning to try to set up a meet. And if we can make it happen, Max, you and your team will make sure we get all the information, but from what Bates said, it won't be easy."

Granger replied, "We'll figure it out, sir."

"Good." Steinberg looked back at Grant. "Pastor Grant, we need your help."

Grant said, "At what?"

"I need you to go to church tomorrow morning at New Jerusalem, and take Trent here with you. After the church service is over, and people have wandered off, you're going to introduce Pastor Schroeder to Mr. Nguyen. And perhaps with your assistance, and on church grounds, maybe you two can get Pastor Schroeder to feel kind of guilty about his apparent partnership with Oleg Rumas, get a confession and find out what else the guy knows."

Grant did not respond immediately. *Good idea or bad idea, Grant? Okay, it's not interfering with the church service, and Schroeder's obviously fallen off the beam.*

Steinberg asked, "Is that a problem, Pastor Grant, formerly of the CIA and Navy SEALs?"

Grant said, "That'll be fine. No problem."

"Good, thanks." Steinberg turned to Caldwell. "As for you, Agent Caldwell, I've brought you in on this meeting due to everything that's happened today. Your actions were exemplary. Also, I spoke to your superior over at NCS, and he apparently wants to be briefed, immediately."

"Right, thanks," she replied.

Stephen detected concern in Paige's voice.

Steinberg concluded, "Who knows, if all goes well, by this time tomorrow night, we might have all of the answers we need. Thanks for your work today people, and let's make it happen tomorrow."

Chapter 62

Stephen and Paige found themselves outside the home of the FBI, once again.

Paige was distracted. "Stephen, I'll talk to you soon. I've got to call Tank. You're alright grabbing a cab, right?"

Edward "Tank" Hoard worked with both Stephen and Paige years ago, and now Paige was reporting to him at the CIA's National Clandestine Service.

Stephen tried to engage her. "Who would have thought when we first met him so many years ago, that Tank Hoard, who had a pretty muscular brain to go with his Schwarzenegger-like body, would wind up as your boss?"

Grant chuckled. Paige did not.

She said, "I know what you're trying to do. But don't bother. I'm going to call Tank, confess my little trysts with Schmidt, tell him our suspicions about Gerhardt's involvement in all of this, and then I'm going to be, at best, suspended, or at worst, be out of the only job, the only life, I've ever known."

Her voice cracked ever so slightly when saying "the only life." Other than Charlie Driessen, probably no one else would have noticed. This was as vulnerable as Paige Caldwell got. Even under the most intense situations working together, Grant could only remember seeing such a tiny chink in Paige's armor perhaps three times, at most.

Grant knew there was nothing else he could say, for now. But he did add, "I'll say a prayer for you, Paige."

"Thanks, I could use it." And she disappeared into the early morning darkness.

Wow, Paige thanking me for a prayer. That's not good. Well, you know what I mean, Lord. Please help Paige, dear Lord. She's unconventional, as you and I well know, but she tries to do what's right, loves this country unwaveringly, and needs to be doing this kind of work. And I continue to hope that her heart is open to the Holy Spirit.

Stephen spotted a taxi, and jumped in the backseat.

When Paige closed the door of her Mustang, she flipped open her encrypted phone, pulled up Tank Hoard, and after hesitating, hit the dial button.

"Paige, you okay?"

"Yes, thanks." She gave a rundown on what happened with Bates, and the plan for tomorrow.

Tank Hoard replied, "Okay, thanks for the update. Anything else?"

"Well, yes, and you're not going to like it."

"I usually don't, Paige, but go ahead."

Paige Caldwell was rarely nervous, or at least, she rarely ever showed that she was nervous. In this case, though, she spoke much faster than usual, sounding almost like a high school girl confessing to her father that she'd gotten pregnant.

Ironically, Hoard's response was not all that different from the father receiving such news. "What the fuck were you thinking? That's right, you weren't thinking. You were doing the Paige Caldwell 'I don't give a rat's ass' thing, again. Well, the rat has finally bitten you in the ass, Paige."

"I'm not sure the rat's ass and biting me in the ass really work together."

Hoard screamed, "For once in your life, shut the hell up! The cute wise ass act is not going to help your case."

Paige breathed in slowly and unsteadily. "Sorry, Tank, really."

"Sorry, shit. Sorry isn't going to cut it this time, Paige."

She asked in the least confident tone Paige Caldwell might have ever used during her adult life, "What's going to happen?"

Tank Hoard apparently picked up on the unusual concept of Paige Caldwell being shaken.

"To be honest, Paige, I have no idea. As of now, you're suspended. Have a drink and go to bed. I'll get back to you when my head clears on this, and after I get through trying to justify to those above both of us why we still need Paige Caldwell at the CIA."

Hoard hung up.

Paige sat in her car on a dark street in Washington, D.C., staring at her phone. She clicked on another number, and the screen read "Stephen Grant." But she didn't hit the dial button.

The screen eventually went as dark as everything around her. The phone fell out of her hand and tumbled onto the floor as her body started to shake. Paige Caldwell struggled to take in air as she wept uncontrollably.

Chapter 63

Stephen was in the elevator at his hotel ten minutes after getting in the cab, and he opened the door to his room less than a minute later.

Though it was in the earliest hours of the morning, Jennifer was still awake, as she promised during a short update phone call Stephen had given her a few hours earlier. She sprang from the bed, and lunged into him. They squeezed each other tightly, and then kissed.

Stephen's rib and arm screamed in pain, but he did not care.

Jennifer stepped back, and looked at her husband. "I haven't decided if you'll be in trouble or not tomorrow with all of this stress you're dishing out to your newlywed wife, or if I'll still be in the current mode I'm in."

"And what mode would that be?"

"That I'm incredibly thankful you're safe and here, and all I want is for you to come to bed so we can hold each other."

"Believe me, after these past eight or nine hours, there's nothing else I want to do. But can you tolerate about five more minutes, while I call Sean McEnany?"

"Sure, but why are you calling him?"

"Sean has helped me before, getting information that I was unable to get elsewhere, and I'm hoping he can help with the current situation."

When Jennifer saw Stephen reach for the encrypted phone Paige had given him, she said, "My God, Stephen, I'm sorry, how is Paige?"

"She was fine during our engagement with Bates. But when I left her, she was shaken."

"Shaken? That does not sound like Paige."

"It certainly doesn't, but she might lose the CIA." Stephen quickly told Jennifer about Paige's involvement with Schmidt, and his likely role in these Belarusian events.

"Stephen, that's terrible. Does she have any chance to stay with the agency?"

"To be as objective as I can, Jen, the odds appear pretty slim." He switched gears, and began dialing McEnany. "I'm going to get Sean, now."

"Don't you think he's going to be annoyed with a call at this time of the morning."

"Funny thing with Sean, I think he's used to it."

The call was answered on the first ring, and then came McEnany's low, raspy voice, "Yes."

"Sean, it's Pastor Grant. Sorry about calling at this crazy hour."

"Pastor, not a problem. And since you're not calling on your usual phone and I believe you're still in D.C., I assume that this is not a St. Mary's evangelism committee emergency."

"No, it's not. I could use your help on a very non-church matter."

"Shoot."

"It has to do with Belarus."

"Ah, I knew Jennifer was testifying on the foreign aid issue, but I'm guessing you've got something else in mind."

This guy is plugged into everything, it seems.

"Yes, I wanted to see if you could get me any information on the links between Anatoliy Snopkov..."

"Well, we're starting at the top, with the president."

"Yes. And Oleg Rumas, their ambassador, and another person, Gerhardt Schmidt. Schmidt is..."

"I know Schmidt, and you already know some of the Snopkov-Rumas history?"

"Right, but there's more with those two than seems to be common knowledge. At least, that's what I think, but I'm working off a nearly two-decades old warning."

"Okay, I'll see if I can bring you more up to date. Obviously, you're not coming back home tomorrow, and I should have something, hopefully, by late afternoon or early evening?"

"That would be great."

"Shall I call you on this line? I assume it's encrypted."

"Yes, it is." Stephen gave him the number. "Sean, thanks, I appreciate the help."

"Get some sleep, Pastor. After all, tomorrow is Sunday." McEnany ended the call.

While he quickly got undressed for bed, Stephen said, "I really haven't figured out Sean McEnany. He's far more than a corporate and government security consultant. He's deeper in the shadows than many I've known over the years."

He slipped into bed, and held his wife.

Jennifer said, "Pastor Grant, I have a confession to make."

"That sounds very official."

"I don't know how official it is, but I feel guilty."

"About what?"

"About Paige, I really was concerned about her safety, and now I'm worried about what she'll do if forced out of the CIA."

"And for this caring, you feel guilty?"

"No. But I also had this feeling of being glad I was not her. I thought about the fact that if life had been just slightly different for each of us, you could be in this bed tonight with her. And I was so glad that was not the case, that I had you all to myself. And I hate to say it, but I had this fleeting feeling of satisfaction that we were together, and she was alone."

Stephen said, "Jen, I cannot tell you how often I think about how fortunate I am that God brought you into my life. I thank him everyday. But we all slip. I falter sometimes in thinking that I am, or we together, are somehow better than others. But if God can forgive the worst of sins, I think He will forgive these emotions that spring from what we have together."

Jennifer squeezed Stephen a bit more, kissed him, and they drifted off to sleep.

Chapter 64

Two FBI agents were listening, with the conversation being recorded.

"What can I do for you, Agent Bates, on this Sunday morning?" asked Oleg Rumas.

Bates' voice was steady. "There are some things bubbling up around the FBI about you and President Snopkov, and I cannot control it."

"But you are getting paid to do just that."

"It's outside my abilities."

"Does it have anything to do with Senator Farrell, the others and the Mexicans?"

"No, at least not at this point. From what I can tell, it's older material focused on the two of you. I pulled down some files and information – all I could. I think you will find it useful."

There was silence on the line. Assistant Director Steinberg stood near Bates listening.

Rumas finally said, "I will get back to you very shortly."

The call ended. Steinberg looked around the room and told everyone, "Now, we wait."

* * *

"Yes, Oleg," said President Snopkov after he picked up the telephone.

"Bates has just contacted me. He says the FBI is poking around our past, and he has information to pass on. He wants to meet. What would you like to do?"

Snopkov grumbled some traditional Belarusian curses. "The Americans have no reason to care about what we did decades ago, Oleg. At best, they suspect our involvement in the Farrell and other murders. This is an attempt to trap us."

"Why do you think this?"

"Think, Oleg, it's the only thing that makes sense. They must have Bates, and he will be under surveillance if you meet. The effort to get the American money is over."

Rumas said, "If that is the case, I need to come home."

"Yes, you do. But first, you must find out how much they know. The meet with Bates has to happen. But you need to neutralize or disengage from the FBI surveillance team, extract everything from Bates, and then proceed with our contingency plan for you to come home. If all goes smoothly, you will be back here in a few days, my friend."

Rumas said, "I don't like this. It's very risky."

Snopkov's deep voice got sterner. "You are a trained operative, with decades of experience. Get this done, Oleg."

"Of course, Mr. President."

"Good, my friend. I look forward to seeing you soon."

After they hung up, Rumas called Bates. "We will meet tonight at eight. The same location as last time."

Bates replied, "Yes, good. Thank you, Mr. Ambassador."

Chapter 65

After the service, in the lobby of the New Jerusalem Worship and Fulfillment Center, Stephen led his trio over to Pastor Bill Johnson.

Stephen and Jennifer shook hands with Johnson, and then Stephen said, "This is Trent Nguyen."

Johnson offered Nguyen a broad smile, a vigorous handshake, and a hearty, "Welcome to New Jerusalem."

Stephen asked, "How is everyone holding up, Bill?"

"They are, well, we all are, still in shock, I think. It's going to take time to heal, and then to see where New Jerusalem is headed without Graham and Margo. In so many ways, New Jerusalem was the Fosters."

Grant glanced over Johnson's shoulder at a new kiosk in the New Jerusalem lobby selling Graham's book *Let God Maximize Your Returns*, with Graham's smiling face on the cover. *I miss the old Graham. I miss what was the new smiling Graham. But he should have known that personality-driven and centered churches are never a good idea.*

Stephen said to Pastor Johnson, "Where's Pastor Schroeder? I was surprised that he was not involved in the service with you."

Johnson lowered his voice, "It's strange. He's re-engaged here at New Jerusalem, but in a different way. He laid out an agenda going forward, at least for a while. I'd be doing the services, youth events and so on, while he would handle all of the administrative work of the church, along with working with the Entrepreneurship & Values people. It looks like he stepped in to Graham's spot there already."

"So, is he around?"

"Yes, just head back to the administrative offices. I saw him in his office earlier."

Stephen replied, "Thanks, Bill. Listen, as time passes and you're trying to figure out the next step for New Jerusalem, please let me know how I can help."

"Okay."

As they shook hands, Stephen pulled Johnson closer, "No, I mean this very seriously. In the coming weeks and months, you're going to need all the help you can get, and you're going to get all kinds of advice, not all of it good or constructive. If you want a sounding board or anything else, just let me know."

Johnson lost his smile in what seemed like a knowing moment. "I appreciate that, Stephen, thank you."

Pastor Johnson then took Stephen by surprise with another of his bear-like hugs.

After Johnson went off to talk with various congregants, Stephen said to Jennifer, "Why don't you head back to the hotel, and I'll catch up in a bit."

Jennifer eyed her husband for a split second, and then said, "Works for me." They kissed quickly, and she whispered, "Be safe."

Jennifer turned to Trent Nguyen. "Trent, it was a pleasure to meet you. Take care."

"You as well, Jennifer."

As Jennifer went to exit the front doors of the Worship Center, Stephen and Trent went out a side door. They walked around much of the building, re-entering via the administrative office entrance.

A young lady at the welcome desk smiled a bit half-heartedly, and said, "Pastor Grant, hello. How are you?"

"I'm well, thanks. How about you, Denise?"

"Basically, trying to hang in there, with the Lord's help."

"That's all we can do. Is Pastor Schroeder around?"

"Yes, he's in his office. You can head back there."

"Thanks."

Stephen led Trent past the various empty desks and offices, as most staff members were still over in the auditorium or lobby with church attendees. They came to Schroeder's office. Through two large windows, they could see Leonard Schroeder looking down at papers on his desk. The door was closed.

Stephen knocked, but did not wait for a response. Opening the door, he was followed into Schroeder's office by Nguyen.

Schroeder was taken aback. "Ah, hello, Pastor Grant."

Grant nodded. "Pastor Schroeder. By the way, this is Trent Nguyen."

"Yes, well, what can I do for you? I'm kind of busy right now with ..."

Nguyen spotted the venetian blinds at the top of the two windows. He lowered each so that no one could see into the office.

Schroeder stood up and stuttered, "Hey, hey, what are you doing? Coming in here like this, what's the meaning?"

Nguyen looked at Grant, and asked, "May I?"

"Of course," replied Grant, who sat down in one of the chairs on the side of Schroeder's desk.

Nguyen looked at Schroeder closely. "Pastor Schroeder, I'm with the FBI." He pulled out and flashed his credentials at Schroeder, who immediately staggered back into his chair.

"Um, what can I, I ... do for you?"

Nguyen sat down across from Schroeder, and said, "I think you know how you can help us, Pastor Schroeder. It looks to us that you have been working with the people who murdered Pastor and Mrs. Foster. Is that right?"

Schroeder merely uttered, "Um, uh, well ...oh, God."

Grant just watched from the side. *This is going to be very easy.*

Nguyen said, "I'm about to arrest you and read you your rights. Just so you know, charges like being an accomplice to murder and treason come with heavy punishments. You'll be lucky to get life in prison. Of course, any information you might provide on who you worked with would help reduce your sentence."

Grant could see that the part about being lucky just to get life in prison shattered what little defense Schroeder might have had. He confessed all, from being approached by Oleg Rumas, to knowing that the Fosters would be murdered, to him then moving up and effectively controlling the Entrepreneurship & Values group in order to guide the money to where Rumas told him to funnel it.

Nguyen had a small recorder on and jotted down notes as well. He asked, "Did Rumas ever mention President Anatoliy Snopkov to you?"

Schroeder thought a moment. "No. Never. Why?"

Nguyen smiled a bit. "'Why?' Pastor Schroeder, that's none of your damn business."

Nguyen got up and walked around the desk. He looked down at Schroeder. Then he grabbed Schroeder by the arm, pulled him out of the chair, turned him around, and slapped handcuffs on him. While Nguyen was reading Schroeder his rights, Grant took a peek between the blinds. About a half-dozen people were now milling about the office.

Nguyen pulled out a small two-way radio, and said, "I've got Schroeder in custody. Jackson, bring the car up close in the back."

A voice came back, "Roger, already waiting."

"Good. Beckett and Strinski get in here and start going through his office, and Henderson and Rivers over to his townhouse."

More affirmatives returned to Nguyen.

Stephen said to Trent, "More staff members are out there now. If you don't mind, I'm going to stay behind and talk with them. The Fosters were murdered, and now they're going to see one of their other pastors being taken away in cuffs. They're going to need ... something. Though I'm not completely sure what at this point. But I've got to stay."

"That makes sense, Pastor Grant. Let us know if you need anything."

Grant opened the door, and out came Schroeder with his hands behind his back, head down, being pushed along by Nguyen. A wave of shock swept across the room, generating gasps and still more tears in a place that should have been tapped dry of such emotion.

Lord, help me answer questions without fully answering questions.

Chapter 66

While the FBI was hauling Leonard Schroeder off, Gerhardt Schmidt sipped cold coffee, and took another look through his binoculars.

His tan Jeep Patriot was positioned to look down the long street to the backdoor and garage of the brick and white-shingled townhouse that Vadim Slizhevskiy rented in Fairfax, Virginia.

The garage door began to slowly rise. A silver Lexus LX SUV with diplomatic plates rolled up. There was one passenger in addition to the driver. Once parked in the garage, Vadim Slizhevskiy, trade minister for Belarus, got out the passenger side, while his aide, Aleksandr Kachan, exited the other side.

Slizhevskiy pressed a button on the garage wall, and the door began its slow descent. He said to his aide, "Thank you for picking me up, Alek. Have lunch and then you can get back to that American girl who has grabbed too much of your attention."

After the garage door touched down, Schmidt said, "Convenient two-for-one sale, as American shoppers might say."

He pulled down the street, did a quick U-turn and backed the SUV up to Slizhevskiy's garage. Schmidt checked to see that his weapon – a German HK45 with a suppressor – was set.

As he got out, Schmidt held the gun down and close to his right leg, partially hiding it. He had checked earlier, and the residents fortunately chose not to install any kind of security cameras.

Schmidt looked into a laundry room, and tested the backdoor. It was locked. He stepped back and aimed the force of his kick on the dead bolt. The lock held, but the door flew open along with a chunk of the doorframe.

With the noise, Schmidt moved quickly, scanning as he ascended the stairs.

He heard Slizhevskiy shout to his aide, "What the hell was that?"

Kachan responded, "I don't know, Minister, I'm checking."

Kachan turned a narrow hallway, and stopped when seeing Schmidt emerge from the staircase. As if not believing his own eyes, Kachan's only move was to push up the thick glasses resting halfway down his nose.

Schmidt wasted no time. He fired off three rounds into Kachan's chest.

Slizhevskiy called out again, "What's going on, Alek?"

"He can't get his fat ass off the toilet," Schmidt whispered to himself with a chuckle.

He turned a corner, moving toward Slizhevskiy's voice. Schmidt spotted the light coming from under the door at the end of the short hallway.

Schmidt exerted less force kicking in that door.

Slizhevskiy, in fact, was sitting on the toilet bowl.

With the gun pointed at him, all the trade minister from Belarus could manage was, "Oh, shit."

Schmidt shrugged. "Apparently." He deposited a bullet into Slizhevskiy's skull, and after the minister toppled off the bowl, two more in his back.

Schmidt managed to get the back door to stay in place, and vanished within two minutes.

Chapter 67

After finishing a small, room service dinner, exhaustion caught up to Stephen Grant.

His day spent at New Jerusalem trying to help Pastor Johnson and his staff wrestle with Schroeder being taken away by the FBI, on top of everything else they'd been through, was long and hard. It felt even longer. Several hours of questions, prayers, Scripture reading, tears and doubts drained him.

Jennifer added, "Oh yes, and that came on top of a week of murder, torture, and being attacked by someone that you had worked with before. I can't understand your exhaustion, my dear."

"You're funny."

"No, I'm right."

Jennifer told him to lay down, while she put the tray of used plates and glasses outside the hotel room door.

"I'd love to, but if I went horizontal, it would be all over. I have to stay awake for Sean's call." Grant checked the clock, which told him it was 7:20 PM. "He's actually a bit late."

On cue, Stephen's phone rang.

Jennifer commented, "Speak of the devil, or in this case, the shadow."

Grant went for his phone. "Is that what we're going to call Sean now: The Shadow?"

Jennifer answered, "Yeah, I think it fits."

He flipped open the phone and answered, "Hello."

"Sorry I'm a bit late in getting back, Pastor. But I had to wait on one confirmation."

"No problem. What do you have, Sean?"

"Rumas and Snopkov were nasty dudes in their Soviet days. They were masters of keeping the average person, or peasant, in line in Belarus, the Ukraine, Poland and East Germany. They helped run a network of spies and snitches from city to city, village to village. And they had a constant inflow of information on those questioning the state and the party, and would regularly make examples of a select few getting a bit too bold in their questions. Between the two of them, they may have had as many as a thousand people killed."

"Dear God. How did we not know this?"

"Even you might be surprised at how much of the terror inflicted by the Soviets went unpunished. After the Wall came down, few had any interest or incentive to track down animals like these two. The more we dig, the more we probably don't want to know about some leaders in Eastern Europe."

"What about Gerhardt Schmidt? Any link between him and either Snopkov or Rumas?"

"Link? Get this, Snopkov and Schmidt are half brothers."

"What?"

"You heard that right. It turns out that they had different mothers, but dear old dad was a Russian general. Apparently, this General Sergey Semigin was screwing women in assorted beds behind the Iron Curtain. As far as we could tell, in addition to six legitimate children, he had at least seven more illegitimate kids."

Who are "we," Sean?

McEnany continued, "And since no one trusted each other in those grand days of the Evil Empire, members of the East German Stasi were keeping eyes on each other. We've found a handful of rather pedestrian files in which it's noted that Snopkov and Schmidt were meeting. Other files confirmed some work that Snopkov and Schmidt had done in rooting out enemies of the state."

"Any more recent contact?"

"The best we can do is put Schmidt in Minsk at least a couple of times a year over the past half decade."

"That's good enough. I owe you big time, Sean."

"Glad to help. By the way, when you get back, we need to sit down and talk about some evangelism committee stuff."

They hung up, and Grant realized that other than Jennifer, Sean McEnany was the only other person that he could speak with about both his former CIA life and his current church life.

Jennifer asked, "The Shadow had what you needed?"

Stephen smirked. "Yes, the Shadow had good information." He sat staring at Jennifer for several seconds.

She said, "Trying to figure out who to call?"

"Right."

He opened the phone, and hit a key.

"You're calling Paige first, aren't you?"

"You know me too well."

After two rings, Paige answered, "Stephen?"

"Yes. I've got information on Snopkov and your friend, Schmidt. Where are you? Can we meet?"

"No time for that. Give me what you have now."

Stephen recognized the urgency in Paige's voice. He gave her the full story in quick fashion.

Paige said, "Shit."

"What is it? Where are you? And what happened with Tank? Are you suspended or what?"

"No time. You need to call this in to Steinberg. Got to go."

Chapter 68

Bates approached the front gate of the secluded 15-acre spread where Oleg Rumas was waiting.

Maxine Granger was talking in Bates' ear. "Take it easy, Bates. You've got the small transmitter on the watch. As we said, I doubt if that's going to reach us once you get in the house. I'm betting these guys have some kind of dampening field. But the digital recording device inside the St. Michael medal hanging around your neck will record everything. Get him talking about Snopkov, and whoever else he's working with."

Following the instructions of Mort Steinberg, she then added, "Remember, this is your chance at redemption."

Bates said nothing in response.

Maxine flipped off the microphone so Bates could not hear. She complained to the tech aide next to her in the truck. "I don't like this. He's not responding, and he'll be naked out there without us being able to see. Even the snipers and assault teams we have ready will not be able to see what's going on inside."

Bates drove up to three guards at the gate, and rolled down the window. "I believe I'm expected."

"Yes, get out of the car." The guard spoke with a strong East European accent. Bates was patted down. His pockets were emptied, jacket and tie removed, along with his shoes and belt, and the watch was taken. Bates told the guard, "Your boss is going to want that thumb drive." The guard looked at the small, black item, and stuck it in his vest pocket. Everything else got tossed into Bates' car, while Bates was ushered into the passenger seat of a waiting Range Rover. In addition to the driver, the well-armed guard with the thumb drive sat in the backseat with an Uzi SMG at the ready.

All of this security went far beyond what Bates had experienced during his previous visit. The SUV pulled up to the early-twentieth-century, wood-and-stone hunting lodge, and Bates was taken inside.

On the other side of the estate, Gerhardt Schmidt had parked his Jeep in a small clearing. He checked his HK45, slipped it into his waist holster, and added a smaller PK2000 SK to his left leg.

Schmidt moved about two hundred yards into the woods, and found the spot that he had marked when Belarus bought the estate. After all, Snopkov had him design all of the security for the facility. He pushed aside two boulders, and there it was – a smugglers tunnel built during Prohibition. It led right into a storage space in the basement of the lodge. Schmidt only told his half-brother about the tunnel, and he made sure that no one was going to discover the underground pathway on either end.

He climbed in and began feeling his way along the dark four hundred yards.

But just as Bates, the FBI and Rumas did not know that Schmidt was moving in on the meeting, Schmidt missed his own tail.

In a dark gray Honda Pilot, Paige Caldwell had picked up Schmidt when he stopped at his D.C. condo in the mid-afternoon. He didn't stay long, in and out in less than 10 minutes, and she had stayed with him, discreetly, ever since.

When she saw him disappear into the woods, Paige grabbed her Glock, and a couple of extra clips. She got out, and moved ever so slowly and quietly in the direction that Schmidt had gone.

She spotted the rocks that had been moved, looked around for any other movement, and spied inside the entrance. Paige listened, heard nothing, and moved inside.

Just two rooms away from the hidden tunnel entrance, Oleg Rumas dismissed two of his men, leaving just himself, Bates and a heavily armed guard in a sound proof room that cut off any remaining chances of communications being received or sent out to the rest of the world.

Rumas and Bates sat across from each other in wood armchairs with comfortable blue cushions.

"So, Agent Bates, what is it that you wish to tell me?"

"Well, first, your guard has the files I spoke of."

Rumas looked over his shoulder, and the guard handed over the thumb drive. The Ambassador dropped it in the inside pocket of the blue blazer he was sporting.

"What will those files tell me, Agent Bates?"

"Based on my quick look, and what I heard in meetings yesterday, one FBI team is looking into activities you and President Snopkov took part in going back a good number of years. They're trying to link the two of you together on some unsavory matters. They seem to be piecing together your days under the Soviet Union initially, and then straight through to today."

"I see. That's unfortunate."

"Is there something we need to be concerned about? Was President Snopkov aware of your ... our recent actions?"

Rumas smiled, "No, that's not what's unfortunate, Agent Bates. Yes, of course, President Snopkov was aware. He directed this entire operation, including the approvals for taking down Senator Farrell and the Fosters. The unfortunate thing is that you take me for an idiot. That you think we do not know that you were captured by the

FBI, and are now trying to get me to say things that they will then use against me and President Snopkov. But that information will never leave this room. Instead, you are going to tell me everything you have learned from the FBI since being taken into custody. And then I will leave here, eluding the grasp of your FBI observers."

Outside the room, two guards stood casually talking, knowing that their boss could not hear them inside. As one laughed at the other's off-color joke, a bullet entered the right side of his skull, and then exploded through the left side. His partner could barely turn in the direction of the bullet, when two shots entered his chest.

Schmidt stepped over the two men, and opened the door.

Bates was the first to see the pistol, and he took his chance. He jumped to his feet, and moved toward the guard. But too much distance existed. The guard had time to wind up, and he slammed the side of Bates' head with the butt of his Uzi. Bates crashed to the floor.

Seeing Schmidt and the bodies in the hall behind him, Rumas had a sudden look of resignation on his face.

Schmidt raised his gun at the bewildered guard, and put two slugs in his chest. He turned his gun on the Ambassador.

Rumas said, "Your brother has ordered you to clean things up?"

"Yes, I'm sorry, Oleg."

"No, you're not. Get it over with."

But a voice from behind Schmidt surprised everyone in the room. "I don't think so, Gerry. I believe we'd like to question Ambassador Rumas about a few things."

Schmidt didn't move a muscle. "Liebling, is that you?"

Paige began to circle into the room. "Yes, and please don't call me that."

"Well, doesn't it count that I saved you and your friend, Grant, from that barbarian Audia?"

"Sorry, but no, since you set me up in the first place. I don't like being used, Gerry."

"Well, that depends on the use, doesn't it?"

"Knock off the shit, Gerry, and put down the gun."

"Sorry, but I still have to kill old Oleg here."

"If you do that, then I will have to shoot you, and trust me, you will not live."

"Well, what do we do, liebling?"

"Gerry, did you not just hear what I said about calling me liebling?" Paige pulled the trigger, and Gerhardt Schmidt tumbled to the floor, lifeless with blood flowing from the hole in his face that used to house his right eye.

She looked at him on the floor, and deposited two more bullets in his head. "You cost me, you bastard."

Rumas stared at Paige dispassionately.

She moved to Bates who was stirring on the floor. "Get up, Bates. We need to get out of here, now. More guards, no doubt, are on their way."

Bates grabbed his head as he got to his feet. "I'm okay."

Paige looked at Rumas, "You're coming with me, Mr. Ambassador."

"You'll never make it."

"We'll see about that."

Paige pushed Rumas out the door and toward the storage room. Boots moved across the floor above them. She shouted, "Bates, move it."

But before he left the room, Bates bent down and took the dead guard's Uzi.

He came into the hall. Boots started down the stairs toward them.

Paige pushed Rumas into the storage room, and looked back for Bates. She saw the Uzi, and that he was looking back and forth to her and to the sounds of the oncoming guards.

Bates yelled to her, "Get Rumas the hell out of here."

"Bates..."

"Go!" He moved the other way, positioning himself in a doorway waiting to shoot Rumas' security team.

Paige entered the storage room. Rumas stood still. She shoved the gun in his face. "You saw what I did to Schmidt. I'd have no qualms doing it to you. So, die now or move your ass into that tunnel."

Perhaps due to the fact that Snopkov had ordered his death, Rumas wasted no time in entering and moving through the tunnel.

As Paige followed, she heard the bursts of Uzi fire behind her.

Chapter 69

Stephen pulled his red Tahoe onto the roadway leading up to the parking lot adjacent to the Tudor-style St. Mary's Lutheran Church building.

In Washington, everything had wrapped up, as far as he was concerned, with the fallout from the murders of Graham and Margo. That included Paige coming to the rescue, in a sense, when the FBI was flying blind. He and Jennifer flew back to Long Island.

They were home by 9:30 Monday morning. He called Barbara and Zack, letting them know that he would be in the office shortly.

Stephen parked his SUV, got out into the early July summer heat, and looked at the church. *It's good to be home.*

He nearly raced up the stairs, and entered the front door. Stephen continued through the narthex to take a look inside the sanctuary. *Home, indeed. Thank you, Lord.*

With Zack's arrival, they had done some moving around of rooms, so that Stephen and Zack had adjacent offices, with Barbara's across the hallway from them.

Stephen casually strolled to his office door, and before entering, called out, "Mornin' all."

Barbara was in his doorway first, and they gave each other a warm embrace.

Barbara said, "I'm glad you're back, Pastor. And I'm sorry about Pastor and Mrs. Foster."

"Thanks, Barbara. It's very good to be back."

After hanging up the phone in his office, Pastor Charmichael appeared next.

Stephen said, "Zack, how are you?"

"I'm good, Stephen, what about you and Jennifer?"

"Considering the circumstances of our extended stay in D.C., we're doing fine."

"Again, my sympathies on the Fosters. I'm glad they got the people behind it all, at least."

"Yes, me, too. Hey, let's sit down and you two can update me on everything going on here."

They didn't sit at Stephen's desk, but instead gathered in the other half of the room around an oak coffee table, with Stephen taking his usual spot in an armchair, and Barbara on the couch. Zack decided to pull over a straight-back chair near the desk.

Barbara provided the administrative rundown, and Zack passed on a few prayer requests and mundane questions that he had received from parishioners.

When the brief reports finished, Stephen said, "While a honeymoon and the murder of a pastor might be legitimate reasons not to be here, I still feel bad about being absent for so much of the past month from our church family. And again, I have to thank you both for carrying the load. It's much appreciated."

They both offered the similar message of "Glad to help" and "You're welcome."

Stephen added, "No offense to you Barb, but you have had to put up with me for many years now."

"Yes, I know. It's my cross to bear in life." She smiled.

"However, Zack, this is not how your early days at your first call were supposed to go. So, here's the deal: You're going to take the rest of today off. We're closed for July

Fourth tomorrow, and then you're going to take Thursday as well."

"No need, Stephen."

"Yes, there is. Take some time to relax, get more acclimated to the area, and have some fun. Jennifer and I are going to a barbecue tomorrow with a group of people I'd love for you to meet. Can you go?"

"Thanks, I'd love to."

"Good. Now, for the other item that you two have been wrestling with – Drew Frazier."

Barbara repeated her previous declaration, "He's a crackpot."

"Thank you, Barbara, for that contribution." Stephen raised an eyebrow at her.

She said, "Sorry." Then she apparently could not resist, "But he is."

Stephen continued, "Anything more than what you told me about regarding Saturday night?"

Zack answered, "No, at least not that I heard. There certainly wasn't anything along those lines on Sunday. Rather, most people again said that they were praying for you and Jennifer."

"That's good, and appreciated."

Barbara asked, "So, what's the plan for dealing with Drew?"

"Jennifer and I spoke about it, and we're going to follow Matthew 18. I think Jennifer wants to talk with him one on one after we get back into the flow here at home."

Chapter 70

Just eight miles from downtown D.C., on 258 acres of land, sits the headquarters of the CIA in Langley, Virginia.

Within that complex, Paige Caldwell sat in the office of Tank Hoard. She lacked her usual style, merely dressed in a pink t-shirt, jeans and white sneakers. She had been waiting for about an hour, patiently – or at least that's how it appeared on the outside.

Hoard finally came in and shut the door behind him.

Few had a presence like Hoard's. His massive, sculpted, muscular body was glaringly evident even under his blue, pinstriped suit. And the fact that he cut his light brown hair so close made his head look even squarer than it actually was.

Paige remained seated, while Tank took off his suit jacket, tossed it on the brown couch, and then sat behind his desk. There was nothing on the desk. It was clean and shiny.

"What's the verdict, Tank?"

"Considering the mess you got yourself into, I managed to get you a better deal than otherwise would have happened."

Paige sat up a bit straighter. "Are you saying that I'm staying?"

He removed his look from her, and looked up at the ceiling. "Not exactly."

Paige sat back in the chair once more. "What the hell does that mean? Either I still have my job, or I don't. There's no such thing as being kind of pregnant."

"Well, in this case, there might."

"Come on, Tank, what's the deal?"

"Okay, you're done as a CIA employee." He tried to quickly add, "But..."

Paige interrupted. "But. There's no freakin' 'but.' You're telling me that after all I've done for the agency and this country that I'm just being cut loose. Tank, you know who I am. This is who I am. And you know how fucking good I am at this work. And what about me pulling the government's cojones out of the fire by getting Rumas? No credit. Nothing. How can you just let this happen?"

Tank raised his voice, which was rare. "First, Paige, I didn't let anything happen. You're the one who screwed up by fucking around with Schmidt. Second, believe me, everyone around here, including me, knows how good you are."

"So, then why..."

Tank raised his hand in the air to stop Paige. "Third, will you shut up, and let me finish what I was going to say?"

Paige gave silent acquiescence with a scowl and folded arms.

"Thank you. As I was saying, you're done as an official CIA employee. The higher ups just cannot get around the sleeping with a former Stasi agent who turned out to be involved in the murder of a U.S. senator, even if none of that information will ever see the light of day. Quite understandable, when you think about it. However, how does contract work with the agency sound to you?"

"Keep talking."

"It's simple really. We still want your expertise, skills and experience. As you said, this is who you are. And as a contractor, you'll not only wind up getting paid more – probably more than me, which is pretty damn annoying – but you'll also have... How should I say this? You'll have far greater freedom and leeway than an agency employee. At the same time, though, if you get caught crossing any lines, the CIA will not be there to back you. You know the drill, you'll be left hanging."

Paige stared at Tank. And then she smiled broadly. "I love it. When do we get started?"

"Pretty much immediately. I've already got a job for you, and I think you'll like it a lot."

"What about my team?"

"That's up to you. But I spoke to Charlie Driessen this morning, and he's thinking about filing his retirement papers. He might be looking for some work once he's mobile. There's also a guy in New York that I'm going to put you in contact with. He'll be invaluable for information and getting you various other assets you might need."

Paige said, "Tank, thanks. I couldn't have walked away, or been cut off from this."

"I know, Paige. Since it's July Fourth, think of this as your personal Independence Day."

Chapter 71

The July Fourth weather turned out to be nearly spring like. The sky was a clear blue, and the combination of no humidity to speak of and a nice breeze made the 80 degrees feel a bit cooler.

Jennifer, Stephen, Zack, and Ron joined the Stone family for a barbecue on the considerable lawn stretching out behind the rectory of St. Bart's.

Stephen marveled at Maggie Stone. She served as a pastor's wife, raised six children spread out from ages 12 to 26, and ran her own small public relations firm. Given all of that work, she seemed to relish entertaining guests, and the more the better. For good measure, strawberry-blond hair that rested on her shoulders, bright blue eyes, thin and fit body, and ready smile made her look like she was in her mid or late thirties, rather than turning 50 later in the year.

The day was restful, filled with barbecued hamburgers, chicken, sausage and corn on the cob, the occasional volleyball and Frisbee, and good conversation with friends. All of that was much needed by Stephen.

Late in the afternoon, Stephen, Tom and Ron were talking and sipping beers when Zack came over after knocking the volleyball around with various Stone offspring, as well as a fiancée and a "very serious," as

Maggie classified him, boyfriend that were being initiated into the Stone clan.

Stephen said, "Zack, how about a beer?"

"Sure, thanks."

Stephen tossed him one from the cooler conveniently located next to his chair. "Grab a seat. We were just talking a little Christian education."

"Good topic."

Ron picked up their conversation, "So, you have not heard anything from Mike since?"

Tom replied, "No, all he said was that he's been thinking and praying about it when he's had the chance to focus, and that his education team is re-evaluating some things."

Stephen said, "Well, 're-evaluating' is hopeful. If they were still set on giving to public schools, then there wouldn't really be anything to re-evaluate."

Tom continued, "He's had to focus on a Corevana game launch coming up at Comic-Con."

Zack nearly spit out his beer. "Wait, are you talking about Mike Vanacore?"

Tom and Ron looked bewildered by Zack's excited reaction, but Stephen immediately understood, given Zack's love of video games.

Tom responded, "Yes, do you know him?"

"Do I know him? No, of course not. But you do?"

"Well, yes, he's a member of St. Bart's."

"Really? Holy crrr..." He caught himself. "That's wild."

Ron asked, "Okay, what am I missing?"

Stephen decided to interject. "Zack enjoys video games, and, as you know, Mike Vanacore has made hundreds of millions of dollars creating and selling popular video games."

Ron said, "Okay, now I'm up to speed. Thanks."

"You're welcome," said Stephen. Then he turned to Zack, "Ron is a little slow on the draw at times."

"Anyway," Tom said to Zack, "Mike Vanacore is about to set up a foundation to support primary and secondary education. His original plan was to focus on public schools, and we recently made a presentation to him over at St. Luke's to hopefully adjust or change his focus to parochial schools."

"That would be huge," said Zack. "I read in passing that he was a Christian, but didn't know any more than that."

Tom added, "Yes, he's been a tremendous presence here at St. Bart's, and is an unassuming, great guy."

Ron said, "Tell Zack about the onerous pre-condition that you had to agree to in order to set up the St. Luke's meeting."

Tom replied, "Knock it off, Ron. Give me a break."

Ron continued, "Well, if you won't tell him, I will. Other than the ugly Hawaiian shirt, the cargo shorts and flip-flops that he is wearing right now, you probably would not guess that many years ago, Tom Stone was quite the radical surfer dude. And it turns out that Mike Vanacore likes to hang ten as well."

Zack chipped in, "Yeah, I know. I surf a little as well."

"Really? Another one?" said Ron. "You'll love this then. Mike would not meet unless Tom agreed to be flown out to California on Mike's private jet in order to go surfing and stay at his beach house."

Zack looked at Tom Stone seemingly with a new degree of respect. Charmichael raised his glass to Stone, and said, "Tom, that freakin' rocks."

"It sure does, Zack." Tom smiled broadly. "Unfortunately, our friend Ron here seems to be falling prey to that sin of envy."

Ron brought the conversation back to the education issue. He looked to Tom and asked, "So, when is this Comic-Con?"

Zack answered, "It starts in a week, and runs through to that following Sunday."

Stephen said, "Not that you're all that interested."

Zack said, "Are you kidding? I've never gone to a San Diego Comic-Con, but would love to one year."

Tom answered Ron, "Mike said that after the Comic-Con launch, he'd finalize things and get back to us."

Chapter 72

It was a little more than a week since the Grants had returned from D.C., and Jennifer had finally set up time to speak with Drew Frazier.

They sat down at a longtime staple on the North Fork of Long Island – The Modern Snack Bar, with its 1950s neon sign, on Main Road in Aquebogue. It was old-fashioned through and through, not only with the wood paneling and Formica-top tables, but with some excellent home-style cooking.

They exchanged uneasy niceties, while looking at menus. Drew ordered the Shepherd's Pie, and Jennifer selected the crab cakes, with the restaurant's famous mashed turnips.

"Whenever I come here, I have to have the mashed turnips. Very tasty." Jennifer smiled, and took a sip of water.

Drew remained standoff-ish. He said, "Mrs. Grant, why did you ask me to lunch?"

"Well, first, call me Jennifer. Can I call you Drew?"

"Yes, fine."

"Okay, to be honest, I'm trying to figure out why you have a problem with me."

"I don't have a problem with you, Jennifer."

"Well, Drew, it looks to me like you do. From what was said at council and what you told Pastor Charmichael, you're troubled by my job, how much I earn at that work, and my family's background. If you'd work with me here and now, I'd like to answer whatever questions you have in each of these areas. I'm not just an economist and daughter of a casino owner, but the wife of a pastor, your pastor, Drew, and I don't want anything to undermine his important work."

For the first time since Jennifer Grant had known Drew Frazier, his face seemed to soften a little. "I appreciate that Jennifer, and I don't want to cause any unwarranted problems. I just have some questions and worries."

Jennifer said, "Well, let's see if I can answer those questions, and maybe ease at least some of those concerns."

For the following two hours, over lunch, dessert – Drew went along with Jennifer's suggestion of the toasted almond cream cake – and a few cups of coffee, Jennifer answered Drew's questions about what her firm did and about her father's casinos. But they soon ventured into more personal waters.

Jennifer told him about the distant relationship she had with her father since college, and how poorly he treated her mother.

Drew then spoke about how shocked he was that his wife had divorced him, and his frustration at not being able to get his own business ideas off the ground. But most painful was his inability to find friendship, even, he felt, at St. Mary's.

By the time they were parting in the restaurant's parking lot, Drew Frazier and Jennifer Grant hugged. And she reminded him, "So, we'll see you at our place for dinner next Tuesday at six-thirty. You're going to love my sword collection."

"Right, looking forward to it."

She watched him as he got into his late nineties Ford pick up truck, and backed out of the parking space. He rolled up to her, and lowered the passenger side window.

He looked at Jennifer, with moist eyes, and said, "Thank you, Jennifer. And ... and I'm sorry."

"Nothing to be sorry for, Drew, I understand. Take care."

And off he went.

Jennifer got into her red Thunderbird, turned the key, and as she lowered the convertible top, called Stephen.

He answered, "Hello, Jen. Did you survive your lunch with Drew? I just realized that it's almost three."

"We wound up having a great conversation. Stephen, he's just a very lonely, sad man."

"Well, apparently you did have quite a conversation."

"We really did. He's coming over on Tuesday for dinner and to take a look at the sword collection. If that's okay?"

"Okay? That's spectacular. I've never been able to connect with Drew. What did you do?"

"I'll explain later tonight?"

"Fair enough. By the way..."

"Yes, I have a quart of lobster bisque and a piece of toasted almond cream cake for you."

"Great. Love you."

"Love you, too. Bye."

With the top down, Jennifer Grant loaded the new Beach Boys CD into the car radio/CD player, flipped over to the "That's Why God Made the Radio" track, and made a right onto Main Road.

Chapter 73

In the three weeks since Paige Caldwell brought to an end the plot by Belarusian leaders, the U.S. administration decided to let stand the original story presented by the Justice Department, including the FBI, and the CIA.

As far as most of the world knew, it was Lydia Garcia's DTO that murdered a U.S. senator, a top Senate aide, and a prominent pastor and his wife.

For his silence, Manny Rodriguez got a new life somewhere in the United States through WITSEC operated by the U.S. Marshals Service. For his cooperation, Oleg Rumas did not receive a death sentence for his many atrocities. Instead, he would spend the rest of his life deep inside a military prison.

Jackie Moss never knew about the wrongdoing committed by Ryan Bates. Instead, she was told that he died a hero, taking on larger numbers singlehandedly to secure the safe escape of others.

And Mort Steinberg was right about Rich Noack. He, along with the rest of his team, could be trusted. And now added to that team was Trent Nguyen.

As for the foreign aid legislative effort, it was allowed to die without a conference committee appointed to iron out differences between the bills that passed each congressional chamber. The subject moved from being hot in political and media circles to falling into oblivion. Elected officials, including Senator Ted Brees, moved on to other issues that would help them get re-elected in November.

Meanwhile, in Belarus, uprisings were mounting as long-secret information about the gruesome past of President Anatoliy Snopkov was becoming public, and circulated on the Internet despite his security forces' best efforts to stop such communications. Snopkov blamed a CIA plot. But that was mocked as the pathetic pleas of a despot, who had a direct hand in the death of perhaps thousands across Belarus, the Ukraine, Poland and the former East Germany.

But as popular uprisings occurred, Snopkov showed no signs of loosening his grip on power. Instead, he readied troops and tanks to move on people in the streets.

Paige Caldwell's team was in Minsk to try to stop attacks on innocents from happening. The U.S. government had made back channel contact with Snopkov's Prime Minister, who assured the U.S. that he saw no value in what Snopkov was doing. At the same time, he was powerless to stop it. But if the U.S. or an ally would be able to stop Snopkov, they would find a far less militant successor in the Prime Minister. Zyanon Lebedko, the businessman who carried weight with the Americans, backed up the Prime Minister's credentials.

Snopkov was now more protected than ever before. The new living quarters were not far from Snopkov's office in the House of Government on Independence Square. His security people had chosen wisely. The only chance that Caldwell's team had was a rooftop gardened patio area where he would occasionally come outside and stroll about, with guards on both sides, however. There were no easy, close shots. In fact, there were no tough shots. Instead, Caldwell's only chances were long distance sniper shots, and then there were only two, maybe three places with clear looks.

This first excursion by Caldwell's team featured two people on Snopkov. Caldwell was positioned in a residential apartment building about a half-mile from the presidential rooftop, and Sean McEnany, the person that Hoard had put her in contact with in New York, was just a little closer in the nearly opposite direction.

Charlie Driessen was monitoring developments in Belarus and staying in contact with both Caldwell and McEnany from Poland – specifically, from a hotel room, with a nurse tending to the needs of his new knees.

Last was a trusted pilot who worked for the Belarus government. But he could be counted on, according to Driessen, to get Caldwell and McEnany out of Belarus when necessary.

For four days, Caldwell and McEnany had not left the apartment each was in. They handed off monitoring Snopkov as needed. And their respective XM2010 Enhanced Sniper Rifles were kept ready, though hidden from the possibility of any prying eyes on the outside.

It was three in the afternoon. McEnany's voice came through the transmitter while Paige was taking a few minutes to close her eyes. "He's up and about."

She responded, "Right. I'm here."

Each looked for the opening that Snopkov, while getting a little air, would step into, and his body language would indicate that he would stay there just long enough for a 7.62 mm bullet to take him down.

Paige spoke softly to the distant Snopkov, "Come on, you son of a bitch. This time. Just for a couple of seconds."

McEnany saw him. Snopkov pulled a cigar out of his pocket, and held steady for a light. McEnany whispered, "Bam." He squeezed off the shot, and through his scope he saw Snopkov go down, and then various personnel moving around frantically.

From the transmitter came Caldwell, "Beautiful. My compliments."

McEnany replied, "Save it for home. You owe me a dinner and several drinks. I've got my own way out. Later."

The transmission ended.

Caldwell changed from the black shorts and gray t-shirt she was wearing into a light blue skirt, white top and flats. She took her phone, camera and transmitter, and slipped them into a small white handbag.

As extra precaution, Paige then wiped down the rifle, night vision goggles and binoculars. She placed them all in the bathroom with everything else she was leaving behind, doused the pile with a little gasoline, lit up an entire matchbook, and tossed it on the pile.

She slipped on a pair of sunglasses, and left the room and the smoke behind.

By the time she exited the building and was getting into a taxi, less than five minutes had passed.

She called Driessen, while the cab driver periodically glanced at her in his rearview mirror.

Driessen answered, "Yes?"

"It's all finished."

"You or him?"

"Well, I'm jealous."

"Ha, him then. Sorry about that."

"Can you let your friend know I'm on my way?"

"Certainly. Hey, this is kind of fun, isn't it?"

"I wouldn't want to be doing anything else."

She hung up.

The taxi driver stole another look. Paige looked at him, formed a kiss with her lips, and then smiled.

Chapter 74

In light of the nice weather and summer vacations, attendance at the early Mass at St. Mary's Lutheran Church was smaller than at other times of the year. It was one of those frustrations that Stephen had to come to terms with early in his career as a pastor.

As the Hymn of the Day was concluding, he stepped up to the pulpit in St. Mary's sanctuary. Given his experiences in recent weeks, this sermon nearly wrote itself.

Grace to you and peace from God our Father and the Lord Jesus Christ. Amen.

Money. Not an easy topic to talk about these days. And it can get a little squirmy in church, right? But don't worry, this is not a sermon on giving or tithing.

Money is especially hard to discuss when facing financial difficulties.

Jobs aren't being created as quickly as they should be. If you want the numbers, check with the economist I happen to be married to after the service.

That drew a chuckle from the congregation, and a smile from Jennifer.

Maybe in your house, someone is out of work. Or, your pay has stayed the same, or even declined, yet the bills mount.

But others here today are doing okay or even pretty well. Though in recent years, I think few have felt truly secure.

So, what do we do about this? Even in this sanctuary at this very moment, one person may be doing fine, while another is in trouble.

Well, first and foremost, we have to realize that no matter what we're going through, good or bad on the job front, God created each of us and loves each of us. Proverbs 22:2 speaks directly to our experience right here in these pews. It says, "The rich and the poor meet together; the Lord is the maker of them all."

That means we should love, respect, and support each other, especially when in need.

And then there is the danger of seeing material wealth as a sign that your faith is strong or it's the right kind of faith. Of course, the flip side of that would be that if you haven't been doing well – perhaps experienced bankruptcy, for example – then there's something not right about your faith.

A dear friend of mine fell into this thinking. He liked to quote John 10:10, which says, "I came that they may have life and have it abundantly."

But that does not mean material abundance. Instead, it's about eternal life through faith in Jesus Christ. Keep in mind that Jesus himself was not a wealthy man, and his earthly life, especially the end, was not exactly what happens to the well-off. The story, of course, was much the same for His Apostles.

Jesus also warns us that money, when not viewed in the proper way, can get us into trouble. In Matthew 6:24, the Lord instructs, "No one can serve two masters, for either he will hate one and love the other, or he will be devoted to the one and despise the other. You cannot serve God and money."

Notice that Jesus says that *we* cannot serve God and money.

Also, it's important to see what Paul actually wrote to Timothy, "For the love of money is a root of all kinds of evils. It is through this craving that some have wandered away from the faith and pierced themselves with many pangs."

Again, take note that Paul wrote that "the love of money is a root of all kinds of evils." He did not write that money is the root of all evil, which is how the quote is usually tossed around.

That's a real difference, isn't it?

Of course, we should not serve money, and we should not love money. It's God that we serve and love.

Money is a tool. And like any tool, it can be used in our service to the Lord and to do good in this world, or it can be used for things that are very different.

Again, Jesus points us in the right direction. Consider The Parable of the Talents from Matthew. Jesus said, "He who had received the five talents went at once and traded with them, and he made five talents more... And he who had received the five talents came forward, bringing five talents more, and saying, 'Master, you delivered to me five talents; here I have made five talents more.' His master said to him, 'Well done, good and faithful servant. You have been faithful over a little; I will set you over much. Enter into the joy of your master.'"

Another servant was given two talents by the master, and returned four. The master, too, rewarded him.

But then there was the servant who merely buried the one talent that he had been given. When the master returned, that servant said, "Master, I knew you to be a hard man, reaping where you did not sow, and gathering where you scattered no seed, so I was afraid, and I went and hid your talent in the ground. Here you have what is yours."

As we know, the master was not pleased. He called the servant "wicked and slothful," and said to "cast that worthless servant into the outer darkness."

The talents in this parable are all about the gifts given by God — gifts, no matter what they may be, that we should be productive with in the service of God.

It's also interesting, though, to see that Jesus used a talent, which was a form of money, to teach this lesson.

No matter how many talents God bestows upon us, they all should be used to His greater glory. That can be here at church. That can be in your vocations. That can be in fulfilling your responsibilities to your family.

The love of money, indeed, is a root of all kinds of evils, including, for example, the sins of both greed and envy.

In the end, we need to keep our focus on the Lord, and use all of the varied gifts that He has given us wisely, as best as we can, to serve Him and to take care of each other. And remember that our ultimate reward will not be in this world infected by sin, but in paradise with Jesus.

Amen.

Chapter 75

Mike Vanacore sat at the head of the long glass conference table, with sunshine streaming into the room.

He was smiling, as was everyone else around the table.

Mike said, "So, I want to thank you guys, especially Tom and Ron. If you had not nudged and helped me, I would not have set up this education foundation to focus on building up and growing Christian elementary and high schools. Tom, you got me thinking, or re-thinking, where my charitable efforts would be put to the best use. And then Ron, I will never forget what you said in our first meeting. Of course, I can't quote you exactly, but you made the point that public and non-religious private schools can talk about love and values, but that your school and other Christian schools can truly explain it all. What the sacrifice and love of Jesus means to each of us, and what it says about how we should treat others. And in terms of right and wrong, you actually can teach students *why* something is right or wrong, moving away from the latest whims in our culture and returning to first principles from our Creator. That's powerful stuff. I've been blessed. So, if I can use my resources to provide a stronger foundation of faith for students who could not otherwise afford it, how could I not do it? Thanks to all of you."

Ron responded, "Well, thank you, Mike. Your contribution to St. Luke's School trust will allow us to upgrade and expand facilities, and most importantly, expand our school population through scholarships. It's an incredible blessing."

Stephen chimed in, "The same goes for the other four Catholic and Lutheran schools on Long Island you chose to support. Each of the schools and churches involved, I know, have contacted you over the past few days, but when the principals at the Lutheran schools heard both Zack and I would be meeting with you, they contacted us to relay further thanks."

"Gentlemen, I am blessed that I am able to do this. Now, I think we need to move on to the other reason – really the main reason – that I brought you to my home here on Laguna Beach. And that's to see if our 52-year-old friend, Tom Stone, can still get it done."

"Can I get it done?" responded Tom. "Just watch."

He stood up from the table, and turned to look out at the majestic view of the Pacific Ocean. "What are those waves at, about four feet?"

Mike and the other three men stood up as well.

Mike said, "Yeah, I'd say that's right."

Tom smiled. "Why so easy?"

He took off his shirt populated by pineapples, and dropped it on his chair.

Ron observed, "Oh, this is getting ugly."

Tom Stone then began running, through the large, open sliding doors, across the expansive stone-floor patio, past the pool, and down the stairs to the beach below. He grabbed one of the boards at the bottom, tucked it under his right arm, and continued his run, which now became more of a trot, toward the water. He high stepped into the water, laid the board down, jumped on and started paddling.

The four friends moved to the wall of the patio to watch from above.

Stone moved just beyond where the waves were breaking, and then maneuvered the board, looking to catch a wave. And after two went by, he caught the third, stood up on the board, guided it along neatly for several seconds, stuck his fist in the air, and then flipped back over the wave and into the water.

After applauding, Stone's fellow would-be surfers went down the stairs, each also grabbing a board.

Mike and Zack were in their element, rushing forward across the sand and into the surf.

Stephen and Ron took their time.

Ron admitted, "I've never done this before."

"Really? Never? Why didn't you tell anyone before this?"

Ron shrugged sheepishly. "I'm a little nervous."

"I bet."

"What about you? Have you ever surfed?"

The two stopped on the sand. Stephen thought he saw a ray of hope from Ron, probably thinking that Stephen would say that he'd never done it either, so let's go back to the house for a couple of drinks.

Stephen whispered, "Once with the CIA, I took on some of the biggest, most treacherous waves in the world at Dungeons in Cape Town, South Africa. Did pretty well, actually. But of course, I can't tell you any more about that. You know, national security and all."

Stephen smiled, slapped Ron on the back, and sprinted to the waves. He could hear Ron yelling, "You know, sometimes I really don't like you."

About the Author

Ray Keating is a weekly columnist with the Dolan Company (including *Long Island Business News* and other newspapers), a former *Newsday* weekly columnist, an economist, an adjunct college professor, and board member of the American Lutheran Publicity Bureau. His work has appeared in a wide range of additional periodicals, including *The New York Times, The Wall Street Journal, The Washington Post, New York Post,* Los Angeles *Daily News, The Boston Globe, National Review, The Washington Times, Investor's Business Daily,* New York *Daily News, Detroit Free Press, Chicago Tribune, Providence Journal Bulletin,* and *Cincinnati Enquirer.* Keating lives on Long Island with his family.

This is his second novel featuring Stephen Grant. The first was *Warrior Monk: A Pastor Stephen Grant Novel.*

Made in the USA
San Bernardino, CA
25 September 2013